Volume 1

Jack the Lad
(Nowt Else for It!)

A childhood in Yorkshire's West Riding
from the mid 1940s

Frank English

2QT Limited (Publishing)

First Edition published 2016

2QT Limited (Publishing)
Unit 5 Commercial Courtyard
Duke Street
Settle
North Yorkshire
BD24 9RH

Copyright © Frank English 2016
The right of Frank English to be identified as the author of this work has been asserted by him in accordance with the Copyright, Designs and Patents Act 1988

All rights reserved. This book is sold subject to the condition that no part of this book is to be reproduced, in any shape or form. Or by way of trade, stored in a retrieval system or transmitted in any form or by any means, electronic, mechanical, photocopying, recording, be lent, re-sold, hired out or otherwise circulated in any form of binding or cover other than that in which it is published and without a similar condition, including this condition being imposed on the subsequent purchaser, without prior permission of the copyright holder

Cover design: Charlotte Mouncey
Cover images: main photographs supplied by ©Frank English
Additional images from iStockhoto.com

Printed in the UK by Lightning Source UK Limited

ISBN 978-1-910077-82-5

To me mam
Florence May English

with best wishes

Charles English

Chapter 1

"What does tha mean, 'mine'?" he asked, half hissing through clenched teeth. "It can't be mine. Look at that neck. It's like a bloody swan, for God's sake."

The ward seemed to stop and fall silent. Heads turned slowly towards this source of aggravation, this unseemly outburst.

"Can't you keep your voice down?" she said through a forced whisper, casting her furtive and embarrassed eyes around the room. "Of course he's yours. Who else's could he be?"

"But he's nowt like me," he went on, only slightly less loudly than before, eyes fixed on the bairn, alarmed to be so close to such an ugly infant.

"He's only been an hour in this world," she tried to soothe. "He probably looks more like a monkey than anything else."

She giggled nervously at the funny she felt might lighten the atmosphere. It served only to make him more aware of what she had produced.

He leaped to his feet, knocking over the chair next to her bed, pacing about urgently for a short while, then stamping out of the ward, the staccato echo from his hobnailed pit boots receding as he left.

She drew the baby closer to her breast, cooing and kissing

its sparsely thatched head tenderly. Why had she married such an unforgiving and boorish man? Her father had warned her. Why hadn't she listened to him? They often say father knows best. She hadn't wanted to believe it, wanted to make up her own mind. He *was* handsome, though, wasn't he? Too late now. Two children: one withdrawn and introverted, and the other newborn. Where to go from here? Only one place: back home, eventually. For now, rest and regain her strength. God knows she was going to need it.

"Is he yours?" chorused Doris and Izzy.

"Well, of course he is," stammered Flo, puzzled at the question, drawing the infant closer. "I…"

"No, not the bairn," explained Doris with a half smile, "yon bugger who's just stomped out o' t' ward."

Blood rushed into Flo's pale cheeks, staining them bright crimson in her embarrassment, to cover her stupidity.

"You want to get rid of *him*, love," said Doris, folding her arms across her ample chest, all the while Izzy's head nodding vigorous assent to her left. "Mark my words, he'll do you no good. Until you do there's nowt else for it but to get on and meck the best of a bad job."

How long had Flo known these two? Just a few hours … and they seemed to know him better than she did. Her dad's words of warning flooded her already confused and racing mind.

"Tha'll niver make owt on him, lass," her dad Jud had said seriously the day before they wed, thumbs locked under his trouser braces. "He's from an unpleasant father. I knew owd William almost all me life, and niver found owt good in him. Even Elizabeth, his wife, detested him. She were a bit like you, really: a decent sort who didn't know what she were getting into until it were too late. Fortunately she had a few years of peace after he died.

"I remember t' funeral as if it were yesterday. She were

asked if she wanted to see him one last time in his coffin. 'See 'im?' she'd snorted. 'See *'im*? No bloody fear. Screw t' owd bugger down, and let's be rid once and for all.' I don't want you to get to that stage," he added.

-o-

The couple of weeks Flo spent in Manygates Hospital getting to know her new son were the most restful and pleasant she'd spent in the ten years she'd been married to her pitman husband: no quarrelling, no aggravation about food, and no unpleasantness about his excesses, his demands, or his meanness. She had developed a rheumatic heart in her early teens, and Manygates was the only specialist hospital in her area in the mid forties that could cope with her type of difficult birth.

Long by any stretch for a second-time mother, her exhausting labour had produced a strapping eight-pound undemanding boy, whom she was determined to name after her much-loved late brother. *His* last moments on this world were spent in a Lancaster bomber over the Netherlands, returning from a raid on Germany's industrial heartland just four years before.

He was the second love of her mother's life to be lost in war: first her husband – Flo's biological dad Herbert, in the war to end all wars – and now Jack. Not surprising, her views on conflict and its perpetrators.

An undemanding baby who needed little sleep, her new son shared many of the characteristics of his namesake from *his* early days. If anyone needed convincing about reincarnation they needed to look no further.

"He's a bonny lad," Flo's mother would say on her daily visits, proud and convinced that *her* son had revisited this world once more. "It's a pity about his sire. But then I suppose you've had enough of that from your dad. He's galled he can't make it. He's on afternoons down t' pit this week and next week."

"Don't worry, Mam," Flo answered, an understanding smile creeping into her face. "He's done more than yon."

"Not been to see you yet?" Marion said, disbelievingly.

"Aye," Flo answered, cradling her resting infant. "Only the once, and then he stormed out. Doesn't believe he's the father."

"What?" Marion gasped, eyes flashing murderously, not believing what she was hearing. "The— Wait till I get my hands on him. I'll—"

"No, you won't, Mam," Flo insisted. "Dad was right. He's not worth it. The only thing I'm concerned for now is to look after my lads. If this one grows up to be like *our* Jack I'll be happy."

"And William?" her mam asked. "How do you think he'll cope, both with a brutish father and with a new brother?"

"There's a lot more goes on behind *his* eyes than we know about," Flo answered. "He's nearly ten, so he'll cope. He always was the apple of his father's eye. He can do no wrong, so there'll be no worries there. Besides, he's the image of him."

"And Eric's rejection of Jack is because…?" Marion asked.

"He doesn't look anything like him," Flo replied. "Can you believe it? Goodness knows what would have happened if William had looked nothing like him either."

-o-

Early January was not the best time to bring new life into a freezing cold world. Flecks of snow carried on a keen northerly wind had been threatening to settle for several days before Flo was due to take home her bairn. She had decided against telling her mother the exact day for fear that she would organise a taxi, which she knew she wouldn't be able to afford.

Manygates was an awkward place to get from – two buses and a five-minute walk – but she knew she would have it to do because she knew her husband wouldn't take time off work to fetch her. Her worry was for her newborn, but she felt in her heart he would be strong enough as long as he was kept warm.

"Are you sure we can't call you a taxi, Flo?" the nurse asked, concerned, as she opened the door on to thicker flurries of snow. "It's wicked out there."

"No," she replied, wrapping her baby in more tightly and holding him more closely to her. "We'll be OK."

Thank goodness for the winter coat and stout boots her dad had bought her for her birthday in November. What would she do without him and his kindness? He would be enraged when he got to know his son-in-law hadn't been man enough to collect them from the hospital. But she'd cross that bridge when she got to it. Her only concern now was getting her child home safely.

The blast of icy air as she crossed Bull Ring and headed for the bus station caused her to wince and to draw her coat more tightly around her baby. Blissfully unaware of the cold and people's stares, he had slept from the hospital in the cocoon created by the warmth from his mother's body and the gentle rocking of the bus journey to the centre of town.

Westgate bus station was almost deserted, which was to be expected for mid afternoon on a Sunday in early January. The deepening slushy snow hunched around the bus stands played its part, too, in creating this ghost town feeling. Had it not been for midwinter in the West Riding you might have seen ghostly tumbleweed balls drifting lazily across the concrete.

Flo reached her stand with difficulty against the freshening wind, trying forlornly to find shelter behind the lone bus stop pole, and hoping she might see her bus chugging around the corner before she froze. Fortunately for her, Sundays in winter didn't generate many stops en route, so she didn't have long to wait.

Recognising her condition straight away, the kindly conductor helped her along to the warmest seat and as far away from the open back as possible.

"Wakefield Road, please," she asked, through unresponsive, almost frozen lips, as she fumbled for her nearly empty purse.

"Because it's snowy and cold today," he added cheerily, "there'll be no charge."

"But...?" she replied, puzzled at what he had said.

"Mothers and new bairns are free on my shift, my dear," he interrupted. "I insist. You can pay double when he's ten."

She smiled at his cheer and generous understanding, which would be in stark contrast to what she would meet when she got home. My, the heat from that engine vent was wonderful, giving her strength to light and stoke the fire when she got in to her own freezing house.

Built at the turn of the twentieth century, number 206 Wakefield Road was one of a long line of late Victorian/early Edwardian terraced houses provided by the local coal board to accommodate its pit workers at a reasonable and affordable rent. Two up and two down plus a scullery, it was then considered to be living in the depths of luxury – particularly when these houses were compared with what they had replaced. However, amenities within *were* sparse – no bathroom, coal-fired blackleaded range, cold running water only, gas mantles to provide lighting, and ... an outside toilet across a cobbled yard. To Flo, however, it was hers, although she relied on her husband to pay the rent.

Husband Eric had a good job down the local mine as a coal hewer, but money for Flo was always short. Her housekeeping was almost always late, as was the rent. This wasn't because she was a bad housekeeper, but often *he* forgot to hand over both. The embarrassment she suffered and warnings *she* received from the landlord and the tradespeople were as a direct result of *his* dissolute and disorganised ways.

"The drink will kill him one of these days," her mother would often say.

"The only way drink will kill *him*," her dad would reply, "is if a barrel fell on his bloody head."

Her key slipped the latch easily, but she hesitated on the threshold before pushing her way in, dreading to feel the icy snatch of the front room and the handwritten rent arrears note on the front mat. Opening the front door slowly, she encountered neither. Puzzled, she snecked the door behind her and moved gingerly towards the kitchen/living room. The door was half open, allowing a welcome waft of warm air to caress her as she approached.

Her baby began to stir, sensing the change of temperature and motion, and, maybe, the approach of food time. Huge yellow flames licked up the chimney at the back of the fire grate as a bright red glow leaped out at her, forcing her to remove coat and boots.

Deeply puzzled, she caught sight of her husband in his favourite chair by the fire – boots off, cleanly and recently bathed. The tin bath was hanging from the wall by the range, dripping slightly from recent use.

"Hello, lass," he murmured drowsily as she moved to put on the kettle. "I've not been back from t' pit long. So I thowt I'd get a fire going and 'ave a bath. Parky out yonder. Bring t' bairn ower 'ere. 'E must be frozen. Cup o' tea?"

Surprised and dumbfounded by this change of attitude, she glanced around to see where this interloper had hidden *her* husband. He had never been this considerate, even when their William had been born. Had he had a personality transplant? It wouldn't last long, she was convinced, but she would enjoy it while she could.

"I've left yer money and t'rent in sideboard for tomorrer," he told her as he brought the huge brown teapot Flo had inherited from her mam's mam and a couple of pint mugs. Pint mugs? How she longed for fine bone china. But with him it was never going to happen. Everything she possessed was utilitarian, and nothing she could share socially. This much she had in common with many of the women she knew. Her next-door neighbour but one, Doreen Green, was the exception. *She* demanded better from her man. *She* stood her ground with him. *She* got what she wanted. It was widely accepted that George was a good man, whom many had wished they had snapped up when they'd had the chance. Not the most beautiful by any stretch, Doreen was still a striking woman, and *he* worshipped the ground she walked on.

"Stopping in tonight?" Flo suggested tentatively, after making a bite and feeding the bairn, knowing what his answer would be.

"Just thowt I'd nip out to t' club," he ventured, "just to wet yon bairn's head, you know. After all, it's not every day a man 'as another son home from hospital. Our William's coming home from your mam's today, by the way, isn't he?"

"He'll have to," Flo replied. "School tomorrow for him. Mr Tomlinson, the head teacher, won't want him off at beginning of t' year. Not when the eleven-plus practice tests are about to start. I want him to do well, and go on to t' grammar school."

"Mecks no odds," her husband replied. "He'll be goin' down t' pit, anyway, so what good's a grammar school education going to do 'im?"

"How many more times?" she snarled, rounding on him menacingly, the carving knife still in her hand. "My lads are not going down t' pit, and that's that."

"Tha's got no say in t' matter," he replied, heading for the stairs. "What I say goes, and that's an end."

"We'll see about that," she snarled defiantly. "They're not going down any black hole. They're going to be properly educated, and come home from work clean and not covered in grime."

"What's good enough for me and my father," he threw back at her as he unlatched the stairs door, "is not good enough for them, eh?"

"There's nowt wrong with them bringing home a regular wage, which they hand over to their wives regularly," she harrumphed disdainfully.

"Ooh … sharp," he jibed. "We'll see. We'll see, won't we?"

With that he clumped upstairs to change into his drinking suit.

-o-

"Mam," a shrill voice summoned her from the front door. "I'm back. Are you?"

"In here, love," she shouted, not knowing how her other son could have known she'd be back. She'd only told her mam.

"Your Gran tell you I'd be back?" she asked as he shot through the middle door into the kitchen.

"This afternoon," William replied as he hugged her, glad to have her back home.

"Your Gran with you?" Flo asked.

"Granddad brought me," William answered, fixing his eyes on his new brother. "Left me at the door. Thought you'd like to be on your own a bit. Said he'd see you tomorrow."

She understood her dad perfectly. He had taken himself away back home so that his inevitable confrontation with her husband wouldn't upset her. He was a big man, her dad, and not averse to standing toe to toe with upstarts who needed correction. He knew she didn't need that sort of aggravation on her first day back.

"Dad back from work yet?" William asked, eager to see his family together.

"Going to his club, love, I think," she answered, hardly hiding her disdain.

"Can I…?" he asked, eyebrows lifting towards the stairs.

"I wouldn't," she replied. "You know he doesn't like to be disturbed when he's getting ready. You might get chance to see him later, depending on whether he gets back before your bedtime."

Disappointment swimming in his eyes, he turned his attention to the new arrival.

"My new…?" he asked tentatively, creeping over towards the new pram.

"Brother Jack," she added, a smile of satisfaction oozing out of her face. "He's asleep, so try not to wake him."

"He's not asleep," William reassured her, seeing Jack's two big green, unblinking eyes looking back at him. "Hello, Little Jack. I'm your big brother, William. Pleased to meet you. Mam, quick … he's smiling at me."

"Probably wind, my sweet," she assured. "It won't last."

"He's still smiling," William insisted.

"Unusual," Flo said, sidling slowly across to the pram. "Perhaps—"

"I'm off," a loud voice burst over them from the partially open middle door. "Won't be too long."

"Dad," William shouted, turning quickly on his heels to head towards the front room.

The outside door slammed before he could get there. He turned back towards his mother, disappointment etching his face.

Unable to hide her feelings, William caught the disdain

she felt for her husband's actions, neither quite understanding why his beloved father didn't want to spend time with him, nor why his mother disliked his father so much.

-o-

The following days for Flo were a blessed release from the drudgery of everyday life with her husband. Her two boys had become the centre of her universe, from which Eric was becoming more and more isolated. He seemed to care only about one thing, and that usually took up most of the weekends he wasn't at work.

She felt sorry for her elder son, who seemed to be becoming more withdrawn because of the lack of meaningful contact with his father. The occasions he took the time to be with his son were few and far between – and, although they picked up the lad's mood considerably, it didn't last long, because there was no carry-over to the next time. The next time was usually so long in coming that the benefits had been long forgotten.

His new son he rarely acknowledged, pleading pressure of work. That lack of contact, Flo was sure, wouldn't affect Little Jack at all. *He* would be the strong one of the family. Of that she was convinced.

Little Jack was so much like his forebear it was uncanny. Even Flo's parents had remarked on it. Her mother had stopped calling him 'our Little Jack', and had begun to use 'my Jack' as her term of endearment. Flo often looked into his face and saw her brother, and his steadfast gaze back seemed to understand what she felt and what she had gone through to have him.

Although this lifted her spirits it also weighed heavily on her mind that her firstborn shouldn't miss out. He was the one she had sacrificed so much to have, and, rightly or not, he needed to be her first priority.

Chapter 2

With the passing days her husband's views on his new son had become entrenched. He insisted that he couldn't be his because of the wild differences between the two boys. William was blond, blue-eyed and becoming physically more like his dad every day, whereas Jack was not only dark-haired and green-eyed but his features could have been passed on from anywhere. It didn't matter that he was growing to look more and more like Flo's brother, obviously inheriting *her* genetic makeup. It was enough that the boy didn't look like him which aroused Eric's suspicions, and *that* turned him against the little chap.

"I can't believe you are so bigoted – or stupid – that you can't see the obvious," she yelled at him.

"Don't thee call me stupid," he retorted, clenching his fists. "Or thy'll feel the back of my hand."

"Going to hit a defenceless woman, now, are you?" she goaded him. "Don't let me stop you, big man. Ever thought of threatening that to my dad? See what he'd do. I dare you."

"He's nothing to me," he hissed, "and neither is yon bairn. You can take the bastard and do what you like with him. He's no concern of mine."

"You bloody swine," Flo screamed, picking up her iron frying pan and making a dart for him. "How dare you!"

Seeing the murderous look in her eyes – and realising he had gone too far – he slammed the front door hastily behind him and headed towards his club, leaving her to calm down. She'd be much quieter in an hour or so, when he got back after a pint or two. Little did he realise how his insults would come back to haunt him.

-o-

"And that's for what tha said about yon bairn," Jud snarled as his fist slammed into Eric's face. Only minutes out of the warm comfort of his club – and with four pints of Courage inside him – he reeled backwards, blood exploding from his nose. "And that's for what tha might say next."

Jud's second punch almost broke his jaw, and dropped him to a bloody pile where he stood. Checking that he wasn't about to retaliate, Jud spun on his heels and made for home, satisfied he had made his point.

"Eee … Bloody 'ell, Eric lad," Ernest Smallshaw gasped when he saw the damage Jud's fists had wrought on his friend's face. "Did tha get t' number o' wagon as hit thee?"

"It were nowt," Eric's muffled reply dropped out of his mouth. "I can manage. Leave me be. I'll be all rayt."

"Come on, lad," Ernest carried on. "I'll get thee 'ome. It's a good job thy only lives ower t' road."

"What on earth's happened to you?" Flo gasped as he staggered in from the road, leaving the door wide open and a trail of blood drops on the oilcloth floor. "Finally wound up the wrong person? Mind the furniture. We don't have much, I'll remind you. Well?"

"Nowt," he mumbled, his swollen mouth and nose making it hard to form his words. "Had an accident coming aht o' club. That's all. Now leave me alone, woman."

"You'll not be wanting anything to eat, then?" she asked, her initial shock and sympathy evaporating rapidly.

"I'm off to bed," he muttered after he had bathed his face in cold water. "I'm on days tomorrer, so I'll be out of your way. Look after me lad."

"Little Jack'll be fine," she replied.

"I said *my* lad," he threw sarcastically over his shoulder as he snecked the stairs door.

Although she found it hard to deal with his snide comments, which were designed to wound, she vowed from this day she would ignore everything he said. By not rising to his baiting she hoped he would become bored with his unproductive sniping, and eventually it would go away. Unfortunately his family wasn't noted for its forbearance. *They* never gave up. This day, however, marked a turning point in their relationship, which was to decline for the rest of her life.

-o-

His snoring through blocked nose and swollen mouth allowed her to sleep only fitfully. Her feelings of utter hopelessness and impotence flooded her conscious and semi-conscious mind. Why hadn't she listened to her father, who knew the family of old? She had had other suitors, but they had largely been warned off by her dad's menacing presence. The only other suitable boyfriend Flo had had was Jimmy Baines, whom she liked, but whose prospects didn't amount to much. He was an ordinary chap, was Jimmy: quiet, shy, unassuming and self-effacing, who really liked Flo a lot. So much so that he had just about plucked up enough courage to ask her to marry him when, seduced by Eric's sugary tongue, she announced her engagement to *him*.

Jimmy was devastated. Flo should have been the girl for him. He rued the day his bashfulness and lack of confidence robbed him of the girl of his dreams. Not one not to learn from his mistakes, he courted and married Elsie Jenkins the year after. The following year she gave him twin daughters, and he became undermanager at the local colliery. Deliriously happy, they moved into a large colliery house down Ash Gap Lane.

How could she have let him slip through her fingers?

She felt her husband move beside her as he gasped for breath. His inner alarm clock never failed to wake him at the appropriate time for his shift at the pit. His one act of decency had always been to try not to disturb her as he readied himself for work.

Like most men of his generation who worked in the local mines he breakfasted on a chunk of bread and butter and a mug of steaming tea, taking his snap of cheese and bread with a bottle of cold tea to be consumed halfway through his shift underground. This Flo always prepared the night before, and left in his snap tin on the cold stone shelf in the pantry.

Slipping his feet into his heavy pit clogs, and snecking the front door quietly behind him, he shuffled across the road to the stop to wait for the early pit bus. Still dark, the sullen glow from the gas street lamps formed faint puddles of light around their bases on the stone pavements. Within another couple of hours or so Albert Makepiece, the local lamplighter, would start his rounds to turn off the lights. It was his job, too, to knock up those workers who didn't possess that all-important inner clock.

Eric's pit mates acknowledged him with a nod and a grunt as they crouched in the Co-op doorway to escape the keen January breeze. Ridges of frozen slush on the road at the pavement's edge had gathered a clean white dusting of new snow, to herald a taste of what might yet fall before their next gathering. Same place, same time every morning shift: same place, different times for all the others.

Eric's mates gave him a cursory glance, nodded, and

looked down again, making no mention of his injuries. It was of no consequence to them. The only thing that concerned them was his ability to do his own shift so they could do theirs. No more, no less.

Flo heaved a sigh of relief on hearing the front door latch, turned over, and immediately fell asleep, knowing that she would need to be up a couple of hours later to set the fire and to prepare breakfast before the elder of her two skipped off to school. Little Jack shuffled in his crib by her side of the bed, still asleep, as he had been all night. William had been a mewling sort of a baby, who needed constant attention day and night. Jack, on the other hand, had slept through almost as soon as he had made this crib his own. He was a good baby, who consumed all the sustenance she offered without demur – breast milk, preparation feeds, rusks, whatever – and, as such, he was happy on it.

William had always been picky, and it had taken her a good deal of trial and error to find stuff he *would* eat. His favourite of all time was fish and chips from Colin Heald's Fish and Chip Emporium, at the end of their row, across the entrance to Goosehill Mount Road. That was a luxury she couldn't often afford for herself. The bairn got it regularly because it was one of the few meals on his menu. She rarely had them.

The scullery latch woke her, heralding William's visit to the toilet. An outside loo – at this time of year – encouraged him to hold on as long as he could. So it had to be urgent … Time to get him ready for school.

Woodhouse County Junior and Infant School was an imposing late Victorian/early Edwardian building which dominated a large stretch of road between Sen Garrett's sweet shop and post office and the clandestine bookie's on the opposite side of Wakefield Road, just a couple of hundred yards from number 206's front door. It boasted a large hall, separate entrances and playgrounds for girls and boys, and six spacious classrooms. The infant section occupied a separate building on the same site. With fields to three sides, and a new housing estate planned within eyeshot, it held an enviable position in the educational hierarchy of this bustling and prosperous mining town.

Being at the heart of the Yorkshire coalfield was the centre stone of this town's prosperity, but that success had come at a price. A whole forest of whining and interminably whirring pithead gearwheels had sprung up, surrounding the town entirely, periodically retrieving blackened workers from the bowels of the earth. In their turn they had spawned a wasteland of barren, grey slag heaps that provided a secondary line of defence against the ever-encroaching greenery of nature.

Like many others, this unprepossessing Yorkshire mining town – with its history in the Domesday Book and its roots in industrial Victorian provincial England – had grown in importance because of its geographical position and the foresight of its forefathers. The railway brought it further prosperity, as had the canals before it, making it singularly one of the most important hubs in the north of England.

"Breakfast's ready," Flo warned her offspring. "You don't want to be late for school."

"Coming, Mam," he called back. "What is it today?"

"Usual," she said, as he skipped through the scullery door after his wash and brush. The stone sink of warm water she had boiled for him to wash in would do for the breakfast pots as well. "Cornflakes, and bread and jam. OK?"

"Yep," he replied, tucking into his cereal. "We got PE today. I forgot to tell you."

"I know," she said, buttering his bread. "Your pumps and shorts are in your bag."

"How did you know that?" he asked, a gasp of surprise

ready to explode from his lungs.

"I'm your mother," she said. "It's my job to know everything. Home for lunch? Meat and potato pie and home-made bread do?"

"Yes, please," he enthused. "There's only one thing I like more than meat and potato pie."

"Oh, yes?" she said, eyebrows heralding surprise. "And what's that?"

"Two meat and potato pies," he laughed, pleased with himself.

"Ooh, 'ark at you," she smiled. "Since when did you have a sense of humour? One of your granddad's, I'll bet."

"How did you know that?" he said with a grin.

"Like I said," she explained. "I'm your mother, and…"

"I get it," William replied with a grin, pushing himself away from the table. "Half eight. Got to be off."

"Coat," she reminded him before he reached the front door. "Scarf and gloves."

"Yes, Mam," he yelled back just before shutting the door. "See you at lunchtime."

"Well, now," Flo said, once her son's echo had sneaked out after him, turning to her other little man. "Food, bath and change, I think, for you, Little Jack. I wonder how long it'll be before we call you Jack, and you're no longer little. Never mind. All in good time, eh?"

-o-

"Flo? Are you there?" a familiar voice shouted from the scullery door.

"Mam?" she replied. "That you? I'm in the kitchen, bathing our Little Jack. What brings you out on such a cold day?"

"Your dad's been barred from St John's Club," Marion replied, a note of anger edging her words.

"Dad? Barred?" Flo asked, not believing what she was hearing. "Why?"

"He thinks it was yon husband of yours as put the word in," Marion said, slumping into an easy chair by the fire.

"Eric?" Flo asked, a frown clouding her face. "What would he have to say that would make any difference? Dad's the secretary, for goodness' sake."

"Your dad – how shall we put it – had a word with him the other night. 'Private matter' is all I could get out of him," Marion said.

"Bloody face? Swollen mouth?" Flo added. "Now it all makes sense, but what's it to do with the club?"

"It happened on club property, apparently," Marion answered, "and yon bugger complained to the committee."

"Well, the…" Flo said. "I'm sorry, Mam, and I'm sorry for all the hard work Dad's done for that club."

"Not your fault, love," her mam answered. "It's probably done him a favour, anyway, because he's decided not to go back."

"Good for him," Flo agreed. "Serves 'em right. They don't deserve a good man like my dad."

"How's my Jack, then?" Marion switched, a smile creeping back into her face.

"Champion, really," Flo answered, happy to talk about her son all day, as she dried him off and put clean clothes on him. "I can't believe how strong he is."

"He's got a grand pair of legs on him," Marion said, pride swelling in her chest and taking her back to the time twenty-six years before when *her* Jack was in the same place. A tear of reminiscence welled in her eye corner, which she caught before it could start its dash down her cheek.

"Aw, Mam," Flo whispered softly, as she clasped her to her chest. "I think about him a lot, too. I can't imagine what it would be like if I lost my Jack. I'd be heartbroken. It was bad enough with *our* Jack."

They hugged each other for a few moments, while the baby – a contented child for whom, at that precise moment, the world was a perfect place – gurgled and kicked happily in his crib.

"Do you feel like a walk down to ours for a spot of lunch?" Marion asked. "It would be nice to have Jack there for a bit."

"Can't, really," Flo said. "William's coming home for his dinner. I promised him meat and potato pie."

"Bring it down," her mother suggested. "We could call off at school on the way and ask them to send him to our house. It would be good to have them together for a bit. What do you say?"

"Go on, then," Flo agreed. "It's still only early, and Jack can have his nap at yours as well as here. *He* won't be home until mid afternoon, so that gives us plenty of time."

By the time they had reached Marion and Jud's home on Church Lane, only a ten-minute walk away, the wind had freshened and was dropping larger flecks of snow. Although it had turned the pavements and roads to white, they didn't remain white for long because of the traffic on both. Mother and child were well wrapped against the bitter cold, but were still happy to see Marion's front door.

"Will Dad say anything more about the club?" Flo asked once all were inside and the door was locked against the winter cold.

"To whom?" her mother asked, shrugging her shoulders in resignation. "He won't say anything to the committee, because he's not going back. And to your husband? It's hardly likely. You know your dad. If he loses it, he'll kill him. No, it's best to let things lie. It's not important any more, anyway."

"I do wish he didn't have to be like this," Flo sighed. "Things could be so much better if he wasn't."

"Shall you be voting for that Alf Roberts again this

coming May?" Flo asked, sliding easily into a different subject.

"Alf Roberts?" Marion repeated. "No fear. Your dad knows the whole clan – is there anyone he *doesn't* know? – and *he* says they're all tarred wi' t' same brush. If his party put up a donkey for election folks round here would vote for it, yer dad says. He's decided he's had enough of successive governments' shenanigans. Mark his words, he says, they'll bring the colliers down in a few years, and then where will we all be? How about a nice cuppa, lass?"

Mother and daughter had always been comfortable in each other's company ... more like two halves of the same, really. Where one started the other always continued ... an easy relationship.

"It looks like we're in for it," Marion observed as she waited for the kettle to boil in her little kitchenette. "Snow's thickening, and it looks wicked out there."

"Aye," Flo answered, "but it's nice and cosy in here. Your house is so much warmer than mine."

"It's all to do wi' doors and windows, you see," Marion went on, mashing the tea, "and thicker curtains. I always said…"

Her voice faded away as the sky darkened and flurries of thicker flakes quickened and swept across an already frozen industrial landscape. Few hardy souls ventured out, even to the corner shops to restock pantries or to fetch essentials forgotten in earlier hurried forays, like bread, slabs of butter, or Woodbines. It was going to be snowy and cold for quite some time to come. They could all feel it in their collective bones.

Chapter 3

"I just can't believe how time has gone on," Flo said to her neighbour, Ada Gittins, as she hung her washing across the yard. "Four months since our Jack's first birthday, and now look at him."

"Never," Ada replied. "You could take him for three any day. I don't know … how do they get to be so big so quickly?"

"Good food, Ada, though I don't know where he gets it," Flo said, bursting into a good-humoured guffaw, which her neighbour shared.

"And your William?" Ada asked. "How's he getting on?"

"Good, I think," Flo replied. "Just waiting for his scholarship results, you know, for the grammar school."

"Same here," Ada added. "Our Peter's having eggs waiting to see if he's passed. I think that's somebody at your front door, Flo."

"Oh, 'eck," Flo exclaimed, scattering her pegs in her surprise. "Who can that be? Rent man's not due for another couple of days, so I don't have to crack on I'm not in. See you in a bit, Ada."

"All right … I'm coming," Flo shouted as she rushed through the front room to the rattling of the door again.

"Don't get your … Mr Tomlinson—" Flo said abruptly, rearranging her tone as she opened the door to William's head teacher. "What brings you here, in your holiday too? Please come in… Can I get—?"

"Thank you, Mrs Ingles, no," he said, seeming a little out of breath. "I've a lot of calls to make today. Another time, perhaps. Just wanted to let you know your William has passed his scholarship for the grammar school, and to ask if he will be taking up his place in September."

"Oh, my gawd," she replied, flummoxed and throwing her pinny in the air. "Is the Pope Catholic? Yes, please. Of course he will, no matter what his father says. Thank you."

"No need to thank me, Mrs Ingles," he replied, a smile of satisfaction and relief crossing his face. "It's all due to William's hard work and to your undoubted support, I'm sure. Could I ask if you know whether Mrs Gittins is home?"

"Yes, she is," Flo assured him. "She's out in the yard. Come through: it's much easier. You'll never find your way otherwise."

"So kind," he answered a little nervously. "If you're sure…"

She left him at the back door talking to Ada, who by this time had assumed her usual stance: hands on hips and head jutted slightly forward. She was a card, that Ada Gittins. Always had a laugh and a friendly piece of advice, which usually spun around not getting mixed up with married men.

Her shrill scream rattled the back window sash, making Flo almost drop her kettle. Spinning on her heels, she saw Ada waving her hands wildly in the air, and Mr Tomlinson beating a hasty retreat towards the snicket in the middle of the row.

"What is it, Ada?" Flo asked, an alarmed frown jumping into her face. "What's he said?"

"He's only gone and bloody well passed," Ada screeched again.

"Who?" Flo asked again. "Mr Tomlinson?"

"No," Ada shouted, grabbing her friend and starting a jig

in among the streams of washing. "Our bloody Peter. He's only gone and passed his bloody scholarship. Starts at the grammar school September."

"Our William too," Flo joined in the screech. "I think this calls for a celebration. Cup of tea, love?"

"Too bloody right," Ada agreed readily. "And I think the occasion calls for a digestive too. Don't you?"

"Have you ever thought," Ada continued, dipping her biscuit into her tea, "how we're going to afford all this? Lovely cup of tea, by the way, dear."

"Rob a bank, happence?" Flo replied. "My Co-op divvy won't cover uniforms and stuff, I know. Can't ask Eric, because he's dead set against either of my two getting a grammar school education. Waste of time, 'e says. Going down the pit, 'e says. Over your dead bloody body, I says to 'im. They're both going. Now the first's there, that only takes one more. I'll get the money if it's the last thing I do. My dad'll help, I'm sure."

"Any more of those biscuits, Flo?" Ada mumbled through a soggy mouthful. "They're very nice. My 'Arry says my two are welcome to it ... as long as they can afford to pay for it. Mine's as big an arsehole as yours, but 'e won't have a say where t' education of them two lads is concerned. They're both going, and that's an end to it, or 'e'll feel my rolling pin across 'is 'ead."

"Good for you, Ada," Flo agreed. "And can I borrow it when you've finished with it? Yours is bigger than mine."

They burst into fits of laughter again at the pictures they had just created, pouring themselves another cup of tea to celebrate.

"Mam!" William's shrill voice interrupted Flo and Ada's five minutes of peace and quiet. "Mam, you in? Can Peter and me—?"

"In here, love," Flo replied. "Come on through. We've got

something to tell you both."

"Both?" William said to Peter. "*We've…?*"

"Mam?" Peter puzzled as the lads shouldered their way into the kitchen. "What are you doing here? What do you want to tell us?"

-o-

In common with most of his mining pals, Eric Ingles wasn't such a good father generally: too selfish, and busy with other things in his life. He wasn't a good husband, either. Most women in Flo's position accepted the status quo that generations before her had bequeathed to her the lot she had to manage. At worst a war of attrition, at best an uneasy truce, her life gave her much less than she expected or felt she deserved. It could have been so much better, but not much worse. Yet the physical violence he often threatened never seemed to materialise. "All mouth and no trousers," her mam used to say, which was as low as he could be in her estimation.

Being a coal hewer at Sharlston Colliery brought its rewards: a very good wage, and four tons of free coal every year. Consequently heating and lighting were minimal drains, from which household coffers found it easy to recover. It did have its slight drawbacks, however. Safety measures below ground weren't as well developed as they might have been, which often resulted in maiming or death. These were ever-present dangers, which were never talked about. They were facts of their working life, which were always there as an accepted risk.

For all his faults, Eric Ingles loved his firstborn, in his own way … perhaps not love in the accepted sense, but a deep regard for the intellect his son displayed, which he could never aspire to. He wondered at some of the stuff William knew or could perform, though he would never admit to it.

Eric never gave anything away willingly, perhaps feeling that his family, including his wife, should have to work for a slice of what he had spent forty hours or more in a black hole a thousand feet below ground to earn. He got a good deal of perverse satisfaction from that knowledge. Only ... William, much to his father's disappointment, never questioned his father's authority. If Eric said 'no', that was always good enough for his son. As far as William was concerned 'no' never meant 'maybe', and he would never revisit his father's decisions.

Eric, of course, couldn't revisit them either. He always had to find other ways to give his lad what he needed, which sometimes taxed both his ingenuity and his creativity. He often wished he could explain things about money to William, and then give him what he had asked for and so obviously needed. He knew his son's demands were never unreasonable or born of a whim, but his philosophy was too entrenched to change at this time in his life. Or was it?

"Mam?" William asked at breakfast during his last couple of weeks at junior school. "My class is going on a trip during the last week of term to Llandudno, and ... I wondered if I could go?"

"What does it cost, love?" she asked as she packed his sports kit into his bag. "If I can afford it, I'll give it to you when I get my housekeeping from your dad."

"I've got a note here from Mr Hardwick," he said, digging a screwed-up scrap of paper from his pocket.

"That's a lot of money," she sighed, not wishing to disappoint him. "And I really haven't got it."

"OK," he replied, accepting what he knew to be the case. "It's just that ... I'll be the only one not going."

"Look," she offered. "Why don't you ask your dad? You never know..."

"I already did," he said, looking down at his porridge.

"He said 'no'."

"Why don't you ask him again?" she ventured. "He's on afternoons this week, and I can hear his boots on the stairs now."

"I don't know," he hesitated.

"Just ask," she urged. "It might be your lucky day."

"Just ask what?" Eric said, as he snecked the stairs door behind him.

"Well," William gulped, "you know I asked you if I could go on the school trip before we finished for the summer, and you said 'no'? Well, I'll be the only one left in our class if I can't go. I know…"

"Tha knows it's a goodly amount of brass, right?" Eric started. "And tha knows I don't 'old wi' such frivolities, as isn't necessary? But … now 'ere's the thing … if tha agrees to 'elp me wi' fetching t' coal in when next it's delivered, tha can go."

"Really?" William said, excitement jumping out of him. "Thanks, Dad."

He leaped from the table and headed for the scullery to brush his teeth.

"Tha'll be needing this, then," Eric reminded him, holding out his hand to reveal a bright new white five pound note. William took hold of it gingerly, a look of awed surprise on his face.

"Anything left from t' cost o' trip…" his dad said, "tha can have for spending money."

"Dad," William shouted, joy overcoming him as he threw his arms around his dad's resisting neck.

"Na, then," Eric warned, not given to such wanton displays of affection. "Steady on. And remember the deal … plus … bring thi mam a stick o' rock back, and a sugar dummy for yon bairn."

That sealed it. His dad *was* the best.

-o-

Summer dominated life in the West Riding. Usually cold in the extreme from November through to the end of January, with a touch of chill until just after Easter, the warmer months were a goal for planning most outdoor activities for the majority of families. Mid June through to late September was the time most people lived for. It was a lifesaver for most mothers of school-age children that the long holiday fell in the middle of this time of plenty. Most young mothers didn't work, considering looking after and bringing up growing youngsters a full-time, unpaid – sometimes thankless – job. Summer was the time *they* could relax a little and enjoy the outdoors, although their burrowing menfolk still had to shut themselves away in the dark, courting danger and fatigue for most of the day, even they were drawn out by the sun and its re-enlivening warmth.

Youngsters loved it. They were at last allowed the freedom to explore, to play, and to be children in an area surrounded by open country and a large grassy central park. Haw Hill Park was immense, serving a growing population of around twenty thousand – of which you could be forgiven for thinking, in the summer, that the majority was under thirteen.

Few of these children had watches, but they all knew when lunch or tea was on the table. William spent most of his days here with his friends. Flo, on the other hand, spent quite a bit of her time at her mam's, largely because she had a back garden with a lawn. This, of course, was heaven for her, with a young, increasingly mobile child, whom she could keep her eyes on and allow to stretch his chubby limbs. The warm weather even seemed to lift her husband's spirits, making him less bombastic and less inclined to drink himself into oblivion. They even spent a small amount of time together.

"I've been thinking," he mused one Saturday afternoon midway through July, as they shared a pot of tea in the backyard.

"Shall I call a doctor?" Flo jibed playfully, which he ignored. His non-response to her funny retort had persuaded her that either he didn't understand her sense of humour or *he* didn't possess one of his own at all.

"No," he replied, deadpan. "Don't you think it's abaht time we had a family holiday? You know, somewhere where there's a bit of sand and sea to paddle in?"

"You serious?" she replied, quite taken aback by the look on his face. "But we don't have the money, surely? And…"

"I've done some extra shifts lately," he went on, "and so we should have enough for a week away. Our Harold's brother-in-law has a caravan at Brid which he lets out during t' summer. I'm sure we could get it cheaper. What do you think?"

"T' bairns would love it," she enthused. "I'm sure we'd love to go, but only on condition it's not going to be a drinking excuse."

"Course not," he agreed. "It'd be a chance for us to 'ave a bit of fun as a family for once."

"Go on, then," she smiled. "When?"

"I thought end of this month or beginning of t' next?" he offered.

"You've got it all planned, 'aven't you?" she laughed. "You owd bugger."

She leaned across and kissed him on the cheek.

"Eh up," he warned, laughing. "None o' that. Don't think you can take advantage."

So he did have a sense of humour, in his own way.

-o-

Bridlington was the east coast choice of holiday destination for most Yorkshire folk – except for those on the far reaches of the West Riding, who preferred Blackpool and Morecambe.

There was a time in the fifties when Morecambe was thought to be an outpost of Yorkshire during August because so many folk joined the mass migration west.

Stationary caravans in East Riding resorts like Bridlington and Scarborough were a cheaper and more popular option to boarding houses for many of the West Riding's working masses. A week in the sun somewhere you could paddle or build sandcastles turned an ordinary geological feature into a wonderland to be explored from morning to night.

Eric's brother Harold had mentioned it to him in passing a short while before – and, in one of his rarer moments of magnanimity – he felt that *that* could be what they needed as a family. He had already settled upon and booked Saturday to Saturday in the third week without telling Flo, making it seem as if she had had the final say-so as to the ultimate destination and time. This was a clever ploy he often used, but one which Flo never tumbled to in all the years she knew him. Although she thought she had worked out what motivated him, she never really got down to understanding what made him tick.

How were they to get there?

"Nowt wrong wi' t' train," Eric answered confidently. "There's one early on. Gets us there by dinner, in time for fish and chips, tea, and bread and butter at Swaleses."

"Swaleses?" Flo said, puzzled, sure he was making it up. "Since when did you know about 'Swaleses'? Never heard of it."

"Ah, well, tha sees…" he began, "I've been to Brid before, long before I knew you, and I believe Swaleses is an old family chip shop with a sit-down part, where you can sit and … eat."

"But," she went on again, "when was the last time we had fish and chips together? Anyway, you don't like fish and chips."

"Ah, but I do," he insisted. "When they're good fish and chips, there's nowt like 'em."

"You won't have them from our local," she argued.

"Well, Colin Heald's are nowt like good fish and chips," he said firmly.

At this point their discussion would usually have descended to a slanging match, where they wouldn't have spoken for days, but now ... it didn't. Did this herald a new era in relations between them? Or was it as a result of holiday euphoria that neither seemed to want to take the bait?

"Then fish and chips it is, at Swaleses of Bridlington," Flo chanted. "Can I assume you've booked the train tickets?"

"Aye, I have that," he said, pulling a fistful of railway tickets from his weskit pocket. "And that's what tha calls organisation. Next Saturday, half past eight."

He delivered this last pronouncement with a growing smile, which was alien for him, but an alien she could put up with. This was going to be the best holiday they'd had. It was also going to be the *only* holiday they'd had.

-o-

"Are we there yet, Dad?" William chimed, as the train pulled into York. He had never been on a train before. The excitement of being pulled by a steam engine which belched out a stream of white smoke clouds, and the tickety-tack tickety-tack rattle of iron wheels across plate-jointed rails, kept him on the edge of his seat forever. He had, of course, been to the seaside already this summer by coach with the school, but the Great Orme and the Little Orme of Llandudno were no match for a *week* at a proper seaside in Yorkshire. Bridlington ... how could you compete with that?

His dad had told him about the *Yorkshireman*, a seagoing tug which had been converted to carry passengers on days out. He couldn't wait for that. Nor could he imagine how wonderful it might be to paddle in the sea. He had been to the swimming baths with school before, but ... the sea. Wow.

"How many times have I to tell thee?" his dad said to him, trying unsuccessfully to keep his overexcitement in check. He wanted the lad to enjoy himself, but such an overzealous attitude could only end in tears. He hoped his lad *would* enjoy the experience. He had never got the chance when he was a lad himself. *His* father refused to spend anything on him or his brothers and sister. Harold, Allan and Blanche neither complained nor even talked about it, but *he* knew. Why wasn't *his* dad like other dads? Why couldn't *they* go to the seaside? They weren't short of money, so why? It was the eternal question, for which there were no earthly answers.

"How long now, Dad?" William insisted again, as the train rattled out of York station.

"Na see thee here, lad," Eric warned him again, "either settle down or..."

"Would you like a cheese sandwich and some pop?" Flo butted in, seeing her husband's ire growing at William's insistence. "If you settle and have a bite – and watch the countryside whizzing by – by the time you finish we'll be nearly there. No gobbling, mind. Come and sit here, and talk to Little Jack a bit. He's just woken up."

"OK," William agreed. "I *am* hungry and thirsty."

"Not surprising," his father added. "Thy hardly had any of thi breakfast at all."

"Look who's talking," Flo butted in. "Bread and butter and a mug of tea?"

"Shows how much notice tha tecks," he replied, a bit of an edge to his words. "It's what I have every time before I go to work when I'm on mornings. Force of habit."

"Sorry," she said, realising she'd been a bit sharp with him. She appreciated full well that he always tried not to disturb her, when *she* should have been up getting *him* off.

"Bit thoughtless on my part."

"It's all rayt," he nodded. "Don't worry abaht it. Soon be there, our William. See t' seagulls waving at thee? Ower there. See?"

"Waving at *me*?" William asked through a mouthful of home-made bread and cheese, and scanning the skies through the smokestack's billowing clouds. "Where?"

His dad started to chuckle wickedly. "Got thee *then*," he said, making his son smile.

"Look," William gasped, "through those hills. I think I can see—"

"The sea at last," his mother assured him. "This must be Bridlington by the Sea, Eric, mustn't it?"

"Aye, it is that," her husband agreed. "And that, my boy, is the North Sea. I learned that when *I* was at school."

"In t' last century, was it Dad?" William laughed, pleased with his funny.

"Cheeky little bugger," his dad laughed, secretly quite proud that his son was as sharp as that. *He* knew very well that the pit wouldn't be for his son. He knew he'd go on to better things in his life than burrowing through the earth, like a giant mole seeking his plunder. He just wanted him to appreciate that he *could*, with his dad's support.

"Are we there yet, Dad?" William laughed, the excitement of his first stay in a caravan in a caravan park in a Yorkshire seaside resort in July overtaking him. Struggling with his suitcase, he tried to keep up with his dad – who was managing two cases – and his mum, who had his brother, Little Jack, in a pushchair.

The caravan park was amazing. There must have been fifty vans of many different sorts, with little doors, even smaller windows, and tiny net curtains to cover what was inside.

"But there aren't any beds," William gasped once inside.

"And it smells a bit musty."

"I'll show you where the beds are when it's time to sleep," Dad said, sounding like someone who knew what he was doing. He had to think on his feet fast so as not to appear stupid. The last caravan he had stayed in was very different, very much older, and a long time ago.

'How different must it be?' he thought, looking around desperately, trying to find clues. He did work it out – with a little help from Flo – and finally sat down with a bump, relieved that the sleeping arrangements were now beyond question.

"Now, then," Eric declared, "time for fish, chips, tea, and bread and butter. Anybody with me?"

"Yeah," William cheered, to the amusement of his mam and the agreement of his father. Little Jack's 'a' sealed the deal, and they all trooped out of the park to find Swaleses.

-o-

That holiday signalled the high point in both the lives of the Ingles family and the relationship of Flo and Eric. Little did they know, as they enjoyed their week in Bridlington by the Sea, that it wouldn't be long before deterioration set in and quickened, leaving their marriage nowhere to go.

Chapter 4

The Ingles family had never been big on celebrating birthdays, something which was to stay with William all his life. Eric and Flo never exchanged either gifts or cards at birthday and anniversary time, mainly because of cost – but partly because Eric could never remember, and Flo preferred to forget. Their children never missed the rituals much because they hadn't been brought up to place too much emphasis on them. They had presents, yes, but not especially memorable ones.

Little Jack's fourth birthday came … and went, uncelebrated except for the usual 'Happy Birthday, Jack', and a special tea from Flo. As he ate most things there wasn't anything she could have done which could have marked this day as something different from any other. Because of its proximity to Christmas Eric had decided it would be expedient to combine the two. So Jack enjoyed a 'double' celebration with combined presents, along with all the special fare. It wasn't a double celebration at all, however. It was simply a cynical excuse not to have to spend good money on presents Eric considered to be unnecessary. This was to become the norm throughout Jack's childhood, where his dad had seen an opportunity to save money at his son's expense because of an accident of birth timing.

Each of Jack's birthdays in early January had been remarkable because of the weather. Cold, snowy and dull, it urged a day indoors – relaxed – with feet up. Only Flo, being a fully-functioning mother of two youngish bairns, could never relax or put *her* feet up. Not one day passed without her doing something for her family. For her children this was usually a pleasure. Not so for her husband. His behaviour had reverted slowly to type: boorish, morose, sarcastic, unresponsive, and given more to going to his working men's club alone. And they were just the better days.

Although ever optimistic, Flo hadn't noticed the gradual slide towards his former behaviour until it was obvious. To be fair, she was a full-time fully paid-up mum, who devoted her life to her children's upbringing and education in their widest terms. Whether her husband – like so many others of his type – had felt increasingly left out, abandoned, or ignored, was open to conjecture and speculation. Unlike many others of his generation, however, he felt unable to cope, which pushed him towards isolation, bouts of drinking … and Dotty French.

Dotty French had held a secret torch for Eric Ingles ever since their time at Dodsworth Junior School, when a precocious childish crush had grabbed her in Class Four. This fascination gripped her more tightly throughout secondary school and into early adulthood, when she fell pregnant by Eric but lost the baby within a few weeks of conception. Ignorant that she carried his child, they drifted apart, and he met Flo Morley.

Feeling that now might be her time, Dotty 'accidentally' bumped into Eric as he climbed the hill to his club shortly after Little Jack's fourth birthday. Their meeting lasted moments, but her clever little seed had been sown. All *she* had to do was provide sunlight and warmth, and stand back to watch it grow.

"Mam?" Little Jack asked through a mouthful of his bread and jam, over lunchtime.

"What is it?" she said, emerging from the scullery, wiping her sudsy hands on her pinny. "Your eternal questions will make my head burst one of these days. Can't you ask your brother? Where *is* William?"

"Gone out," Jack replied without looking up.

"What? In this weather?" she snapped. "He'll catch his death."

"Said he was calling for Peter, and they had to go somewhere," Jack mumbled.

"Where?" she asked, not really needing an answer.

"Don't know," he said. "I asked if I could come, but he said I was too young."

Flo smiled and returned to her washing.

"Mam?" Jack shouted five minutes later.

"Yes, love, what is it this time?" she said, sighing, as she returned to the scene of food devastation on the table.

"Why is it always cold and rainy on my birthday?" he asked deliberately. "And why don't I get presents like Gordon Gittins next door, and Allan Smith the other side, and Allwyn—?"

"OK," she interrupted sharply, "I get the picture."

She took a sharp intake of breath, pulled out a chair next to him, and looked into his steadfast gaze. She had never seen such deep eyes before, feeling it was almost like looking into his soul.

"Well," she started, "it's always this sort of weather at this time of year. It's called winter, and that's when you were born. Besides, your granddad always says that whatever weather greets you on the day you are born will always share future birthdays with you."

"Granddad always says funny things," he replied, honest and insightful as ever. "And so far it's true."

Flo looked at her little son, brows slightly raised, always astounded at his perceived wisdom for one so young. He was one of the calmest and quietest children she had ever known, where nothing seemed to faze him – except for when his father came into the room. When *he* was there Jack never spoke, never took his eyes from him, seeming to want to shrink into invisibility until *he* left. Only then did Little Jack breathe out softly, almost with relief that he hadn't been noticed.

Eric's feelings about the boy hadn't changed, despite having tried to rationalise them in his own way. Even if Jack *was* his he felt he must have been a throwback to a previous generation, and he could experience no feelings for him at all. This confused his simple mind (where sons took after their fathers in all aspects) significantly. As far as he was concerned the child's mother had the easy job. All she had to do was bear the infant, and make sure he was fed and cleansed regularly.

"I know I'm supposed to be going into the nursery soon," Jack said as he eased himself from the table.

"Yes, love, you are," Flo said calmly. "Is there something bothering you about it?"

"Well," he started slowly, brows knitting in deep concentration, "do I have to go in this weather? I mean, you know I don't like snow and cold, and…"

"You don't have to go anywhere just yet, silly," she reassured him. "In a few weeks, after Easter, when it's a bit warmer. You'll enjoy it then."

"Did you go to nursery, Mam?" he asked.

"Well … not really," she replied, stumped by his question.

"Then, how can you *know* I'm going to enjoy it?" he continued simply, his deep green eyes filling her mind with doubts. How could this … this four-year-old have such depths of thought so far beyond his years? She knew her husband had doubts about his origins, but even she was beginning to wonder if he was a changeling. She knew in her heart he *was* hers, but what she didn't know was how far back in *her* family line he stretched. Heredity was a powerful concept. Knowing Little Jack hadn't inherited from his father's stagnant gene pool made her all the more wary about how deep his own pool was.

"I don't really know, love," she answered, deciding honesty was the only way. "I just think you will. Anyway, Gordon Gittins is already there, and his mam says he loves it. They do all sorts of interesting things that you can't do at home, she says."

"But," he insisted, "how do you know *I'll* enjoy them too?"

"You'll just have to suck it and see," she insisted.

"Suck what and see?" he asked again, after a moment or two's deliberation. "Do we get sweets as well, for going?"

"No," she sighed. "It's just a saying. It means you'll have to see whether you like it or not."

"And if I don't?" he added.

"You're going, anyway," she insisted. "It's the big school soon after, and you *have* to go there, so you might as well get used to it."

End of discussion.

Jack was quiet for quite some time as he played with his toys on the clip rug in front of the hearth. Flo stood at the kitchen table finishing off the remains of last week's ironing, the black metal of the spare flat iron glowing sullenly in the fire grate close to the hot embers that would give it life. She wondered about her little boy. How would he cope among the other rougher children, what with his incessantly inquisitive mind that sought answers which seemed to question authority itself? She knew instinctively there *was* no questioning of authority, but she felt that the way he sought those answers might be misconstrued and, consequently, might antagonise. If only she could explain to them what he was like: that he was a good, obedient boy, who wouldn't cause them a moment's trouble.

The front door latch rattled ominously. Little Jack froze in mid play, his wary eyes sliding towards the middle door. Two choices: it was either his brother coming in for tea or his father returning from the pit after his shift at the coalface. He knew it wouldn't be his brother, because he always came in at the back. So it had to be...

"This bloody weather," Eric grumbled as he burst through the door, and, stumbling forward, he collapsed into his chair.

"You're early," Flo shouted from the scullery, as she tidied away her irons and ironing basket. He grunted as his clogs clattered to the floor.

"You all right?" she asked, coming back into the kitchen. "Bloody 'ell. What's happened to you?"

The shock at seeing the state her husband was in frightened Jack, who crawled out of the way, whimpering softly.

"Where's your coal muck?" she gasped. "And that bloody bandage on your head. What's going on?"

"New showers at t' pithead," he muttered, head in hands.

"I gathered there'd been a change in bathing arrangements," she added caustically, "but it's the bandage I'm asking about. Well?"

"There was a roof fall towards end of t' shift," he answered quietly, "and I hit me head. It's nowt much. Just a scratch."

"'Ang on a bit," she said more forcefully. "Me dad's on your shift: your gang. Right?"

He didn't answer.

"Well?" she insisted, one of her flat irons still in her clenched fist. "Was me dad involved? Is he all right? So 'elp me, Eric Ingles, if you don't speak to me, tha'll 'ave need o' yon bandage."

"Yer dad were caught," he muttered. "Buried along wi' ten others. They're diggin' 'em out now."

"Oh, my God," she shouted, dropping the iron on to the floor. Tearing off her pinny and reaching for her coat, boots and headscarf, she lurched for the door.

"Look after t 'bairn," she ordered. "I'm off to tell me mam."

"I'm not looking after 'im," he shouted back. "I'm off to t' club. Tha'll have to look after 'im thissen or teck 'im wi' thi."

"Mam," William's shrill voice burst in as the back door slammed shut. "I'm back. What's for tea? I'm starving."

"You'll have to see to your brother," his dad said. "I've got to go out. Your mam'll be back shortly. Get summat to eat out o' the pantry, to put thee on," his dad told him. "Thi mam'll get thee something when she gets back."

"Where's she gone?" William asked, puzzled and concerned that neither of his parents was going to be in. And what about *his* tea? The front door slammed and snecked itself, and the explanation he sought stayed within.

"Well, our Jack," William said, matter-of-factly, "we'll just have to make do until our mam gets back, though goodness knows where she's gone. Bread and jam sandwich OK?"

"Yes, please," Jack answered, finally breathing a sigh of relief and venturing a smile once he was sure his father had gone. "My fav … fayvr … I like it best."

-o-

"Dad," Flo said quietly as she sat by Jud's bed in Pinderfields Hospital. His black, sunken eyes were all that could be seen of his face, which was swathed in a sea of hospital-yellow bandages. Tufts of iron-grey hair poked here and there through chinks in this haphazardly wrapped dressing.

"Dad," she urged gently. "Can you hear me? It's me, Flo.

Me mam's here as well."

His eyes flickered and opened slowly, to close again, waves of pain dictating his levels of consciousness and response.

"Eric couldn't come," she went on. "He's—"

"Don't thee *ever* mention that bastard's name in my presence again," he groaned, eyes flashing open for an instant, exhaustion closing them almost immediately.

"I don't understand," Flo said quietly, a profoundly puzzled look descending upon her as she turned to her mother.

A harshly guttural voice flooded the room and said,

"Probably because yon bloody 'usband o' thine was the cause of all this."

"Who are *you*?" Flo asked, jerking around to face this new assailant.

"It's Alf Todd," Marion butted in, "one of your dad's oldest friends…"

"And his workmate," Alf added respectfully. "I were one o' the lucky ones. Them of us who lived owe our lives to this man here. He saw what was wrong in an instant when t' weight came on, scattered us, and took the full brunt himself. We're lucky most of us were only slightly injured, and only a few ended in here. He's a hero, he is. Deserves a medal for what he did. I'm only sorry we couldn't save Big Joe."

"Sorry," another – much gentler – voice interrupted, "you'll have to leave now. Mr Holmes has to be prepared for theatre. There are a lot of internal injuries and bleeding that have to be attended to."

"Theatre?" Marion said, a sharp note of panic edging her voice. "What do you mean, 'theatre'?"

"He needs an operation to make him better, Mam," Flo assured, as she ushered her out of the ward.

"I think it would be better if you all went home," the theatre nurse advised them. "Can we can contact you?"

"Contact?" Marion said, rounding on the nurse. "You bloody well won't. I've had enough of your 'contacts' to last me a lifetime. I'm staying here."

"But ... you can't," the nurse protested.

"Oh, yes, they can," the quietly authoritative voice of the ward sister intervened. "They can stay in the visitors' day room, nurse, for as long as they need to. I'll take them there now."

"What about your bairns?" Marion asked Flo, concern overcoming her.

"I've arranged for Ada Gittins to have them until I get back," Flo answered, once she'd settled her mam into a chair and brought her a cup of tea. "They'll be all right. Their father'll be at his club, where he can rot for all I care."

She turned towards Alf Todd and said,

"What did you mean when you said my husband was the cause? How was he the cause of that terrible roof fall that nearly killed me dad?"

"I don't want to speak out of turn, missus," Alf replied, uncomfortable he had been put on the spot, "but…"

"I'm sure what you have to say, Alf, won't leave these four walls," Marion assured him. "Come on, now. I think you owe it to my Jud."

"Eric Ingles is responsible on all our shifts for making sure the roof props are fixed and firm, which can give us the maximum warning of a possible collapse should weight come on," Alf started. "I think it's enough to say that he didn't do that job as it should have been done."

"And how do you know that?" Flo asked.

"I've worked down this colliery wi' Jud here for forty years or more," Alf assured them, "and I can tell thee when mistakes have been made. And, believe me, there've been many over t' years. This was a 'mistake' as shouldn't have happened."

"Are you saying it was deliberate, then?" Flo asked, becoming more and more disquieted.

"I'm saying no more," Alf said sharply. "You can draw your own conclusions. Management will niver find anything. They don't have either the will or the incentive to have a full enquiry."

"So if it's true," Flo pressed again, "he'll get away with it?"

"We have our own ways of sorting stuff out," Alf finished. "Look, I'll have to go now … back at work tomorrow. I'll call in when he's out of theatre. All right, Marion?"

"Is he likely to be at club, do you think, Alf?" Flo asked finally.

"Aye," he replied, as he turned to the door, "or wi'—"

"With?" Flo turned, eyes flashing.

"I've said too much already," he replied, face reddening as he strode out of the room.

"But—" Flo shouted, to be cut off by the door slamming and the rapidly disappearing rattle of his pit clogs on the marble floor as he beat a hasty retreat.

Flo and Marion looked at each other, aghast and dumbfounded at what they had been witness to.

"Go on then," Flo said. "Say it."

"Say what, love?" Marion replied. "What yon gets up to is none of my affair unless it affects me and mine. My only concern right now is for that good man in there. And I don't know whether I'll be taking him home any time soon … if at all."

"It's late, Mam," Flo said as they both nodded in the visitors' day room, "and those chairs are hard. I think we ought to go home and come back tomorrow. We can't do any good here without being able to wash and clean up. Besides, I need to see to my lads. They'll be wondering what on earth's happening. 'E won't have told them anything, and I can't rely on 'im to see to them. I've got to go home."

"Aye, lass," Marion agreed. "Your Dad'll be out for quite some time, and we can't do anything here. I think we both need a proper sleep as well. No buses at this time, though."

"It's OK," Flo assured her. "I've arranged for Mr Lee to pick us up."

"What, Mr Lee the taxi man?" Marion asked. "Won't he be expensive?"

"Not really," her daughter said, slipping on her coat. "I was at school with their Theresa, and did some babysitting with their Alice when they needed to get away. I *will* pay him, but for the very odd occasion he does it at cost."

"It shouldn't be too busy at this time," Marion said, stifling a yawn.

The first minute or so in the night air woke them up and refreshed their lethargic and jaded senses. Too much longer, and glaciation would set in – lips turning blue, ears beginning to ache, and losing sensation in fingers and feet. Mr Lee pulled into the hospital car park just as discomfort in the cold began to surround them.

-o-

"I'd best be off," he said, tightening his belt. "They'll be back soon, and I need to be there as if nowt's happened."

"You can stay a bit longer, can't you?" she replied, straightening the bedclothes and patting his still-warm side of the bed. "I was just getting … comfortable."

He could make out every detail of her slim, firm body under the single white sheet inviting him back to revisit her warmth and comfort. They had known each other for many years, since junior school, and had been here before. Only last time their encounter was a one-off fumble in the local park after hours, when they were scarcely out of childhood. This time she wasn't about to let him slip through her fingers. His wife would never understand what they felt for each other, and *she* was under no illusion what it would take to keep him. She was prepared for all that. She had waited almost fifteen years for this moment, developing her allure so that the way into her affection wouldn't also be the way out.

"I really will have to be away this time," he insisted, dragging his trousers back on again, and sliding his warm feet into his unwelcomingly cold pit clogs. "We have to be more careful from now on. I don't want things to become … complicated, just yet. I've one or two things to sort out, a few more scores to settle, and then… I'll si thi later."

A clatter of clogs on the wooden stairs, a quiet click of the back door latch, and he was gone. She smiled, patting her unnoticeably rounding belly gently, and thinking about the time when *he* would be *hers*.

Chapter 5

"Jack Ingles, would you come here please?" the head teacher's strident voice echoed across the nursery school playground.

A quiet huskiness crept upon her from behind.

"Yes, Miss Cordle."

"Oh," she gasped, turning around sharply. "You startled me."

"Sorry, Miss Cordle," he replied. "I didn't mean to."

"Do you know," she said earnestly, taking his proffered hand, "you are about the politest little boy I've ever had the pleasure to meet?"

"Thank you, Miss Cordle," he replied, walking with her back into the building. "Where are we going?"

"We're just going to my office to do a little reading test," she answered, a smile lighting their way.

"Why?" he asked, genuinely intrigued as to why she needed to test his reading when she knew he could read. Although there were precious few books at home appropriate to his intellectual and chronological needs, somehow he had picked up enough incidentally to show his worth. It wasn't often Miss Cordle came across a youngster with such untapped potential that she could recommend his jumping into the lower ranks of the junior section. Class One's teacher, Mrs Gunn, was always delighted when such a catch fell into her lap.

"I know you can read well, Jack," the head teacher went on, "but I need to know how well that is before I can recommend you to move up to the big school. Do you know what that means?"

"Yes, Miss Cordle, I do, only—" He stopped mid sentence, as if unsure where this conversation was taking him.

"Go on," she encouraged, "only…?"

"Well," he went on after gathering his thoughts for a moment or two, "will it cost us any more? Only we don't have much money, and my mam's finding it hard to make ends meet, you see."

"It won't cost you anything at all, I promise. But I need to know just how much you are able to understand what you read. Do you understand what I am saying, Jack?" she explained

"Yes, Miss Cordle," he replied. "You want to see for yourself if I am good enough to stay in the big school once you've sent me there. Do I have a say?"

"Of course you do," she answered, not quite able to believe that she, a head teacher of twenty years, was having such a mature discussion with a five-year-old. "Would you be unhappy moving into Mrs Gunn's class?"

"Is that John's mam?" Jack asked, as if settling something in his own mind. "And is he moving up as well?"

"John in your class?" Miss Cordle asked. "Yes, it is – and yes, we hope so."

"Then it's all right. I'll go," Jack decided, quite matter-of-factly, after a moment of thought.

"Excellent," Miss Cordle said emphatically, pleased Jack had made his decision. She couldn't help looking back to the days his brother William had spent with them in the nursery and reception. Now *he* was a very different child altogether.

Quiet, almost introverted, they could get hardly any response from him at all. No, Jack was an entirely different animal, whose potential far outstripped that of his brother.

"Now," she went on, "there's just the matter of that reading test. If you're ready…"

-o-

"Miss Cordle?" Jack asked at the end of school.

"Yes Jack," she turned to face his puzzled frown. "What can I do for you?"

"Did I pass?" he asked, quite pointedly.

"Sorry?" she puzzled, not quite sure what he meant.

"Did I pass the reading test you gave me earlier?" he insisted. "You know, the one about the animals in the zoo … the question you asked me about the rhinoceros. The one you thought I wouldn't be able to spell…"

"Oh, yes," she answered, smiling at being reminded so politely and yet so pointedly, "I do."

"Well, did I?" he continued, unabashed and not to be diverted. "Pass?"

"I couldn't really tell you now," she said, trying to employ the diversionary tactics which would have stopped any other five-year-old. Not Jack, unfortunately. "You see, we've quite a lot to get through and to consider."

"There're only five of us," he advised her. "I spoke to all the others, and I could tell you who would be OK in Mrs Gunn's class and who wouldn't."

"Mmm," she mused, having learned an object lesson in being straight with a bright five-year-old. "Tell you what, young man, I'll tell you first thing in the morning. OK?"

"Am I in trouble, Miss Cordle?" he asked, a little perturbed by her response.

"Trouble?" she asked, surprised by his question. "What makes you think you might be in trouble?"

"Well," he continued, "my mam always calls me 'young man' when I've done or said something wrong. So I wondered…"

"No," she laughed, "but I will make sure I see you first thing, to give you a letter to take home for your mum and dad."

"No good sending it to my dad," Jack said, as he turned to go home. "*He* doesn't care *what* I do. Goodbye, Miss Cordle."

-o-

"Going out again?" Flo asked William. "But you've hardly touched your tea."

"Not hungry," he said, throwing his coat over his shoulder. "Besides, I'm seeing my mates, and I'm late already."

"You'll be even later when you've finished your homework," she insisted.

"Haven't got any," he said, making for the door.

"Stop right there, young man," she ordered. "You're telling me you've no homework? With your GCE exams next year? I don't believe it. It's the fourth time in as many weeks you've used that excuse."

"It's true," he insisted. "No maths and no French."

"Then you won't mind if I drop in at that grammar school of yours to talk to Mr Holdroyd and Mr Machin, will you?" she said, looking him in the eyes.

"Can't you just leave the lad alone?" her husband butted in, as he slumped into his chair to remove his boots. "'E's already said 'e's not got any 'omework."

"Stay out of this, you," she rounded on him. "Since when have you taken any interest in your sons' education, or even your sons in general? I *know* he's got work to do, and I intend to make sure he does it."

"Teck thissen aht, William, lad," his dad intervened, trying to undermine her authority with her son.

"No, Dad," William said, standing his ground and pulling himself to his full six feet. "Me mam's right. I *have* got homework, and I have to do it. I was just trying to get out of it because I don't like doing it."

"Do as I tell thee," Eric ordered. "Or…"

"Or what, Dad?" William asked calmly, standing his ground between his parents. "You'll do the same to me as you did to Granddad?"

"What did tha say?" his father growled, clenching his fists as he got up and walked towards his son.

"Everybody knows what you did in the pit when Granddad was injured," William said, anger rising in his throat, "and everybody knows about Dotty French … except for me mam."

"Why, thou little—" Eric raised his fist to strike his son, the son on whom he'd once doted but had alienated badly over recent months. William had realised he had lost him as a father, and now he needed to step up to look after his mam.

"Strike that bairn once," an angry voice boomed from the scullery door, "and I'll break every bone in thy body. I'm still big and strong enough to see thee off."

William's granddad strode into the room – his huge knotted, clenched fists hanging loosely by his sides, ready.

"Get out of my house, Jud Holmes," Eric ordered. "Thy has no place nor business to be here. If thy doesn't, I'll…"

"Tha'll what?" Jud goaded him. "Best thy could do, Mr Big Man, is to run off to be with thy floozy, and leave *my* family in peace. Tha's caused nowt but trouble since tha raised thy ugly face."

"This is my house, and I pay the rent," Eric insisted. "Where are they going to live if I go? Who's going to pay for them, eh? Thee? I thowt not."

Eric backed off as Jud moved forward threateningly.

"Dad," Flo intervened. "It's all right. I can handle him.

Don't get yourself bothered. He's not worth it. I know where to come if there's trouble."

"You sure, lass?" Jud said, making certain they were going to be safe. "Tha knows where I am."

Moving to the scullery door, he turned once more towards his son-in-law, and, raising his finger in warning, he said,

"Just one finger, yon, and tha's got me to answer to."

"Dotty French?" Flo said, rounding on her husband once her dad had gone. "Who's this Dotty French, and what is it everybody knows but me, even our William?"

"It's nowt," he blustered, settling down in his chair again. "They've got it all wrong. There's nowt goin' on. Anyway, where's me tea?"

"Tha's getting nowt from me until I get a straight answer," she shouted, knowing from his attitude he was lying.

"Bugger that, then," he snarled. "I'm off out. Don't wait up."

"Then door'll be bolted," she yelled, as he made for the outside. "Perhaps your fancy piece will put up with you, because I won't."

William put his arm around his mother's shoulder and pulled her sobbing body towards him. Throughout all this Little Jack had crawled under the table, pulled his knees up to his chest, screwed his eyes tight shut, and put his fingers in his ears. This is how he stayed until his dad had gone out and his mam found him.

"Why is Dad so horrible to us, Mam?" Little Jack asked, as he munched his way through the meat and potato pie she had prepared for tea. "Why doesn't he like us?"

"I don't know, love," she answered, a sadness tingeing her voice because her son had felt the need to ask such a fundamentally obvious question. "Perhaps he's tired, or not well, or perhaps…"

"He's found somebody else he likes better?" William interrupted, a strong feeling of betrayal overwhelming his emotions. *He* had loved his dad unconditionally. Why couldn't his father have done the same in return?

"That's a question to be left for another time, my son," she said, proud of this young man who was growing into a man almost before her eyes. "Thank you for sticking up for me with your dad. That took a lot of courage. I'm sure he loves you in his own way, and…"

"He has a strange way of showing it," William snapped, pushing his half-finished plate away and making for the back door.

"What's the matter with our William?" Jack asked. He had never shared his brother's sense of conflict about his father's feelings, having understood and come to terms with his antagonism towards *him* from an early age.

"Just a bit upset, that's all," she answered, not too confident in her own response. "He'll be all right in a bit."

"Is William leaving his pie?" Jack asked, still unsure as to whether his brother would be back.

"Probably," she said, uncertain where he was going with this questioning. "Why?"

"Is it going to be thrown away?" he ventured, eyes lighting up. "Only … if it is, can I have it, please?"

"I'm sorry, my sweet boy," she said, twigging his ulterior motive. "I've some more in the oven if you'd like it."

"No, thank you," he insisted. "Don't want to waste it."

"Course you can have it," she replied, sliding William's almost untouched pie on to Jack's plate. "Do I take it you like my pie?"

"Yef, fang you," he mumbled through another mouthful, the gravy beginning to trickle out of his mouth corners. Jack had learned lessons from an early age which would support him pragmatically in many family issues throughout the rest of his life, giving him the power to shut off from situations where he might get hurt. Consequently he never became too involved in the emotions of family conflicts, of which there were many in this household.

-o-

These particular infidelities were quite rare in close communities where living from day to day was hard. Even though intimacy in its widest sense wasn't the overriding factor in family life it was the feeling of working together that cemented most relationships. This glue occasionally became loosened, but husbands and wives were proud of their achievements through earlier hard times. The only thing to disrupt this harmony amidst disharmony was death – and this, because of the nature of colliery work, was an all too frequent bedfellow.

Jud Holmes had been badly injured in the roof fall, needing several operations to rectify, rearrange and repair his internal organs. Although strong in spirit and body once again, the doctors had declared he wasn't fit for coal hewing any more. This was a blow only to his pride and his pocket. The one he soon got over, and the other he and his wife soon learned to live with.

At sixty-one he was a towering man, to whom life still had a lot to offer. He was given a much lighter job at the shaft bottom, looking after the needs of the pit ponies that were stabled underground during their working week. Because his duties were not as onerous or as lengthy as before the accident he had a great deal more leisure time to indulge his twin passions of going on holiday to Torquay and Blackpool with his wife – and of spending the rest of his leisure time in his allotment, much to his wife's chagrin. She was his gatekeeper, reminding him when he had spent enough time there, both to safeguard *his* health and *her* sanity.

After an argument about his allotment time he had always been used, on returning, to throwing his cap into the house through the kitchen door. He knew that if the cap came back out again he was still in trouble, and it would take much more than a bag of potatoes or a pocketful of home-grown tomatoes to placate his wife. Generally, though, their marriage was strong. It had had to be.

He had been given the option of early retirement on health grounds, with an enhancement of the pension he had taken out many years before to ensure hardship didn't become an early caller. Marion said 'yes', but Jud still seemed unsure. Marion would undoubtedly get him to agree, if only to stop her nagging about it. He *had* decided to accept the coal board's offer, but he would spring it upon her in his own way, in his own time.

"Jud," Marion shouted at the bottom of the stairs, one cold and rainy Monday morning. "Half past seven … time to get up. Tha's going to miss thi bus if tha doesn't get a shake on."

"Jud," she shouted a quarter of an hour later. "Come on, now. Time's moving on. Breakfast'll soon be in the bin … Jud!"

"Where is that dratted man?" she muttered as she bustled up the stairs five minutes later. Bursting into the bedroom, she skidded to a halt … to see her husband fully dressed in his decent clothes, with a suitcase packed, by his side.

"Jud?" the question caught in her throat. "What's thy doing? Suitcase? Is thy going somewhere without me?"

He turned towards her, a huge grin on his face.

"I feel like I've got a terminal case of retirement coming over me," he said, reaching out to flick a crumb from the corner of her mouth. "So I won't be going to t' pit today … or any other day, for that matter."

"But …" she stammered, "what does tha mean? Retirement

as in … *retirement*? No more Sharleston Colliery, where tha's worked since tha were a lad? That sort of retirement?"

"Aye, lass," he agreed. "What does tha think? Can tha put up wi' me at home all the time?"

"Aye," she said, "as long as tha doesn't spend *all* thi time in yon allotment. And, what's yon suitcase for?"

"I'm going on holiday," he answered, a bigger smile creasing his eye corners, "to Torquay."

"Oh, aye," she said, not too sure how to take his answer. "On thy own? Without me?"

"Course not," he said, drawing her closer to him. "I've got the tickets here." He patted the breast pocket of his jacket and moved towards the wardrobe. He opened her side, drew out her suitcase, and dropped it on the bed.

"Tha's not packed *my* clothes, I trust," she said, her stern warning carrying its own menace.

"Would I be likely to rummage about in *thy* drawers, Marion, lass?" he said. "But tha'd better hurry up. Everything's organised. Taxi'll be here in a couple of hours, so tha'd better shake a leg."

"Is this your idea of a joke, Jud Holmes?" she said, not sure. "Because if it is…"

"Just three things to say, Marion," he began. "One: I have finally retired, from today. Two: our wedding anniversary's next week. And three: taxi'll be here in one hour and fifty-five minutes, to take us to Gillard's Coaches down Altofts Road in town. Nothing else for thee to worry about. If tha wants to stop here, OK, but I'm going to Torquay for two weeks, with or without thee."

"Two weeks?" she squeaked excitedly. "Two weeks?"

"One hour and fifty minutes," he advised calmly, as she skipped into the bathroom. "I'm just off to water me hanging baskets out at the back. Jim next door'll do 'em while we're away. So come on. We're almost there."

"Have you told our Flo?" Marion's voice rang out from the bathroom.

"Certainly have," he replied. "I even offered to bring her and t' lads along but she declined, saying she couldn't leave her home. Didn't know whether there'd be one there for them when they got back. One hour and forty minutes…"

"Oh, give up with your countdown," she told him.

"Taxi clock starts ticking when he gets here," Jud advised her. "I'm not made of money, tha knows."

"Enough to take us to Torquay on a whim, though," she laughed.

"Hey," he retorted, "It were no whim. I've been planning this for ages."

"And you let me believe I had to *persuade* you to retire?" she said. "You bugger. Just you wait…"

This was the first time in many a long while she had heard him giggle, like he used to in the times before Flo became mixed up with Eric Ingles. Oh, for the return of those times. Hopefully, in retirement they would be able to rediscover some of the magic they had shared, seeing as how the endgame was gathering pace.

-o-

That selfsame day Eric Ingles had crept back to his home, all apologies, and swearing it was all lies and would never happen again. Flo took him back for the good of her boys, not believing any of his promises. Any feelings she once had for him died the day he raised his hand to her sons.

If she had refused to entertain his return she knew he would have had no compunction about setting them out on the street, either throwing them out or giving up his house and moving in with his whore.

No. She would bide her time in the hope that better days were around the corner. She wasn't sure how, but she felt she was due a slice of good luck. It could only be a matter of when.

Chapter 6

The months following Eric's return from his self-imposed exile were difficult for the Ingles family. Relations were very strained as the adults didn't speak to each other, and the father barely said two words to his sons. However, Jack felt more at ease because he didn't feel any antagonism from his father directly, and school gave him the stability he craved and needed. He also had a much larger share of his mother's attention and affection. He quite liked his brother's company on the odd occasion they shared daytime space, but the ten years between them was just too wide for them to enjoy a really meaningful relationship. Little did William realise that his brother's intellect at almost six was little short of his own at almost sixteen.

Despite appearances to the contrary, William was finding extreme difficulty with his studies. His mock GCE exams in February had been an unmitigated disaster, and he had performed well in only one of his eight subjects, much to his mother's concern. She put it down to the atmosphere created by his father's shenanigans with Dotty French, but worried secretly that it might be something more fundamental. She couldn't find out for sure, because she only had his teachers' platitudes at parents' evenings that what he had suffered was merely a blip. Consequently, they would see to it that matters improved for the exams that mattered.

His father, of course, was interested only in his failure, to prove that *he* was right. They would go down the pit: William first, to be followed by his brother, Jack. It couldn't be any other way. They would show, after all, that they were no better than he was.

Flo had an inkling that her husband wanted to prove a point as far as her sons were concerned. Even though he still refused to acknowledge him as his, Jack bore his name and lived under his roof. To remove all possibility of being forced into doing something he didn't want to do he would have to leave home at sixteen. His grandparents, of course, wouldn't allow that to happen, even if it meant taking in the lad themselves. Flo, however, vowed she would do anything to thwart Eric's evil plans, and by that she genuinely meant *anything*.

"Mam?" Jack asked at the end of a particularly trying day.

"Yes, love?" she answered, putting down her darning to give him her full attention, knowing a serious question was coming her way. "What is it?"

"Will Dad still be living with us when I am as old as our William?" he asked. He always used his questions in a general way, so that you had no idea what their real purpose was – a simple request, or having a much deeper meaning.

"I should think so," she replied. "Why do you ask?"

"I remember, a long time ago, he said William and I would go down the pit when we were old enough," he continued. "Do you remember?"

"Yes, love," she puzzled. "I think I do."

"Well, William's old enough now," he pointed out, "but he's still at school. Does that mean he won't be going to be a coal miner, then?"

"Of course he won't," she answered carefully. "Heaven forbid."

"Does that mean as well then that I won't, either?" he asked carefully. "Because I *don't* want to be. I want to be a teacher, like Mr Hardwick at school. He's good. I can do that."

"If that's what you want to be," she assured him, "then that's what you shall do."

"Does that mean that Dad tells lies?" he asked again, quite disarmingly. "Or does he say all that to try to make us frightened?"

She couldn't believe the depth of reasoning she was hearing from this little chap, with whom she hadn't had a moment's trouble since that cold day at the beginning of January all those years ago. This little one deserved the best of everything, but unfortunately one of his parents didn't even come close.

"Your dad's a silly man sometimes," she confided. "Sometimes he says things he doesn't mean, and then finds it impossible to say 'sorry'. He needs our understanding and pity more than anything else. I love you – and would never tell you lies, for any reason."

"Then," he added after a pause, "do you like Dad to be here with us, or do you wish he wasn't?"

His deep yet disturbing questions would be the death of her. But how could she not respond with truth and honesty after all she had said?

"Your father and I don't get on, I think it's safe to say," she started, after a good deal of deliberation. "It's been the case for a long time … since just after William was born, really. I wish with all my heart he was happier, then we could start being a family again. Both you and your brother are very important to me, and to your gran and granddad too. I only wish your dad felt the same."

Her mind whizzed back fleetingly to their holiday in the caravan at Bridlington, not long after Jack's appearance on the scene. That was what Eric was like when they had married, and that's what she would like back again, even now. Yet did she want it for herself, or for the sake of her sons? She didn't think she could separate the two.

"Even though I wasn't very old," Jack carried on, "I really enjoyed that holiday we had in the caravan in Brid."

Quite astounded at what he had just said, she turned slowly.

"You were only eighteen months old," she gasped. "How could you possibly remember that?"

"I remember digging, and crawling on the sands," he went on, "and I remember William tripping and falling in the sea. He was very wet, and I remember Dad took me to the water. I thought he was going to throw me in, but it was just for a paddle."

"How on earth…?" she marvelled.

"I don't know," he said finally, finishing off his tea. "I just … remember. I can also remember our bedroom window being blown in that same winter, and the glass all over my cot. That's why you moved my cot away from the window later."

"Well, I'm shocked," she said, looking at him through wondering eyes. "Sometimes I can't remember the day before, let alone so far back."

-o-

"Man from the council came round this morning," Flo told her husband as he was finishing his dinner. An afternoon shift always meant he had to eat late, which didn't bother him as he didn't have to put up with children around him.

"Aye," he answered, "and what of it?"

"He said all the houses in Scarborough Row were to be pulled down," she went on, "and the site cleared."

"Oh, aye?" he said, looking up to find his mug of tea. "And

why have they told thee and not me? Last time I looked it were my name on t' rent book."

"Could it be something to do with you being at work during the day?" she replied sarcastically. "And I just happened to be here when he came?"

"All right, sarky bugger," he replied, put out that he hadn't thought of that. "And where do they propose we live? In a tent?"

"They have offered us a brand-new two-bedroomed council house," she said, unable to contain her excitement. "It's got a garden back and front, and an inside bathroom and toilet. Oh, and by the way, hot water, and ... electricity. What do you think about that?"

"We're not going," he said blankly, as he set down his empty mug. "I'm not having them telling me what I can and can't do, and where I can or can't live."

"Well, you're wrong," she took great pleasure in telling him. "They can. And what's more, you don't have to come if you don't want to. I can have my name on the rent book, so you can stay here and be pulled down with all the other useless rubbish, if you wish."

"Now watch thy mouth," he threatened.

"Or you'll what?" she returned quickly, calling his cowardly bluff. "The first three streets have been finished, and we've been given the choice. Time we had a bit of good luck."

He slouched across to his chair, cursing and snarling as he went, not acknowledging the lovely meal she had just prepared for him.

"Me and the lads are going," she insisted, "and you can't stop us. Come if you want, but – don't forget – any shenanigans about keeping me short of money so I can't pay the rent ... the money can be taken out of your wage packet direct. Good, isn't it?"

-o-

"Jack?" Flo shouted as she finished drying the pots in the scullery.

"Mam?" came his immediate answer close behind her.

"You've got an uncanny knack of making me jump when I least expect it," she said, patting her chest. "It's still quite pleasant out, so how do you fancy a walk?"

"A walk? Where to?" he asked, not quite sure why she was asking. "Are we going to the shops? To Grandma's? Into town? To…?"

"OK … OK," she said, holding her hands up. "I get the point. What would you say if I suggested a walk to … nowhere in particular? Just … a walk?"

"OK," he agreed. "Just a bit of exercise. Sounds fun."

"Just a walk," she sighed. Why was nothing ever straightforward with her son?

The early evening was fresh but not too cold as they headed past her husband's club up towards the new estate. Rows of brand-new houses had sprung out of once-green scrubland, providing new, modern amenities for families who had spent generations in Victorian housing with no level of modern living beyond the era for which it was built. These houses were up to date, with gardens back and front sufficient to provide growing space for either flowers or vegetables – or even, indeed, both. A government-backed local council initiative, that recognised the need to drag the housing stock into the twentieth century, it was proving to be a popular concept.

"Jack? You see that garden gate over there – the one that's green?" Flo said, pointing to the first of a set of two semi-detached houses. "The green one?"

"They're all green, Mam," he replied. "But I see the one you mean."

"Do you think it might be a good idea to close it," she

suggested, "to stop dogs and other creatures from getting in, perhaps?"

"Yes, Mam," he answered, dutifully doing what she suggested.

"There's a good boy," she said when he got back to her.

"Did you know," he began again, "that *that* house is in fact empty? So perhaps it wouldn't matter if dogs got in. Next door's gate is open as well, and, as there's no fence between the two, perhaps I should close that one too? To stop the dogs getting in that way."

"Well," she said, ignoring his last remark, "would you like to live in a house like that one?"

"No, not really," he answered, after a moment or two in thought. "I like it where we live now. It's home."

There were times when she felt like she was banging her head against a brick wall with Jack. There was always a sensible if unexpected response to anything she might ask him, which always provided her with minor problems she had to think around. She had brought him up to be always truthful, but sometimes she wished he wasn't *so* straight. She was sure, too, that his teachers shared the same feelings about him: a good student, but occasionally *too* logical to be real.

"Well," she replied, a little concerned by his response, as they made their way back to home and tea, "that's unfortunate, because we *have* to move."

His inevitable question, after a moment's consideration, was only to be expected.

"Has Dad decided he doesn't want to live with us any more?" he asked, a little apprehensive as to his mam's reaction. "We can…"

"We have to move because our houses – all our houses – are to be pulled down soon," she interrupted, "and our town council has said we can have the house where you just closed the gate."

She looked at her son, puzzled at the slight smile creasing his mouth corners. Normally such a serious little boy, she had never seen spontaneous humour taking him over before.

"So you asked me to close *our* gate so that dogs wouldn't get into *our* front garden?" he said. "I like that. Come on, Mam. I need to go home and pack me stuff."

His purposeful march back towards Scarborough Row brought a smile to her face and relief to her mind. She knew it wouldn't have been difficult to persuade him, but now she didn't have to. Her other son hadn't needed any persuading at all. Too many recent unhappy memories in their present home, along with the outside toilet and a lack of privacy, had led him quickly to grab this new opportunity. Yet, at sixteen, he didn't know how long it would last for him. He was unsure down which path the next two or three years might lead him. University was out of the question, he was definite about that. Academic work held no joy for him and, by the same token, neither did working at the coalface. He would have to wait until his exam results pointed him in some sort of direction, and only then would he have a general idea which doors might open – or, indeed, close.

Strangely, Flo worried about William's future much more than she did about her younger son. There was something about Jack that allayed her fears. Intuition? Guidance from elsewhere? She didn't know. She just felt he would be all right, even at five.

"Mam?" Jack asked, as he tucked in to his bread and jam sandwich.

"Yes, love?" she replied, as she finished preparing her husband's dinner, accepting that he would neither appreciate nor thank her for what she would offer him. "What's troubling you?"

"This new house," he went on, "will Mr and Mrs Gittins and Peter and Gordon be coming as well?"

"Not to live with us," his mother replied, her attempt at humour bearing no fruit at all.

"I know that," he answered. "There won't be enough room for them as well. No … will they be having their own new house, like ours?"

"Why do you ask?" she replied. "Would it make any difference?"

"I like Gordon," he continued, "and I'd be sorry if he didn't live close by. I don't have many friends. In fact he's the *only* friend I have, apart from Trevor Durant and Terry Churchill and Joyce Jones."

"Joyce Jones?" Flo queried. "Who's Joyce Jones? Never heard you mention her before."

"She's the girl I sit next to in Mrs Gunn's class," he finished off, flicking the crumbs from his mouth. "She lives with her dad, because her mam left them a little while ago. Why would she want to do that, Mam? Would you ever leave us?"

"What a question!" she exclaimed. "What do *you* think?"

He thought for a moment and then said, quite deliberately, "It seems to me that when older people ask you a question to answer *your* question, they either don't know, or don't want *you* to know. That bread and jam was good."

"I could never leave you, my sweet boy," she said, drawing him to her bosom and kissing his spiky head. "Joyce Jones? She your girlfriend?"

"Well," he said pragmatically, "she's a girl, and she's my friend. So I suppose you could say she's my girlfriend."

How to be put in one's place by the straightforwardness of a five-year-old…

"Well?" he asked again. "Will they?"

"Will they what, dear?" Flo said, puzzled at this new line of questioning.

"Will the Gittinses be coming to live near our new

house?" he sighed.

"Oh, the Gittinses," she said, finally tracking back his questioning. She should have known he wouldn't have forgotten what he had originally set out to ask. "Yes, next door. Happy?"

"OK," he said, without any show of emotion. Job done. He had the answer he sought.

-o-

"Have you any brothers and sisters?" Joyce asked Jack at morning play, over the gate separating the boys' and girls' playgrounds.

"Our William's my brother," Jack replied, "and he's at the grammar school. You?"

"I've two brothers," Joyce said, "but only one of them lives with me and my dad. He's got the same initials as you, but the other way round."

"Ingles Jack?" Jack said, puzzled.

"Initials," she insisted. "I.J. Ian: Ian Jones … initials. Get it?"

"Ian Jones," he agreed. "Course I do. Why doesn't your other brother live with you and your Ian and your dad?"

"Because he lives with my mam, Dotty. Her real name's Dorothy – Dotty for short," Joyce told him quietly, "and he's not my full brother … and he's not called Jones."

This puzzled Jack's straightforward, logical brain. How could she have a brother who wasn't really her brother, and who had a different name?

"How…?" he started after a lengthy pause. She could see he was trying to work it all out, so she interrupted his quandary.

"You see, he's not my dad's son," she burst in, "and my mam's gone back to using her maiden name."

"What's 'maiden' name, then?" he asked, entirely confused.

"Her name before she married my dad," Joyce explained. "She's called Dotty French, and her new baby's called Eric. *We* don't have anything to do with her now, nor the baby. My dad says it's a bastard, though I don't know what that means. I thought it could only be either a boy or a girl. I didn't know there was something else it could be. When's your birthday?"

"January 4, 1946," he replied, precisely.

"You can't go back to that year every time you have a birthday," she laughed. "Your birthday is 4 January."

"No," Jack insisted, a frown beginning to deepen in his brow. "My birthday, which means the *one* day when I was born, was January 4, 1946. I've only ever had one birthday, and that's gone. I don't celebrate it any more. You could say that I'll be six on 4 January next, or…"

"I get it," she interrupted. "You are strange, Jack Ingles, but I do like you."

-o-

"Mam," Jack shouted as he shouldered his way through the scullery door. "Mam, I'm back."

"Back from where?" she called from the kitchen. "South America?"

"No," he replied without question, "from school, of course."

Flo smiled at this strange little boy for whom life was black and white, and for whom every question had a straight answer.

"Have you had a nice day?" his mam asked, as she peeled flour and pastry gloves from her hands and wrists.

"Yes, I have," he said. "I talked with my girlfriend, Joyce, at playtime today."

"But I thought boys and girls have separate playgrounds at the big school, haven't they?" she puzzled.

"The junior school," he corrected her, "has, but we talked

over the dividing gate. It's so silly having two playgrounds, when all they would need to do would be to knock the dividing wall down. It would be so much bigger and better. She told me about her brother Ian, and her baby not-brother."

"And what does *that* mean?" she frowned. "There's no such thing."

"Joyce's mam left her family," he went on. "I told you the other day. Do you remember?"

"Yes, I do," Flo said, sitting down on the settee.

"Well," he explained, "Joyce's not-brother is her mother's son, who is not her father's son. Her mother's called Dotty French. That's her maiden name, which means…"

"I know what it means," she hissed, fearing the worst. "Go on. And…?"

"Joyce's not-brother is called Eric," he went on, "and he's a bastard."

"Jack!" Flo gasped. "Where did you learn such language? You've not to…"

"Joyce's dad said it, so I looked it up in our school dictionary," he continued, "and it means little Eric hasn't got a father. Does that mean, then, that *my* dad hasn't got a father, either, because Granddad says that *that's* what Dad is?"

Chapter 7

"It's a good job we haven't got much stuff," Flo said as Jim and Harry Turnbull loaded the last of their belongings into the wagon prior to moving off to their new home. She remembered the date, because 15 March was her brother's birthday. He would have been thirty-two. The day wasn't lost on her mam and dad, either. They never went out on that day, just celebrated what might have been had he not been taken. Such was the devastation wrought on many lives by the horrors of war. For Marion it had been a double blow. She lost her beloved Herbert, Flo's natural dad, in the Great War – and then her son, Jud's lad, in the second. Her bitterness against the Hun was complete, understandable, and knew no bounds.

Once again, her husband was nowhere to be seen. 'Work', he had said, but Flo neither believed him nor cared. Had he been killed in the war she would have had to do what she was doing now, anyway. But he didn't fight in that last war. Exempted occupation: he was a coal miner. He wasn't allowed to leave to fight, he said. He couldn't explain, however, how some of his shift mates *had* enlisted and fought for their – his – country. 'Coward', Jud called him, along with other stuff too strong to share.

Eric had always boasted that he was in the Home Guard

in London, and how he had saved numbers of people during the Blitz. Yet Flo couldn't understand how he was allowed time off from his vital work down the mine to be there, but wasn't allowed to be called up to defend his homeland.

"Just two or three more boxes, Jack," she said to her son. "Have you packed all you need to take?"

She had kept him off school because it would have been a nuisance to collect and take him back at lunchtime, as Jack wouldn't have agreed to stay to school dinners. He didn't consider they served real food in school. It arrived – already cooked – in large silver-coloured metal boxes from a central kitchen by the town hall, which served all junior schools in the area. This mystical process led Jack to believe it wasn't real food, because it wasn't possible to put uncooked stuff into a silver box – and then, magically, it came out as proper food.

"Yes, Mam," he answered. "All my toys are in that little box over there. It's got Fred, my bear, my glass marbles, my cigarette cards, my two little Dinky cars, my little bagatelle and my squeaky mouse. I haven't got anything else. You threw out my six pieces of string, my torn kite and my box of magnets last week. Remember?"

"All right," she sighed. "You've told me that one six times already. We can't keep everything. We don't have the space. Stuff does become old and dirty, too. I'll buy you some more stuff later on, when we're settled. OK?"

"OK," he replied, satisfied with her answer. He wasn't a demanding child, unlike some others she knew. Mary Brighton's little lad, Simon, seemed to get all the toys going every year, but then *his* dad was an undermanager at the colliery. He was a spoilt brat, was Simon Brighton. Jack's gran said so. Every toy he had he played with once, became bored, and then discarded it. Jack, on the other hand, could indulge in meaningful and constructive play for hours with three lengths of twine and a couple of acorn cups.

"Where's our William?" Jack asked.

"He has to be in school today," she said. "Some exam or other, practising for his GCEs in May… He'll be back at the usual time."

"How will he know where to come?" Jack asked, becoming a little concerned for his brother's welfare. "We won't be here."

"He knows already, silly," Flo laughed. "We *have* told him, you know. Besides, he's been to look at the new house and realises that that's where we'll be by the end of the day. If he doesn't you'll have the room to yourself."

"But…" he started, worried now that he wouldn't see his brother again.

"Only kidding," she assured him.

"Mam," he growled, a nervous smile beginning to dither at his mouth corners.

"All right, Missus," Jim Turnbull shouted from the front door. "Is that everything?"

"Yes, Mr Turnbull," she shouted back, making for the front of the house, looking around as she did, to check the rooms. "It's all clear."

"Well," he said as she entered the front room, "it's half past eleven now, so we have to return to our depot to fill up with fuel. We'll be back at your new house in three quarters of an hour or so. OK?"

"Perfect timing," she answered. "It'll give us just enough time to finish up and lock up here, and put the kettle on at number 44."

"Champion," he grinned. "Up to an hour, then?"

She snecked the door after him and turned again towards the kitchen. It seemed strange and eerie in this empty room, a room they had used more this day during the removal than they had done all the time they had lived there. Her outdoor shoes clicked on the cold oilcloth as she retraced her steps to her son. Her kitchen was still warm from the embers of the fire dying in the grate of her once-beautiful blackleaded range. Although it had been in daily use for as long as they had been in number 206 she certainly wouldn't miss the cold and damp scullery, and she was desperately looking forward to her new home's hot water and inside bathroom.

The news that her husband had likely fathered another bairn by this Dotty French had been a bombshell, but one she had half expected. It had, of course, galvanised her resolve that she didn't need Eric Ingles in her new life. She had carried through the threat of having her name on the rent book. He *could* live in their new house as a lodger for the sake of her children, for sure, but he would have to accept the new arrangements and he *would* have to pay. She didn't care whether he had his floozy on the side. That was no concern of theirs.

"Hello," a familiar voice echoed through from the front room. "Anybody home?"

"Mam?" Flo queried, a surprised smile growing on her face. "What are you doing here? I thought you were away?"

"No, love," Marion said, almost hugging the life out of her grandson. "Got back the other day. Came to give you a hand … Your dad'll meet us at the new house."

"That's good of you," Flo replied. "You didn't have to."

"And yon?" Marion asked, eyebrows leaping to the top of her forehead.

"Working, *he* says," her daughter answered with no show of emotion, "but I neither believe nor care."

She had to be careful what she said, as she didn't want to upset her son. The less he knew about his pig of a father the better. He would get to know the truth about his dalliances soon enough.

"Come on, then," Marion urged. "Let's go and make a cup

of tea, and get this young man a bite to eat. I've something I want to show you."

"But we've no time to be going to yours, Mam," Flo insisted. "Removal men will be at the new house in an hour, and…"

"You worry too much, Flo Ingles," her mother said, breaking into a wicked chuckle.

"You're up to something, I can tell," Flo said as they made for the new estate. "And why are we going towards the new house? I can't even boil a kettle there. All my stuff's packed in Turnbull's wagon … Mam?"

Marion crossed her lips with her forefinger, and marched purposefully on to Garth Avenue, the new housing estate where her daughter's new life would begin.

"Mam, hang on a bit," Flo urged. "We can't keep up with you."

Much to the surprise and puzzlement of her daughter and grandson, she strode past Flo's home, stopped by the front gate of number 37, and waited for them to catch up. As Flo started to ask why they had stopped here the front door opened, and the huge frame of her dad appeared on the threshold.

"Mam?" Flo drawled, as she closed on her mother. "What's Dad doing there?"

"We've moved," Marion and Jud chuckled. "Welcome to our new home. Coming in?"

"We thought you needed a bit of backup," Jud said, as they sat around the kitchen table, a mug of hot tea in their hands and a crumby plate in front of them.

"I can't believe you have done this," Flo stammered, tears welling in her eyes.

"Come on, lass," her dad put his arm around her. "We've done it to be nearer to you and the little 'un here. There was a lot to do at the other house, and the landlord wasn't keen.

So here we are – a brand-new house, and nearer to you into the bargain. What do you think, young Jack?"

"Can I stay here with you, Granddad, please?" Jack said with feeling.

Like a bombshell, this set the three adults back on their collective heels. It was totally unexpected. They didn't understand why he felt like this.

"Why, love?" his mam asked gently after a moment of indecision. "Is there something troubling you?"

Jack was quiet for a while, his little eyes looking out into his grandparents' back garden. It contained only the rudiments, really – a lawn and a few shrubs – but it was a world away from what he had been used to.

"Empty and cold …" he started, "the new house. I liked our old house because it was warm, and I was used to it. It's warm here, and … I might have my own room, mightn't I?"

His folks looked at each other, eyebrows raised in silent question.

"Yes, of course you can, love," Marion reassured him, as she sought the OK from Flo. "You can stay here for a few days until everything is sorted at yours. All right?"

"OK, Grandma," Jack said quietly. "Thank you. I feel better now."

"But in the meantime," his granddad said, "shall we go and help your mam sort out your new house? Then you can come back here to sleep. Shall we go up and have a look at your new room?"

"Yes please, Granddad," Jack enthused, brightening up considerably.

-o-

The next few weeks passed uneventfully, largely because Flo had been left to her own devices to organise her new home. William was an enormous help: lifting, carrying and moving without demur. He felt like he was becoming the man of the house, with his father only a bit player in their particular drama. Eric they hardly saw. He had requested afternoons for the whole of that month, and he spent his evenings after work and weekends either at his club, in the garden or elsewhere. Apart from cooking his food and sharing the same bed their paths hardly crossed.

This suited Flo well. She cringed inside whenever she allowed herself to think she slept not six inches from this … this whoremonger. And, of course, she never let him lay a finger on her again. Her mam was unequivocal about the unsavouriness of this man, who was unworthy of *her* daughter and her wonderful boys.

It was a delight for Marion and Jud to spend more time with Jack – who had begun to blossom and develop in his granddad's company, helping him more and more in his allotment. They had also taken him occasionally to the seaside for the odd day or two. This was a whole new world for him, which brought new, funny – and interesting – people of all shapes, sizes and attitudes into his orbit – all of whom indulged him because of his grandparents, but yet liked him for himself.

As if to try to prove he was worthy of his place in the household Eric had begun to spend a lot of his spare time in the garden. The front was walled, hedged, and planted with a few simple shrubs and flowers, because he hadn't really much idea. The one person who knew most of what there was to know about horticultural matters was his father-in-law, Jud Holmes, but he wasn't about to approach him cap in hand. He had asked a few of his workmates, but all they would say was,

"Thi father-in-law is the best there is. Why doesn't thy ask him?" They often walked away chuckling to each other, because he wasn't well liked at work – unlike Jud, who was.

"Why doesn't thy teck thissen off to another pit?" Alf Todd and Frank Greenside had asked him. "Tha knows tha's not liked hereabouts, and it'd be a lot easier for thee to get on, particularly after what thy did to Jud Holmes, a man worth ten o' thee."

"Get out o' my bleedin' face, Alf Todd," Eric replied. "Or…"

"Or what?" Frank Greenside interrupted, pulling his six foot six, eighteen-stone frame up to its full height. "Tha's a bloody coward, Eric Ingles, and as such not wanted round here. Tha should take thissen off while tha's able."

"And what's tha goin' to do if I don't?" Eric replied, his bravado overstating itself.

Frank clenched his knotted fists and edged towards him, ready to strike him down.

"Steady, Frank," Alf advised, staying his huge arm. "He's not worth it. He'll get his comeuppance soon enough."

"Si thi, Eric," Frank threw over his shoulder as the two men strode away. "Enjoy thy life … what's left of it."

Eric had never been one to be concerned about friends, because he had never had any. Even his siblings weren't close. His father and mother couldn't stand him, and they perhaps were the closest he had to fans. His parents couldn't abide each other either, and so he had very little chance to succeed with outsiders. His family seemed to be a random group of disparate individuals thrown together by an accident of nature. Perhaps the greatest influence on *his* outlook had been the attitude of his father to his own family in general, and to him in particular.

His father William was an old pitman who never spent a penny on anything unnecessary. He kept them all alive – just – and laid out nothing he didn't have to, much to his wife's eternal shame and distaste. She had been married before, to a reasonable man, and it hit her hard when she realised her mistake after his death. Born out of wedlock, Eric had been mistreated by his father from his meagre beginnings in every way. He had unfortunately inherited most of his father's traits – characteristics he would use to his advantage without compunction, but which would serve him ill ultimately.

His brother, Harold, was entirely different. A good if ordinary human being throughout, he devoted his life to his own family despite his upbringing. Very different from his brother, Harold worked for a local engineering firm and played the violin for fun. The only thing they had in common was their upbringing. Yet it was this that bound them. Although Eric thought little about him Harold would have nothing said against his youngest brother, and many thought that his sense of loyalty to this uncaring and heartless man was seriously misplaced. He had nothing to do with his other two siblings at all, because of some senseless dispute when they were young. Allan and Blanche lived their own lives according to their own values, which were a million miles away from his.

-o-

"You know my feelings about you, lass," Jud answered his daughter.

"But, Dad," she went on, "back garden's a bloody mess, and 'e's not the first idea what to do wi' it."

"After what he's done to this family," Jud interrupted, "I wouldn't pee on him if he was on fire."

He stopped for a minute, gathering his composure and turning over his options so as not to disappoint his daughter too much.

"I tell you what," he turned to her, knowing only too well that her husband wouldn't accept what he had to offer. "If he comes to me and asks my advice, I'll consider it."

"But you know he'll never do that," Flo sighed,

exasperated.

"My last offer," Jud insisted, "and it'll stand for as long as it takes him to realise there are them as knows more about some things than 'im. Take it or leave it."

Flo realised that she would have to hope Eric might grow some sense and knowledge about gardening quickly, or their back garden would remain a wilderness. Yet there still might be a way. Harry Gittins – their new next-door neighbour, from Scarborough Row – had an allotment, she recalled. Ada was always going on about how good he was and what lovely stuff he grew, both flowers and veg. Perhaps Ada might have a word with him, and try to get him to have a word with Eric. Harry Gittins was one of the very few people who still talked to him. 'Give him a chance', is what he would say. He was never one to damn anybody out of hand, Harry Gittins wasn't. His wife Ada didn't share his bonhomie, after what he'd done to her good friend Flo. Her view was that castration and throttling weren't too extreme for him.

"Are you leaving yon back garden, then?" Flo asked her husband one Sunday morning in early April. "Only from what I can see, bulbs are growing up and flowers sprouting in all the gardens around ... except for ours."

"Give me time, woman," he snapped. "I'll get round to it ... soon. I've done a lot that tha's obviously not noticed."

"You mean 'soon' as in 'before you go to t' club at eleven this morning'?" she said sarcastically. "Or 'soon' as in 'sooner or later'? And we all know what that means."

"When I'm good and ready," he growled. "Thy knows nowt about gardening, so button it."

"It seems thy doesn't, either," she goaded. "If tha doesn't do summat about it soon I'll ask council to do it for me ... useless bugger."

He spun round on his heels, fists clenched, and a

murderous glower in his eyes.

"And don't think your threatening posture cuts any ice with me," she added with startling confidence. "We both know you're all wind and watter."

He thrust his hand deep into his pocket, drew out a silver tanner and slapped it on the table. "That's all tha's getting from me today. Use it to pay thi council men."

He turned again and slammed the back door on his way out. Not looking where he was going in his heated haste, he banged his head on the coalhouse overhang and cursed it all the way down the path to the gate.

"Serves you right, you bad bugger," Flo laughed. "Pity it wasn't a good bit harder."

She was learning to be less forgiving and more confident in her dealings with her husband, although it still wasn't second nature to her. Most of the time, however, she felt used, let down, and betrayed. The fact of her life was that she had two boys – whom she adored – to a man she detested, who had fathered a child by another woman and who preferred drinking with his cronies to being with his family. From that fantastic week in Bridlington, when Jack was eighteen months old, how could things have deteriorated so badly? Her dad's prophetic words crowded her mind, telling her that she should have listened to him.

"Mam…" A quietly husky little voice drew her out of her reverie. She jerked her head round to see her Jack studying her, a quizzically worried look on his face. "Are you all right? I thought I heard a noise, so I came to see. Was it Dad going out to his club? It *is* eight and a half minutes past eleven."

"Yes, my sweet young man," she replied, drawing him to her and kissing the top of his head. "I am, and it was. I think he was a bit annoyed because he banged his head on the way out."

"Will you tell him off when you see him again?" he asked,

after a moment's silence.

"And why would I do that?" she replied, a puzzled smile on her face.

"Well," he answered, "the other day Mr Tomlinson smacked Jimmy Smith for swearing at Miss Joliff, like Dad just did, and he threatened to cane him. Will you cane Dad when he gets back, then, Mam?"

Chapter 8

"And when is it going to happen?" she demanded forcefully. "You've said all this before many times. I'm beginning to think you're trying to fob me off – trying to keep me sweet."

"I'm not, lass," he insisted. "I can't just up and leave them like that, although I know you'd like me to. If I walk out I'll still have to pay for t' house and upkeep. If I stay for now there'll be less to pay out, and more money for yon bairn and you. That's got to be sense, hasn't it?"

"Does that mean, then, that we'll never live together as man and wife?" she said, toning down her aggression towards him. "And that *your* son will never have *his* father to look up to?"

"Course it doesn't," he tried to reassure her, as all cheating husbands before him had tried to do with their mistresses. "We *will* be together, I promise, but not just yet."

Dotty French wasn't sure how much she could trust him or how far she could push him. She knew Eric Ingles was a slippery character and had no compunction about lying and cheating his way to getting what he wanted. *He* would be able to walk away from his responsibilities, but *she* couldn't. Life for her and little Eric would be unthinkably bleak without his support.

"We're all right together, aren't we?" he urged. "You've everything you need for yon bairn?"

"Everything," she agreed, "except for his dad. I need us to be able to walk out together with our heads up. I don't care what anybody else thinks as long as the three of us have each other and the rest of the world can see it. It's not as if Flo doesn't *know*, is it?"

"Just a bit more time is all I ask," he said, an uncharacteristic pleading undertone edging his request.

He put his arm round her shoulders and drew her to his chest, nuzzling her neck while fumbling with the buttons at the back of her dress. She breathed heavily for a few moments, but then stiffened and pushed him away.

"No," she insisted very firmly, knowing she was risking everything by rejecting his advances. "Not until you commit yourself to both me and our son."

"But…" he gasped, disappointed and surprised she had taken this stance.

He knew he couldn't live without her and his new son, and he knew he had loved her, in his own way, since that first encounter when they were teenagers. He *knew* he would have to find a way round his present situation or lose her again, like he had all those years before. Last time, through his inertia and indifference, he had let her go to another man – whom he knew well, and with whom she had had two children. He had regretted his inability to stand up for her then, and for many years after. He wasn't going to make the same mistake again. She *would* become Dotty Ingles, but he'd no idea how or when.

He lifted his sleeping son from his crib, kissed him on the forehead, and handed him back to his mother. A look of intense pain flickered across his eyes as he reached for the door. Then he was gone. That ominous click of the door's latch seemed to echo in Dotty's mind for an eternity as she dissolved into shoulder-convulsing sobs, burying her face in her bairn's shawl. Not knowing whether she would see Eric again, or whether she would even be able to keep a roof over her son's head, she felt she could no longer bear the uncertainty of their relationship.

-o-

"Is it dinner time yet, Mam?" Jack's gruff little voice filled the kitchen as Flo turned the meat in her oven. Although cooking with *this* range system was not an exact science she had learned to cope with its vagaries and idiosyncrasies over the last few months. She had honed her skills with the range at number 206 over several years, but this one was temperamental and difficult at times. She had had several significant failures, which her husband had been quick to beat her with, but she had noted a good deal of progress lately.

"Won't be long now," she assured him. "Hungry?"

"A bit," the little lad answered, and added tentatively, "but will Dad be having his dinner with us?"

Sunday roast dinner was Jack's favourite, but only if his dad didn't eat with them. He loved Yorkshire pudding, gravy and beef, and could eat up to bursting. Worrying that his father's anger and frustration might be taken out on him, he would eat little if his dad was early from the club.

The rattle of the gate and the heavy, regular footfall on the path down by the house froze the little lad where he stood. A look of apprehension and fear overcame his once happy smile, and his feeling of joyful anticipation for his favourite dinner was swept away by his father's early return. Expecting the worst, he shrank into the corner chair by the pantry door, hoping to become invisible once again.

"Club run out of beer?" Flo jibed, as the back door swung slowly inwards. Realising he was a full two hours earlier than usual for Sunday dinner, she knew instinctively something had not gone according to his simple routine plans. She wasn't, of course, going to give him the satisfaction of thinking she cared, so she didn't ask why. But she felt, after many years of his verbal abuse about her Sunday dinners, that she had to record her displeasure this time.

"Dinner won't be ready for half an hour, at least," she said, ready for his slurred, drunken response.

"I've not been to t' club," he said quietly, slumping into his usual chair. "Didn't have the stomach for it."

"You poorly, or summat?" Flo asked, a surprised smirk creeping up on her face at what had never happened before. Usually Sunday was his main drinking session of the week – afternoon and evening. Mealtimes were unwelcome interruptions. He got up, not wishing to encourage an altercation, and made for the stairs door.

"I'm going into t' garden for half an hour," he said. "Let me know when tha's got dinner out."

Flo was gobsmacked. She had never come across this before. Sunday lunch always became a battle ground over his drunken behaviour and his dislike of her cooking. According to him it was so poor he couldn't eat it, when she knew it was the four or five pints of Tetley's best bitter in his stomach preventing him from doing justice to her excellent cooking. This he knew, but wouldn't admit. The conflict had been quietened by an unexpected and silent ally that she wouldn't be able to fathom. She didn't care, as long as she might enjoy the sort of Sunday most other families had come to expect.

The gate clicked again, and lighter footsteps heralded William's arrival from his mate's.

"Hello, Mam," he said as he breezed in. "Dinner ready? I'm starving."

"Are you ever anything else, William Ingles?" she smiled. "I'd rather keep you a week than a fortnight, sometimes."

"Dad back from his drunks' club yet?" William asked dismissively.

"He's back," she answered quietly, pointing upstairs, "but he's not been drinking. Don't ask why, because I've no idea."

"Just one thing to say, Mam," William said as he was about to sit down for his dinner. "I've just found out—"

"That you need to wash your hands before dinner?" she interrupted.

"But…" he protested.

"Your little brother's watching you," she went on, trying to guilt-trip him. "Do you want it on your conscience for the rest of your life that you taught your brother not to…?"

"OK," he grinned. "I get it. Here I go, to wash my hands before my dinner. You watching, Little Jack?"

"I washed my hands already," Jack chipped in, "before you came in."

"Oh, so you have got a voice," William teased.

"I've always had a voice," Jack replied. "Although you couldn't understand me until I could say words."

"Always precise, eh, little man?" William teased further.

"Leave him be, William," his dad ordered, as he shouldered his way into the room. "He's only little."

"That 'little lad'," William insisted as he began to climb the stairs, "is cleverer than all of us put together. Mark my words."

"Dinner'll be in a quarter of an hour," Flo shouted after her son. "That goes for you, too, Eric. Food'll be on the table if you want it. If you don't I'm sure someone else will."

-o-

"That meal was excellent, Mam," William said as he pushed away his empty plate.

"You're such a polite young man," she said, a smile of satisfaction decorating her face.

"I enjoyed it as well," Jack added, as he finished off his last bit of Yorkshire.

Their father pushed away *his* empty plate, but said nothing. He knew it had been good but he couldn't bring himself to admit it, out of either guilt or embarrassment. It was significant to Flo that his plate was clean.

"I'm going up to have a nap," he said quickly as he made for the door.

"Don't want any home-made apple pie?" Flo offered.

His 'no' was drowned by his sons' eager 'yes, please', 'you bet', and 'make mine a large one'. Eric was so much out of his depth and out of place here that he felt he had to escape. He had never experienced the general give and take of real, normal family life, because his mind had always been dulled by drink. Was this all he had to look forward to with *this* family? Wouldn't he be better off with Dotty and little Eric? Merged images of both families crowded his mind as he dozed into oblivion.

"Studies going OK, William, love?" Flo asked as her boys polished off the remains of her apple pie. She really loved to watch them tucking into her home-made food. Best start in life she could give them, she always thought.

"Yes, Mam," he agreed, his mind more on his food than his answer.

"Any thoughts on what you might be doing afterwards?" she asked, thinking more long-term.

"Well," he said, plate wiped clean and all traces of custard removed from his mouth corners, "straight after, I'm going to Germany."

"Germany?" she said, startled, an extremely puzzled look invading her face. "What on earth made you think of Germany? What for, and who's going to pay for it?"

"The grammar school's organising an athletics exchange

with a secondary school in Bochum," he explained, "and I've been chosen, as the best shot-putter, to represent the district. It won't cost you anything, as it's been funded by several local businesses. All I need is a bit of spending money, and I've already got most of that from the Saturday jobs I've been doing over the last year. I've not got it from pocket money, though … because Dad doesn't give me any."

"Well," she shrugged, "you'll have to ask your dad. I don't know what he'll say. It's a big thing."

"He won't have a say," William insisted. "Chance of a lifetime, so I'm going, and that's that. Three weeks away in May/June, and then, because it's an exchange, we bring back a party from the school in Germany. The only thing we have to do is offer accommodation to the visiting students in our homes. Will there be a problem with that, Mam?"

"Your dad *will* have his say, but there won't be any problems as far as I'm concerned, love," Flo agreed.

"I thought we might offer the lad coming over with me his own room at Grandma's," William suggested. "What do you think?"

"Not going to happen," Flo said quite definitely. "You know her feelings on Germans."

"But the war's been over for seven years," William insisted, "and these young people had no more to with that than we did."

"We'll sort something out, certainly," Flo assured him, "but it won't involve your grandma and granddad. Sorry love, but they won't have anything to do with him."

"And what won't they have anything to do with?" Eric asked, as he sidled through the door. He listened to William's explanation without interruption and, uncharacteristically, added simply, "Tha can please thissen what tha does, as long as it doesn't cost me owt."

Mother and son looked at each other in surprise as Eric

made for the door, his old clothes on, ready for a foray into the wilderness that was the back garden.

"And is that it?" William said, as shocked as his mother. "No argument, no bombast, no objection? Something wrong with him?"

"I don' t know whether he's sickening for something or what," Flo replied, "but he's been like that all day, ever since he came back from the club without his usual barrel of ale inside his gut."

"Do you know what I think, Mam?" Jack said gruffly.

"What can you know, our Jack, that we don't already?" William smiled indulgently. He wasn't about to repeat his one honest admission about his clever little brother, but he *was* prepared to listen to anything *this* smart little chap had to say. He didn't say much, but what he did say was often uncannily close to the truth.

"Dad's been to see Dotty French and her son Eric today," Jack said disarmingly simply. "Something's been said, and it's made Dad unsure about something. He usually frightens me, but not today."

"How can you possibly know all that?" William guffawed at the impossibility of what his brother had just said. "You're guessing, aren't you?"

"No," Jack replied, no trace of defensiveness in his face. "I don't know how, but I just know."

"It's like he's a clairv … clairver …" Flo said, searching for the right word.

"Clairvoyant?" William suggested.

"Somebody who can see the future," Jack added quietly.

"How, at six years old, can you possibly know that?" his mam gasped. "I've got corns on my little toes older than you."

She looked at William for an answer, but all he could do was shrug his shoulders in resignation.

"There's been a change in Dad's ways today," Jack

finished off, "and that means better. I'm going outside for a ride on my bike. Is that all right, Mam?"

"Course it is, my sweet boy," Flo agreed, "but don't go too far."

"I might go down to Grandma's for a bit," he added as he unlatched the back door. His dad was cutting and slashing the waist-high grasses and weeds in the far corner of the garden so he didn't see Jack's little frame slide into the wash house side door, whence he retrieved his bike and slid out again. All the time he was in full view of his father he never took his eyes from his form. A residual fear of him was very much apparent.

Eric stopped and raised his head when he thought he heard the gate click. When nobody materialised after a few moments he got back on with his backaching chore, which did nothing for him emotionally. It *did*, however, allow him the time to think about what Dotty had said earlier.

"Hello, lad," Jud Holmes greeted his grandson. "It's nice to si thi."

"It's nice to see thee as well, Granddad," he replied with a chuckle. Although he spoke properly all the time, he loved to play at using his granddad's broad West Riding dialect. Jud broadened and deepened it even more when Jack was about, realising how much he enjoyed their repartee.

"Wista bahn, lad?" Jud asked, a grin on his face.

"Ah'm bahn to si Grandma," Jack returned immediately. "'Ow abaht thee, owd man?"

"Not so much o' the owd," Jud laughed. "If tha dun't mind."

"Is there anything I can do to help you, Granddad?" Jack asked, dropping back into his normal delivery.

"Aye, lad," Jud replied. "Tha can nip inside and gi' thi grandma an 'and to meck a pot o' tea, if tha wants."

"OK," Jack agreed. "I'll shout you when it's ready."

"Champion," his granddad said, rubbing his huge hands together. "And 'ow about a piece of that nice Victoria sponge thi grandma's just med, eh?"

"Aye, please," Jack said, clapping his hands in glee at the thoughts of her Victoria sponge.

"What's all that noise about, our Jack?" Marion said, as he bowled through the door. "My, but it's good to see you."

"Good to si thi, anorl," he said, dropping back into his granddadspeak.

"That'll do with your granddad's twang, I think, my lad," Marion corrected. "It's OK with him, but don't do it anywhere else. You speak so nicely usually."

"Sorry, Grandma," Jack replied.

"Now, then," she went on, "would it be a pot of tea you'd be wanting, and a piece of my sponge cake? Or you could have seed cake if you wanted?"

"Don't like seed cake, Grandma," Jack said, pulling a face in his mind. "But I do like sponge."

"I know, lad," Marion chuckled. "I know what you like. I was just having you on."

"Jud," she shouted. "Tea's mashed. You—?"

"I'm here, lass," he interrupted, not two paces behind her.

"Oh, for goodness' sake," she yelled, almost jumping out of her skin. "Don't do that. It's a good job I didn't have the cake in my hands, or you would have been scraping yours from the wall."

Little Jack threw up his hands in glee, cackling as he did so. He always liked his grandparents' house. It was so much fun with his granddad, even though Jud's practical jokes often got him into trouble with his wife. Their house was so much better than his, because it had a better garden, a better view, and a back gate to the field beyond. He had realised already that from here to the back entrance of school was a lot shorter than walking round the road to his own house.

He had yet to trial it, though.

"How's yon cake, Jack?" Marion asked. "Any good?"

"It's the best, Grandma," he said, his answer muffled by a large mouthful. They sat in front of a roaring fire which, in these houses in this predominantly coal area, had to be running throughout the day. It not only acted as the sole source for heating and hot water but it was their means of cooking and baking too. A small beige half-moon rug sat in front of the hearth, covering a red paisley patterned carpet. A small glass-topped coffee table held their mugs and plates.

"Any news from yours, Jack?" Marion asked. "I've not seen your mam for best part of a week."

The wireless played softly in the background, to the sounds of *Sing Something Simple* with Jack Emblow and The Cliff Adams Singers, which was Jud and Marion's favourite Sunday listening.

"William's going to Germany for three weeks soon," Jack said, as he finished his cake, "and when he comes back he'll be bringing his German friend with him. Me mam's not happy, but Dad doesn't care … Says he can please himself as long as *he* doesn't have to pay."

A stunned silence descended as Marion and Jud looked at each other, growing billows of anger beginning to cloud their faces.

Chapter 9

Whitsuntide was never going to be an easy time for William. He hated exams, and everyone seemed to think that these exams would dictate the paths he might tread for the rest of his working life. He would have preferred to have become a paid athlete, but there was no such thing … as yet. It had been mooted and discussed for some time, but athletics was still a gentlemen's amateur sport. So what would he become? How would he earn his keep? He had no idea.

His dad still offered him the only way out, as he saw it. But William wouldn't have listened to him even if it *had* been the only way. No. Something would turn up. He might even pass all his exams and float into something lucrative that he would enjoy for the rest of his working life… Pigs might fly.

Throughout his school life his limited ability had been compounded by a serious lack of effort. He hadn't grasped the need for study in this hotbed of achievement, and would have loved something – anything – to tie him to his aspirations for the future. His reports highlighted consistently his unfulfilled potential and his lack of real purpose in most of his areas of study. His English teacher, Mr Hewson, pinpointed the problem:

A lad with obvious potential, he assiduously refuses to prove me right in all my assumptions.

Although not as politely put, most of his teachers agreed with this sentiment.

It was obviously his cavalier attitude towards study and his exams which set him apart from his fellow students. However, it was the opposite force which set him apart from his fellow athletes. He was big and strong for his age, and a natural athletic champion. The best shot-putter for his age by miles in Yorkshire, he invested a great deal of time and effort in his training for this event. If athletics had been important enough to include in the examination curriculum he would have been top every time.

Unfortunately it wasn't, and William languished in a never-never land of false hopes and wasted time. The one high spot on an otherwise low-key calendar was the athletics trip to Germany, which he couldn't wait for.

His PE master had told him whom he would be staying with and whom he would be bringing back to stay. Pieter Muller lived in Westphalia in a professional family, where both parents worked. They had communicated once or twice in English, because William knew no other language, and both had shared their excitement at the six weeks they would spend together.

Flo still had serious reservations about the whole event. She knew trouble would be quick to follow from her mam and dad, and would be viewed as a betrayal of all her family. She would be damned if she supported her child in his chosen path, yet damned if she didn't. She felt in all conscience she must support him to achieve *something*, at least. Her mam would come round eventually.

Little did she know that Little Jack had taken a hand in helping to smooth the process. Understanding that his grandma wouldn't put up with a German in her house, he had volunteered to give up his bed at home to Pieter Muller so he could stay with his grandparents instead. Three weeks … what bliss. His grandma thought he was very clever and unselfish to suggest this wonderful solution. She didn't know the half.

Still, she wouldn't tell her daughter and other grandson just yet. There was plenty of time for that later.

Jack, too, was looking forward to those six weeks in the summer: three in a bedroom on his own, and three with his grandparents. There was a God.

-o-

Jack was a very self-sufficient little boy in that he needed no one else's input into his life but his family's. His mother was the pivot of his existence, without whom nothing else seemed to make sense. Although a very able little boy with huge potential, his mam was the lynchpin around whom the rest of his world revolved. Unlike most other children of his age he showed his feelings not as emotional outpourings but through his pragmatic logic and intelligent questions – many of which were not questions at all, merely observations. However, his observations were insightful and sharp, verging on the inexplicable and unbelievable.

School was good for him because it gave him a learning structure and a sense of purpose. It took his acquired knowledge and turned it into usable chunks, which he was able to assimilate. He was intelligent enough, though, to be able to adapt and use it flexibly to fit any circumstance. It didn't remain compartmentalised for long.

An enigmatic little boy, his teachers were astounded by his quiet yet accurate reasoning. He could seem to be quiet and unresponsive for much of his time in class, then surprise his teachers by the depth of reasoning he was able to display far beyond his years.

This difference didn't endear him to everyone. There were youngsters who found him to be queer, mainly because they didn't understand him and his ways. Norman Carter was in the older end of Class Five, making him around ten years old. A stocky, bullheaded boy – with an IQ somewhere below Jack's knees – he was your typical bully who preyed on children younger and smaller than him, whom he knew wouldn't be able to stand up for themselves. Devious and sneaky, slithering under the teachers' radar with his underhand dealings, he was clever enough not to be noticed.

"Well, if it isn't smart-arse Ingless," he growled at the beginning of morning playtime as he cornered Jack by the outside toilets. Gripping him by the shirt front and the scruff of his neck, he pushed him backwards into the corner of the wall which divided the junior school from the infant school. "Think you're so clever and better than all of us, don't you, Ingless? What do you think, Dennis?"

An easily led numbskull of a sidekick called Dennis Bott had just arrived, sensing there was fun to be had at the expense of this poor sap.

"I'm not called Ingless," Jack said. "It's Ingles. My name's Ingles."

"Well, I'm going to call you Ingless," Norman Carter menaced, "and if you don't say now what your new name is, you'll be sorry. What's your name?"

"My name's Ingles," he replied, not about to change his name for anyone. "Jack Ingles."

"Why, you—" Norman Carter threatened, clenching his fists menacingly.

"Carter," his name rang out loudly from the boys' entrance, "come here."

Mr Hardwick had been watching the bully's antics as soon as he had emerged from the toilet. He had taught his older brother Joe two or three years earlier, and he was the same nasty piece of work. He had reduced him to pitiful blubbering on a number of occasions, but this new one was different – a much harder nut.

"I've been watching you," the teacher warned once the boy was in front of him.

"What, sir? Me, sir?" Carter started, claiming to be the hard done by innocent that he wasn't. "What for, sir?"

"You know well what I'm talking about, lad," Mr Hardwick insisted, jabbing the boy in the chest with his finger. "That young boy you were trying to terrorise has done nothing wrong to you, so leave him alone."

"I was only talking to him, friendly like, sir," Carter protested. "Ask him."

"I'll do just that," the teacher said, knowing well how Little Jack would respond. "Jack … Jack Ingles. Could you come here, please?"

Little Jack had been watching and listening to how the teacher dealt with the bully, knowing well what a bully was and how he should be dealt with.

"Me, Mr Hardwick?" Jack said gruffly, as he approached. Dennis Bott had slunk away, not wishing to become involved.

"Yes, Jack," the teacher said. "Was our friend – Norman Carter, here – being friendly towards you just now?"

Jack thought for a moment or two, and then, choosing his words carefully, he said,

"No, Mr Hardwick, he wasn't. He is a bully, who threatened that I would be sorry if I didn't agree to changing my name. My name's Jack Ingles, not Jack Ingless. His friend Dennis Bott was there as well, though he didn't say anything. He just laughed, as if he was afraid of Norman Carter here."

"Why, you—" Norman Carter threatened, unable to control his anger.

"I might remind you, Carter," Mr Hardwick went on, moving his face closer to the lad's face, "that we don't like thugs and bullies like you in our school. I might also remind you that young Jack is three or four years younger, and a lot smaller than you. He does, however, have an older brother, who is a good deal bigger and stronger than you. He's called William, and is a district athletics champion."

"Think I'm afraid of that?" Carter replied insolently.

"I'd watch out if I were you," Mr Hardwick warned, "if you know what's good for you. He won't take kindly to his little brother being threatened like that. What I find amazing is that you are so stupid to do this to someone who lives just the other side of the road from you. Now clear off. I'm watching you."

Norman Carter slouched away, muttering almost inaudible threats and dire consequences on the little lad.

"You OK, Jack?" Mr Hardwick asked.

"Yes, Mr Hardwick," he answered, without any visible emotion. "Thank you, Mr Hardwick."

-o-

"So you thought you could get away from me, did you, Ingless?" A gruff and threatening voice attacked Jack from behind as he rounded the last corner to his house. A rough hand gripped him by the shoulder, and another slapped him at the back of the head. "Now we'll see what you and that toffee-nosed brother of yours are made of."

"Get off me, Norman Carter," Jack shouted. "How many times does that stupid brain of yours need telling? I'm … called … Ingles. Jack Ingles. Get it?"

"No," Norman Carter guffawed. "But you—"

Suddenly the bully was lifted from his feet by an almighty blow to his head. A look of abject fear and surprise washed over his face as William Ingles planted his foot firmly on Carter's chest, pinning him to the floor.

"So you're the brave little boy who's been plaguing my

brother," William snarled. "Not much to you, is there? You're about as brave as your brother Joe, whom I flattened similarly when *I* was at Woodhouse. I've got a lot bigger since then. And where's your brother now, eh? Going to ask him to come out and take his chances with me again? Didn't think so. He grew some sense, and I reckon he'd give you a worse duffing over than I have for picking on someone much younger and smaller than you."

"I'll tell me dad," Norman Carter squealed. "I'll tell me mam."

"You can tell who the hell you like," William said more quietly, with a great deal more menace. "But, if you as much as look at my brother again, I'll knock your bloody block off. Get it? Get … it?"

He pressed down on the lad's chest with a good deal of his fifteen stones behind it, before Carter's pathetically squealed "Yes" persuaded William to pick him up by his jersey. Drawing the bully's tear-stained face closer to his, William said,

"Just remember: I'll be watching you. Come on, Jack, let's have some tea."

He hoisted the young lad on to his broad shoulders and made his way back into number 44. Jack turned round once to see his tormentor slinking back through his gate, and pulled his tongue out at him before they rounded the corner of the house.

"Why didn't you tell me before?" William asked as he set his brother down by the back door. "I'd have given him what for much earlier."

"I thought he would go away if I ignored him," Jack explained, in his usual pragmatically precise way.

"Never works with bullies, my son," William advised. "It's always best to meet force with even greater force. If he troubles you again just let me know. But I don't think he will."

"But how did you know?" Jack asked in awe of his big brother. "And why aren't you at school?"

"Exams coming up soon," William said, "so study day. Good job, too, I'd say."

"Thank you, William," Jack said. "I like having a big brother. One day I would like to be like you."

"You're welcome, little man," William replied, and, in a rare moment of candour, he added, "Just promise me one thing … You will carry on as you are, and don't change anything? You'll be a lot better than me in your schooling. I just know you will."

"Hello, you two," Flo said as they trooped into the kitchen. The room was warm, greeting them with the welcoming smell of fresh baking. "Cup of tea and a mince pie or two?"

Flo knew that the way to their hearts was through the baking she produced regularly, and mince pies and sponge cake were their favourites.

"Did I hear a bit of a kerfuffle outside just now?" she asked, as she filled the giant brown teapot with leaf tea and boiling water.

"Just reminding yon Norman Carter that he needed to be friendlier towards our Jack," William explained, throwing a wink at him.

Jack smiled. He knew that *that* would be their secret, and that if he ever needed to call on his brother again he could.

"Problems?" Flo asked.

"Not now, Mam," Jack answered, a smile of satisfaction and anticipation parting his lips. "Your baking smells divine."

"Divine, is it?" she laughed. "I swear sometimes you've eaten a dictionary for breakfast."

"Dad home?" William asked, more out of politeness than interest. He had discovered a deep adolescent dislike of his father, following his threats towards his mother and their Jack. The issue with his father's illicit affair and sired child had added an overlayer of disdain and disgust. He once idolised his dad … how certain human frailties can change perceptions forever. Eric was still his dad, and in that there was a lot of happy history. It's just that he was no longer the god he had been.

"No idea. Don't care," his mam answered as she poured out three teas and dished out a plateful of warm baking. Her kitchen was a wonderful place. Primitive by any standards, with a fired range and one gas ring, the baking she produced there, however, was nothing short of magical – and the yardstick by which all future offerings would doubtless be judged for her sons. The mouth-watering smells would linger in this wonderland for days, reminding them that *their* mam was the best.

"He's either at work or … elsewhere," she continued. "He works so many extra shifts these days – he says – that I've lost track. *We* never see any extra brass, though."

"Never mind, Mam," William cut in. "One of these days *we'll* look after *you*."

"Won't be in my lifetime, I fear," she added prophetically. "Anyway, enjoy your pies. Tea won't be long."

Chapter 10

Since her serious bout of rheumatic fever at fourteen Flo had been carrying a ticking time bomb of an illness. She had contracted the illness from no one knew where, had been close to death, and had escaped – by the skin of her teeth – with a diseased and shrunken heart. She had been looked after by her parents throughout, who had tried to make her life as normal as possible in an age where this disease – like many others – usually ended in death, sooner rather than later. Although she never shared it with anyone – not even her husband – she understood the likely prognosis only too well. She had been advised not to have her two children.

"But what would life be without children?" she had always said. So, against all the odds and the collective medical wisdom, she met head-on and survived two difficult pregnancies. Now the busy and uncompromising life with a ne'er-do-well husband was beginning to take its toll. She had no idea how much time she had left, but her dearest wish was to see her boys off her hands, leading productive lives of their own. Then she would face whatever was going to happen.

She had never allowed her condition to dictate the course her life might take, and she never considered she was any different from anyone else. However, her mission had always been to do whatever she could for her children. She had been cautioned by parents and countless specialist medics to be careful with her life, and that so many things might shorten it prematurely. Yet here she was, close on forty years old, with two young, growing children whose lives would mean something after she was gone. She felt an enormous swell of pride when, in her quieter moments – though few and far between – she could look to *her* next generation, and the things they might achieve.

"Mam", Jack said, the Saturday morning before school was due to finish for its two-week Whitsuntide break, "are we going on holiday the week after next?"

"Whatever gave you that idea?" she retorted, putting down her mid-morning cup of tea and the newspaper her dad had left two days earlier. "Holiday? Since when have we been able to afford a holiday? You know full well that—"

"I heard Grandma and Granddad talking last Sunday," he replied, simple and straightforward as ever. "They thought I was listening to *Sing Something Simple* on the wireless, but I heard them whispering. Granddad doesn't whisper as quietly as Grandma, and I put two and two together."

"Hark at you," Flo laughed. "Anyone would think you were four times your age."

"Well, are we?" he insisted quietly.

She had promised herself that she would always tell her boys the truth so, under direct interrogation from her perceptive – and nosy – younger son, she said,

"To tell you the truth, Jack, Granddad has offered us – you and me – a week in Blackpool with them, from the second week of your Whit school holiday. Should we say 'yes'?"

"Of course we should. It would be rude not to… Fantastic," he whooped, dancing up and down. "But what about Dad and our William? Are they coming?"

"Your dad can't get the time off work," she answered, knowing that Jack would understand the whole story, "and our William will be in Germany on his school athletics trip. So it's just you and me and Grandma and Granddad. Will that be all right?"

"Yes, Mam," he replied, "it will."

Flo realised that knowing his dad wouldn't be coming would be a huge relief to Jack. Had Eric been there this little boy's holiday would have been ruined. A week in Blackpool… He had heard so much about it that he couldn't wait.

"How are we going to get there, Mam?" Jack asked again, after lunch.

"Where, sweet boy?" his mam replied from the front room, knowing what he meant. She liked to have him on a bit, which she thought he knew and shared. You never could be too sure with Jack, though.

"You know where, Mam," Jack smiled, understanding the game she was playing with him. "To Bridlington, of course."

"Bridlington? But…" she gasped, darting a glance at him. "Ah, you wicked boy. Playing me at my own game, eh?"

They both laughed, enjoying each other's company without interruption. He was a lovely boy, she felt, and learning so quickly.

"Are we going by train to Central Station?" he asked. "And then to Mrs Ridge's at number 52 Central Drive?"

"How on earth did you know that?" she asked, dumbfounded that he knew something she had only just found out.

"Granddad's not-very-quiet whisper to Grandma," he answered, a grin splitting his face. "We have to make sure he doesn't know *we* know, or it might spoil his surprise. You know what he's like."

He loved his granddad – and his grandma too, of course. For her Jack was becoming a daily reminder of the Jack she had lost only eight or so years before. They would never get back the joy of those years, but Little Jack might fulfil a higher purpose.

"Does Dad still live with us, Mam?" Jack said, throwing his curveball into the conversation unexpectedly. "Only I've not seen him for ages."

"Would you be upset if I said 'no'?" Flo asked, knowing already what the answer might be.

He sat for a few minutes, fiddling with his small store of toys before he ventured his answer.

"Not sure," he said at last. "I feel sorry that he doesn't want to be with us. I feel sorry for *him* more than anything, I suppose. I don't like the way he treats me sometimes, but I thought that about Norman Carter before our William had words. If Dad never came back I don't think it would bother me too much."

Flo hadn't expected such a thoughtful response. She felt he might have said 'no' without too much concern for his father. How could anyone not want to spend time with a child like Jack, who was rapidly becoming his own person with an opinion on most things?

"Is it all right if I go out to play with Gordon Gittins next door? He's got two big swings in his back garden, and he says I can share."

"Course you can, love," Flo replied. "Just watch out for the weather. It's forecast showers. You know the rhyme about May showers, don't you, our Jack?"

"It's April showers, I think, Mam," Jack corrected her as he opened the back door. "April showers bring forth May flowers…" she heard him reciting as he skipped down the path. Although the fence was low enough between the two gardens she knew Jack would never climb over. He would skip down his own path, open and close both gates and skip down the Gittins's path only as far as their side door. He would wait there for permission from Gordon's mam before going any further. He had an inbuilt sense of propriety and belonging, had Little Jack, and of where he fitted into this expanding world of his.

-o-

"'Ow many times do I have to tell thee, lad, that tha's getting nowt from me for any trip to bloody Germany?" Eric snarled.

"How mean is that?" William returned quickly. "I only asked for a measly few quid, because I've got most of what I need from my Saturday job savings."

"You should have thought of that when you said what you had to say the other week," he said, turning his back.

"Thanks," William said sarcastically. "Some father you turned out to be."

"Just be careful what tha says, lad," Eric rounded on him. "I *am* thi father. Show some respect."

"Or what?" William threatened, pulling himself to his full height. "What respect have you ever shown me mam, me or our Jack? You're no father to me. As far as I'm concerned you don't exist. I'll go and have a word with Granddad. He's twice the man you are. He'll help."

William turned and stomped out, leaving his father red-faced and fuming.

"Well done, husband," Flo said as she walked into the kitchen. "Only the second time he's ever asked you for anything and you blow him away. How to alienate your own son, eh? Going to do the same with your other son? Your Eric?"

"None of your bloody business *what* I do," he said.

"Well," she replied, as he headed for the door and escape, "I hope, when you need it, *your* children offer you the same sort of comfort and support you have given to *them* … and then you can't complain."

The door rattled on its hinges as he flounced out, leaving Flo with a satisfied smile on her face.

She was worried about William. Out of a quiet, sickly child she had watched this colossus grow. Although still quiet and introverted in many ways he had begun to embrace what life was about for a rapidly developing young man. He hadn't yet, however, even started to grasp the urgency of organising his future through his academic studies. His naivety in trusting in the native wit he didn't actually possess would be his undoing, she felt sure. Yet how could she, an ordinary lass for whom a grammar school education could never have been an option, tell *him* how to conduct himself in a modern educational world? William – like so many other youngsters of his age – believed he knew everything, only to find at some important time that crucial knowledge and experience were severely lacking.

Flo had almost given up, realising that the only redemption for her son would come through his desire to succeed. She hoped he wasn't heading for a rude awakening with his exams, but she feared the worst. She hoped beyond all hope that he wasn't providing a stick for his father to beat him with.

After a dodgy start May turned into a scorching month, where shrubs and trees came into bloom early and were gasping for water by the middle of the month. Teachers were glad to leave airlessly hot classrooms behind them for a while, and William's examination nightmare overwhelmed him. It was only when he emerged from his first exam that he realised just how inadequate his preparation had been. Overnight the maths that he enjoyed in class had become an alien language, and the geography he felt he knew most about had turned into the geography of the outer solar system for what use it had been to him.

He knew from the off that he was destined to fail …

just how big a failure he would discover in mid August. There was nothing he could do now except his best, rely on good fortune, and look forward to Germany. Perhaps he might stay there. Perhaps all this might be scaremongering. Perhaps the earth might open and swallow him up. There were always resits in November and the following May. He couldn't worry about that too much now, because he had an important three weeks to plan and train for.

Little Jack took everything in his stride, as usual. Although supported by hardly any books at home his reading leaped ahead in Mrs Gunn's class. He could often be found at playtimes – and he had stayed in school the odd dinner time – crouching behind the open bookcase in the classroom, his face buried in some book he wouldn't have had any chance to acquire at home. His life was also clear of that worrying lump that was Norman Carter, who glowered when he saw Jack but never approached him. The power of a much bigger older brother, eh? Jack too was looking forward to a break from the mundanity of ordinary life.

He'd never been to Blackpool before. He'd never been to stay anywhere alien since Bridlington, which he had loved, even at eighteen months old. So the opposite coast would be an adventure to treasure. Unlike most other children going on holiday he had looked it up in the school's outdated encyclopaedia, and was in awe of the Tower and the three piers he was going to see. People like Jack didn't get opportunities like this very often, and so *he'd* decided he wasn't going to miss anything, from the steam train ride from his local station into Central Station Blackpool to dipping his toes in the Irish Sea.

"Looking forward to our holiday next week?" his mam asked him over tea once school had closed its doors for Whit. "Not long now, our Jack."

"Have you ever been to Blackpool, Mam?" he asked her.

"No, love, I haven't," she answered. "But I do know a little bit about it. Shall I tell you what I know?"

"It's OK, Mam," he said simply. "I already know about the Tower and the South and Central and North Piers. I'm looking forward to donkey rides on the beach, and to watching a Punch and Judy show. I've already paddled in the North Sea, so I should like to do the same in the Irish Sea."

"Oh, I see," she said smiling. "Did you notice my joke there, Jack?"

"Yes, Mam, I did," Jack replied, seriously, "but it wasn't funny."

-o-

In the lives of West Riding working folk, holidays almost always stretched for one week from Saturday to Saturday. The traditional time of year for mass migrations to either coast was late July into August – the months when schools were closed and youngsters had the least disruption to their education.

Jack loved his schooling, and wouldn't have wanted to miss any of it. He had become convinced, of course, that his mam's original assurances had been correct, which surprised her to hear it from his lips.

"You were right, Mam," he said, as they were packing their things the day before their trip to Blackpool.

"I'm your mother, Jack," she laughed. "I'm always right. But, what am I right about today?"

"*Nearly* always right, Mam," Jack replied quite seriously. "But do you remember when you tried to persuade me I would enjoy nursery?"

"I think I do," she said, frowning slightly. "Why do you ask?"

"Well," he went on, "I didn't."

"Oh," she said, taken aback slightly by his unexpected

answer.

"But I did – I do – enjoy what came after nursery," he finished, quite pleased with himself. "I don't think I would have enjoyed junior school as much if I hadn't gone to nursery first, though. There … packed."

His little rectangular suitcase contained all his toys, which took up only one corner, one pair of shorts, a sock, his outdoor coat and a school library book whose pages were loose and in the wrong order.

"We're going to have to look at your packing, sweet boy," Flo smiled. "I think you're going to need more than this for a week at the seaside, don't you?"

"Yes, Mam," he agreed. "But I don't really know what I'll need. Will you help me, please? And will you tell me why?"

"Of course I will," she said, quite taken by his interest.

They went through all his dress needs and put his clothes in one by one very carefully, while he looked on, until his case was packed to the brim. He had a last look before his mam snapped the lid shut, and he said,

"Job's a good 'un," before he put the case to the floor.

"Don't tell me," she said, raising her eyebrows, "you got that saying from your granddad."

"No, Mam," he replied, matter-of-factly. "Mr Hullock, our caretaker, always says it when he's done a repair in school, whether it's a good one or not."

"Just out of interest," she said in return, "how can you tell whether it's a good one or not?"

"If you'd ever seen Mr Hullock working in school," he answered, "you'd know."

They both laughed at the picture conjured by Jack's words and the faces he pulled as he mimicked the caretaker. He was a caution, that Jack, and no mistake.

"You'll need to be in bed in good time tonight," Flo warned. "Up early in the morning, to prepare for a long train journey. I'm sure there'll be lots of families following us."

"Why would they want to follow *us*, Mam?" Jack asked, not understanding why anyone might want to follow them. "Is it because they can't find their own way?"

Flo laughed at her little boy's confusion about the use of certain idiomatic phrases, and explained what the expression meant. He wouldn't get it wrong the next time.

-o-

The last few days had been frenetically busy for Flo. She'd had to get William ready, packed, and off on his athletics trip, sort out washing and ironing for *her* holiday, and tidy the house. She had not seen her husband for several days. In fact he was spending so much time either at work, in bed, or elsewhere, that she didn't know whether he lived there with them any more. She couldn't tell by his clothes because he never had many, anyway – not that she cared, but it would have been nice to have had a share of the extra cash he was earning to replace stuff in the house and her youngsters' clothing. Fortunately, she had an account at the local Co-op where she did much of her daily shopping. Dividend time came round once a year, usually in time for Christmas, but the divvy didn't seem to go far. Still, there were others who were much worse off than her.

"You up, Jack?" Flo shouted from the bottom of the stairs. "It's seven o'clock, and you need to be … getting … yourself … up."

Her voice slowed and drifted off to a whisper as she beheld a ghostly little figure, fully dressed in his new short pants, bright T-shirt, and sandals, his suitcase in one hand and his tatty book in the other.

"I'm ready, Mam," he said. "Can we go now?"

"Breakfast first," she said, only just able to contain her mirth. "We're not going anywhere until we've eaten. Have you brushed your teeth and hair?"

"Yes, Mam," he replied, taking the stairs steadily.

"Then down here quickly, and we'll have a bite to eat," she said. "I've done some sandwiches, buns, and a flask of tea for the train, so it's a bacon sandwich for breakfast and a cup of tea. OK?"

"Yes, please," he said, eyes lighting up like Blackpool Illuminations. "I love bacon sandwiches. I don't think I've had one before, though. Are they as good as they sound, Mam?"

"Haven't I made you a bacon sandwich before?" she gasped, throwing her hands in the air in mock horror. "Then, I'll make you one every week from now on. Agreed?"

"Yes please, Mam," he answered, entering into the spirit of their repartee. "But you don't *have* to. I can always wait until I'm grown-up, and then ... I can get my wife to make me one."

"You are such a funny boy," Flo said, roaring with laughter, as he took his first ever mouthful of bacon sandwich.

"Bacon's from a pig, isn't it, Mam?" he said, his words muffled.

"Yes, I think it is," she said. "Why do you ask?"

"Well," he said after careful deliberation, "if *I* eat too much, would you say I was making a pig of *myself*?"

"Course not," she said, a quiet smile of satisfaction growing on her face. This was the little boy who was quiet and almost introverted in his earlier life because of a lack of self-confidence ... and now look at him, making up his own funnies and having the brass neck to share them with an audience. "I'd say don't grunt while you're eating."

They both laughed while they ate, enjoying each other's company and glorying in the time they had together.

"That's rayt," a gruff and aggressive voice burst into their world, freezing Little Jack to his chair and stopping him in mid chew, "enjoy yersens while others work to keep you here."

Eric Ingles had finally shown his face after four days. A heavily bristled face and red-rimmed eyes showed he hadn't slept for some time.

"Well, well," Flo said sarcastically, keeping her back to him, "so you *are* still alive then."

"I hope you both enjoy your holiday, being looked after while I'm stuck here working to pay for it," Eric snarled, sarcastically.

"Your choice," she butted in. "*Our* family here hasn't changed from what it was five years ago when we all enjoyed our stay at Bridlington. *Your* new family is what's changed everything. And, by the way, you haven't paid for the holiday at all. That's down to me dad."

Jack hadn't moved since his dad had appeared unexpectedly. His half-eaten sandwich remained poised in his hand, his shoulders slumped, and his eyes fixed on the table before him. If he could have slipped into the shadows and become invisible he would have done so.

"I'm goin' to bed," Eric growled as he made for the stairs. "Don't meck any noise when you sneck the door behind you."

"We'll be gone in half an hour," she shouted as he disappeared, his clogs clattering on the stairs as he went. "Just don't meck any mess for me to clear up when we get back."

She couldn't make out his mumbled reply, which was probably as well. It probably wouldn't have been complimentary.

Little Jack breathed out slowly, softly, as if he had been holding his breath the whole time his father's presence threatened. He continued eating his sandwich and lifted his baleful green eyes towards his mother's.

"Can we go, Mam?" he whispered. "Can we go soon,

please?"

"Yes, chick," she soothed. "Yes we can. Half an hour at most. Granddad's arranged for Mr Lee to pick us up at theirs in time for us to catch the eleven o'clock train. I think we have to change the train somewhere or other."

"Change it for what, Mam?" he asked, the last bite of his bacon chasing itself around his mouth in its haste to reach his stomach. "Change it into a bus? Or a motor car? Or...?"

"No, love," she smiled, still surprised by his youthful naivety about worldly things. Because he often came out with some amazing stuff she tended to overlook the fact that wasn't yet seven, and much of what he did was for the first time. "Our train won't take us direct to Blackpool, so we'll have to get off this one at some other station and catch one that will."

"What will happen if our first train is late and we miss our new one?" he asked very pointedly. "Will we have to come back home? I don't want to come back home, Mam."

"Don't worry," she assured him, stroking his spiky head. "It's not going to happen."

She knew full well why he didn't want to come back from his holiday before it had begun. If he could be assured that his dad wouldn't be here he wouldn't mind so much. If his father came in on him unexpectedly he could become invisible. But walking in with him already there he would stand out, exposed. *That* he wouldn't be able to cope with at all.

"But..." he carried on.

"Time to brush your teeth and wash your face," she insisted. "We need to get our stuff together."

She started clearing the breakfast things away and tidying things up. She loved this new modern house, where she could wash up without having to boil buckets of water in her blackleaded range. It was magical, running as much hot water as she needed simply by the turn of a tap. She often thought back to the hard old days of filling a tin bath in front of the fire, and – worse – having to empty it at the end. Pity she couldn't wash away her outdated, unnecessary husband in the same way.

One day, perhaps. One day.

Chapter 11

"Granddad," Jack shouted, as he dropped his little case in their porch by the side door and rushed through into the kitchen. "We're here."

"Aye, lad," his granddad said, stepping aside smartly from this human projectile that was his grandson. "I can see thy is. Now quieten thissen down a bit, or t' neighbours'll want to come wi' thi. I can't afford to teck all t' street. I'm not made o' brass, tha knows."

"All rayt, Granddad," Jack replied, a joyful glint in his eye, dropping into his granddad's broad West Riding twang. "Ah know tha's not med o' money, so ah'll shurrup, if that's all rayt wi' thee."

They all burst out laughing at this comical piece of theatre that only Little Jack could perform. The sound of a sixty-year-old Yorkshire pitman's dialect oozing from the lips of a child a tenth his age brought tears of mirth to their eyes.

"Well," Jud said, "I've been looking forward to this adventure of ours for some little while now. I've a feeling, weather permitting, it's going to be a rayt good do."

"I do believe tha's rayt, owd cock," Jack replied, quick as a flash. "I 'ope tha's browt enough brass for t' ice creams and stuff."

Their renewed guffaws were interrupted by a rap at the door.

"It's Mr Lee," Flo said, as she gathered their belongings and ushered her pocket-sized entertainment to the path outside. "Toilet, Jack, before we set off."

"Been, Mam," he replied. "Ready to go." He had learned by now when to react to his granddad's dialect and when to shut off. Flo had noticed this, and had marvelled at how quickly he assimilated and reacted to situations. Would that he could do that with regard to his father.

-o-

"Are we there yet, Mam?" Jack asked, as he watched the billowing smoke streaming out behind the speeding engine, reminding Flo of similar questions asked by her other boy several years before. Only that time it was a journey to the other coast, and Jack was only a baby.

"We read a poem the other day at school," Jack went on, "about a train. It was called 'Night Mail'."

"And what made you think of that, sweet boy?" his mam asked, interested to try to understand his thought processes.

"Well," he replied after a moment or two, "it's about a mail train rushing through the countryside at night to make sure the post will be delivered the next day."

"Mail train?" his granddad asked, recognising the lad's eagerness to share his learning. "How does it work, then?"

Happy to take centre stage and astound his family with what he had learned, they all sat back either side of the table, smiling while he gave them his lesson for the day. Entirely comfortable with an eager audience, Jack missed no detail from the lessons he had enjoyed in his class only a few days before.

"Can you remember any of that poem?" Marion asked. "I never had the patience or the memory to learn poetry, and now I wish that I had."

"I can remember a few lines, I think," Jack said, his eyes half closing and his chin dropping to his chest in concentration, "but not enough to be of any use now. If you're interested, Grandma, I can write it out for you when we get back home."

"Thank you, Jack," she smiled, genuinely pleased. "That's very kind of you. I'd like that."

> *Jack settled back in his comfy seat,*
> *Excitement driving his shuffling feet;*
> *A studied look in his little green eye,*
> *As he watched the fields go streaming by;*
> *And listening to the clickety-clack*
> *Of wheels racing over the jointed track.*

-o-

"Are we there yet, Granddad?" he asked quickly, knowing what the answer would be.

"Not far off, our Jack," Jud said with a smile, understanding the lad's excitement, "but…"

"I can see it," Jack gasped in awe. "The Tower. It's just … there."

"Well spotted, that, man," his granddad said, clapping softly in congratulation.

The train slowed, allowing an acrid smell of sulphur dioxide to seep into the carriage through half-open and ill-fitting windows with casements worn through constant use. Platform 2 slid under the carriage steps almost imperceptibly, encouraging the engine to stop … now.

Jack knelt on the seat and pressed his nose against the window, occasionally looking both ways up and down the platform.

"What is it, Jack?" Flo asked, concerned that something

was bothering him. "What are you looking for?"

"We've arrived," he said, a note of disappointment tingeing his words, "and I don't see him."

"See whom?" his grandmother asked. "Have you invited somebody else?"

"No," he said, as close to irritation as anyone with *his* easy-going temperament could be. "It's Mr Lee. I don't see him."

"Do you mean Mr Lee the taxi man, by any chance?" Flo queried.

"Yes, of course," Jack urged. "He's the taxi driver, and he should be here to pick us up."

"He doesn't work like that, I'm afraid, our Jack," Jud laughed. "He lives in our town, and wouldn't follow us here just to give us a lift to our digs. Besides, Central Drive is only a very short walk away. We will be there in five minutes, once we get off this train."

"Mrs Ridge will be waiting for us with a cup of tea and some cake," Marion said. "So come on. Let's get a shake on."

-o-

Number 52 Central Drive was one of those late Victorian mews houses which would have sold for a fortune had it been in the capital. Here, though, they *did* look splendid, set on four floors plus attic – and each boasting ten double and two single bedrooms, with a shared bathroom on each floor. Not purpose-built, they harkened back to an era of moneyed people enjoying the bracing therapeutic advantages of a comfortable life by the sea.

Mrs Ridge had been a landlady for more than twenty years, from the time when music hall theatre had been approaching the height of its popularity. In that time she had attracted some of the best-known acts of the day to stay in her digs.

"Marion and Jud Holmes," Mrs Ridge announced as they all trooped through her glass and brass front door, at the head of fourteen wide marble steps and a brass balustrade. "How good to see you again. Your daughter Florence, I take it? And who's this little chap, then?"

"Jack," his little voice piped up with some confidence. "I'm Jack Ingles, my grandma and granddad's grandson."

Stunned by his forthright and convoluted explanation about his relationship with the grown-ups surrounding him, she about-faced and led them to their rooms on the ground floor at the back of the house overlooking the garden. Their two rooms were the only ones on this floor, in a quiet alcove where they would be the only ones to share the bathroom. This suited them fine.

Her attention to detail was what made Mrs Ridge stand out above all the others in the area. Almost all her guests were annual returners, making it extremely difficult for newcomers to break in. Mostly accepted by invitation only, hers was an exclusive club where loyalty was rewarded with good accommodation – and care in familiarity.

"What do you think, Jack?" Flo asked her son, who wore a puzzled and unsure look on his face. The room was bigger than his at home, and boasted two large single divans. There was a sink in the window wall's far corner, and a view over Mrs Ridge's back garden. "Is something wrong?"

"I thought we might be able to see the sea," he replied, once he'd thought through his answer. "It's only a … garden."

"None of these houses has a sea view," she explained. "In Blackpool most of the guest houses are not on the sea front, so you can see the sea only from outside. This is what we're going to do. You can't build sandcastles, paddle in the sea, and ride donkeys from inside, silly."

"OK, Mam," he replied, a little happier with her explanation. "Then can we paddle in the sea, now, please?"

"Give us chance to unpack a bit – have a bite to eat – and then we'll go out," she reassured him. "OK?"

"Yes, Mam," he smiled, and rubbed his hands together. "That'll be fine. Do you think Granddad will want a paddle with me?"

"I'm sure he—" she started.

"Just what I were thinking missen," Jud said as he opened the door. "Would ta fancy a paddle, owd cock, in t' sea?"

"Aye, ah would that, me owd Granddad," Jack laughed, answering him in like. "Shall we teck us shoes and socks off an' splash abaht a bit in t' salty watter, like?"

"I'm all for it if thy is," Jud answered, as if talking to one of his old pit pals.

"Well, nar," Jack added, "let's ger off then."

"What did I say, Jack?" his mam laughed.

"OK, Mam," he agreed apologetically. "Soon. Is that all right with you, Granddad?"

"Spot on," Jud acknowledged, while mouthing a 'sorry' to Flo. "See you in ten."

"When we've been to the beach," Jack asked, once his granddad had gone, "can we go to the Tower, and then to South, North and Central piers? And then—?"

"Whoa, Cowboy," Flo said. "Steady now. We've got another six days to do all that. We can't do it *all* in one day. Or would you like to do it all tomorrow, and then go home?"

"No, Mam," Jack agreed. "Tomorrow, the Tower; the day after, Central Pier; the following day…"

"We'll see," she said hurriedly, throwing her hands in the air. "Let's not make any hard and fast lists or diaries for now, shall we? We'll do whatever *we* think is good to do. Is that all right, chick?"

"Course it is, Mam," Jack replied, which brought a smile to her face. "Whatever you say."

-o-

"Hello?" her little voice sounded a mite fearful. "Hello? Who's there?"

"Come on," Eric's heavily hoarse whisper cut through the darkness at her back door. "Open up, will you? It's me."

"I know who it is …" Dotty insisted, "now. I didn't before."

"What's thy afeared about?" he asked pointedly. "There's nowt to be afeared of round here."

"You never know," she said, locking the door behind him. "I'm not exactly the woman everyone wants to be seen with. I never did win any popularity polls, but now … And Little Eric doesn't have any friends, either."

"'E's nobbut a bairn, for God's sake," he hissed. "'Ow on earth can you base your life on whether a baby has any friends or not? You can't be serious."

"You don't know what it's like," she said, "being an outcast. It's all right for you. You can creep in and out of here when *you* want, without anybody seeing or knowing. Well, I've news for you, Eric Ingles. You can't any more."

"What does that mean … can't?" he asked, a warily puzzled look on his face. "Is tha trying to say what I think tha's saying?"

"I'm sick of being your quiet, invisible little whore …" she snarled, "someone who'll come running at the click of your fingers. Well, no longer. Choice time, Eric."

"What does tha mean, 'choice'?" he said defensively.

"Time to choose," she repeated, courage welling up inside, "between your present family, and … us."

"Tha can't do that," he argued. "I…"

"Oh, but I can," she insisted. "Make your mind up, Eric, or the next time you want to see your son *we* won't be available. Now go."

"*Too* bloody right," he growled. "And don't thee expect anything more from me, because…"

"What have I ever had from you but grief and

embarrassment?" she threw at him as he made for the door. "Quiet, compliant little Dotty will do as I want. She'll be grateful she's got me. She will be *grateful* when that door closes behind you. You *will* choose your – our – son, or you won't see him again."

Always one to cut his nose to spite his face, Eric refused to dance to her tune. He would wait her out, and she *would* come round. How could she not? They had known each other since childhood – and although their paths diverged for a while their bond had always been there, waiting to be recemented … hadn't it? This was unlike him. Doubts in his ability as a man had begun to fester. One door had been closed with Flo and his sons, and now another one was dithering on its hinges. What now? His club held his answer, he was sure. All he had to do was wait. He was prepared. Yet the bottom of a pint glass could hold his interest only for so long, and then…

-o-

What had she done? Was it her who had just turned away the only man she had ever really wanted since that first inept fumbling as a teenager? Shouldn't she have been more patient, more understanding? Pride and self-respect were important to her, but at what price? Damn … damn … shouldn't have been so impatient … should have waited a bit longer.

He was taking her for a mug – someone to use and not commit to, surely. The sex was amazing, but that wouldn't last forever. Then what? No. She had done the only thing she could. He had left her no choice. She would bide her time. It was the only way. She had shown him she wouldn't be messed about. But … what if he didn't come back? What if she had given him the easy way out? She *knew* Eric Ingles. He was stubborn. Yet she could wait only for so long, and then…

-o-

"Mam?" Jack piped up at the breakfast table, which overlooked the back garden. The circular table was large by any standards, and was covered by a brilliant white cloth, which Mrs Ridge changed every day. Fastidious in the extreme, it was important she ran a clean house. Her business depended upon it. Her life depended upon it, too.

"Yes, chick?" Flo answered, in the low, quiet voice people always seemed to use during a conversation in busy rooms. "What is it?"

Jack, of course, didn't follow such conventions, because he had neither known about them, nor would he have understood if he had. He *was* only six, when all said and done.

"I can't see any porridge on the table over there," he answered, a little concerned that his usual breakfast wasn't on offer. First breakfast of the week, and he had seen a fault in the system already. "And why are you whispering? Have you caught a sore throat?"

"There's plenty of other stuff you like, I'm sure," she answered, a slightly embarrassed cough announcing a little increase in volume. "What about cornflakes or Weetabix or … Wheaties?"

"What's Wheaties, Mam?" Jack asked while sipping his orange juice through a brownish straw, which wasn't easy. Straws never lasted long because they always unravelled and turned into a chewed mush before the glass had become half empty. "Is it another name for porridge?"

"No, it's…" she stammered, aware that everyone else in the room was looking at her and her son. Jack was the only child in the guest house at that time, because Mrs Ridge didn't do … children. She had relented this once as a favour to Marion and Jud. So Jack was on trial. He didn't know it, but his success at being invisible would decide whether this would be his one and only visit to 52 Central Drive. "On second thoughts, how about an egg and…?"

"Bacon and tomatoes and beans?" he interrupted. "They're my *second* favourite breakfast."

"But, you've never had that before," she hissed, puzzled as to where that had come from.

"Well," he went on after a few moments of thought, "if I *had*, it *would* have been my second favourite."

The adults in the room burst into great guffaws of warming laughter, which left Flo a little embarrassed again until she realised they were laughing *with* him and not *at* him.

"Why are they laughing, Mam?" he asked, his nose wrinkling in its usual puzzled way when he was unsure. "Is it because there's no porridge?"

"It's because you're such a funny little boy," she smiled, nodding at the other guests. "Egg and bacon and fried tomatoes it is, then. No beans, thank you very much."

-o-

"What's it to be, then, young 'un?" Granddad Jud asked Jack once breakfast had been dispatched and digested. "Does tha know, I fancy a walk on the sands, and a paddle. I don't know what thy wants to do."

"A paddle would be just the job, Granddad," Jack replied. "But we'd better be careful not to traipse through any of that 'funny' sand on our way to the sea."

"Funny sand?" Flo puzzled, not knowing where her strange little boy had heard that one. "I've not heard that one before."

"Well," Jack started, "it's not really sand at all. It's poo, you know."

"Jack," Flo said, shocked to hear him telling about something he'd never found the same fascination with as many others of his age. "That's enough."

"Sorry, Mam," he said quietly but firmly. "I've no wish

to offend you, but it does get pumped into the sea when it's been made clean. Mr Tomlinson did a lesson on how we clean up our messes, and what we do with it when it's been sorted. Sometimes it comes back with the tide and covers parts of the beaches. I think it's clean by then, but I still don't want to put my feet in it."

"I'm rayt glad tha told me about that, our Jack," Jud added. "And I were just going to have an ice cream, too."

"I'd like one, Granddad," Jack enthused, "and then I'd like a paddle, a donkey ride, and to watch Punch and Judy."

"Couldn't have chosen better missen," Jud agreed. "Now where's yon ice cream van?"

Chapter 12

The beach was crowded with every known shape and size of humanity vying for their own square yard of sand upon which to soak up the hot Fylde sunshine. Ridiculous windbreaks with their vividly striped three yards of deckchair material swinging loosely between flimsy sticks tried vainly to shield modesty, while inadequate sand-impregnated towels hovered above trembling knees and attempted to hide the switch from soggy costume to sandy underwear. Knotted handkerchiefs swayed like fields of grotesquely shaped daisies wilting in the waterless wastes of some breathless and airless desert.

Pink, bloated bodies threaded their unsteady way between glorious sandcastles surrounded by deep and treacherous moats … and snoring heads marked the whereabouts of half-buried bodies, their tacky tin trays barely preventing cups and jugs of tea from sharing the same untimely fate as those buried, half-cooked piles of flesh.

Gaily striped deckchairs spilled on to the front, nestling in their own little piles of shifting sand … their ranks growing as more people sought to rest their aching limbs, their heartfelt 'oohs' and 'ahs' resonating with their nodding neighbours. Noise covered all, like a gigantic bubble, where the clanking and scraping of tram wheels mingled with countless swazzle-induced calls of 'That's the way to do it', from Punch and Judy shows ... Blackpool in all its common glory.

"They're not real, you know, Granddad," Jack said as they sat on an old green weathered bench on the front, feet on the metal barrier before them as they ate fish and chips from the paper.

"What're not?" his granddad said as his muffled voice tried to force its way out of a mouthful of battered cod.

"They're just puppets, really," Jack went on, throwing a couple of cold chips into the air for the seagulls to catch.

"What's tha talking about, Jack lad?" Jud asked, still not quite following his grandson's tale.

"You know," he said, "Punch and Judy. They're made out of wood and cloth. I like the crocodile when he tries to eat the sausages. They're not—"

"Aye," his granddad interrupted, "I know ... not real."

"I *was* actually going to say that they're not what crocodiles would eat usually," Jack sighed, wishing people would listen *and* follow what he was saying. "But I suppose beggars can't be choosers."

Flo smiled through her lunch. A lot of Jack's sayings came from her dad, she had noticed.

"Such old-fashioned language for such a young boy," her mam would say. There was always a touch of quaintness about him that she never saw in William, or in any of the other children she knew. Trust her Jack to be different.

"I noticed tha sat at t' back o' t' crowd while other children were in a group shouting," his granddad observed after a while. "I thought tha liked it, didn't tha?"

"I do," Jack answered slowly, "but I like to *watch* and *listen*. Those others make too much noise, which blots out the good stuff, and that's why I like to sit out. There's no point being there if you can't hear properly. Besides ...

sometimes … they … smell."

The adults cast furtive glances at each other, trying not to laugh, their faces aching with suppressed grins.

"Is it Blackpool Tower this afternoon, Granddad?" Jack asked, finally breaking the silence. "Or Central Pier? I know tha's not med o brass, Granddad, me owd flower, so I'm prepared to pay my way with some of my saved pocket money. What's it to be?"

This time they could contain themselves no longer. Jud's face split in a huge guffaw, and Flo and her mam laughed until tears rolled down their cheeks as they moved to four vacant deckchairs nearby. All the time a slightly puzzled look flickered around Jack's eyebrows … Funny creatures, these adults.

"Central Pier, I think," Flo said, once their mirth had subsided. "The Tower will take quite a long time, and tea at Mrs Ridge's is at six sharp. Another day for that, maybe?"

"Right you are," Jack agreed, turning and looking up at the fifty-eight-year-old brown iron structure just yards from their backs. Looking at it now, he couldn't imagine climbing to the top … all those iron bars. It was going to take all day, not to mention the strain on his skinny little legs and his delicate little hands. Was it a mistake he would grow to regret, and should he not mention it again? The doubts and worries began to cloud his thoughts about all the other things he wanted to do. Perhaps he should let his mam decide…

Ready to go, but not impatiently so, Jack glanced at his grandma and granddad to see if they were as ready as him. Granddad was asleep, shallow breaths creeping out of his slightly open mouth. His grandma had a distantly wistful look in her eyes, as if she was thinking about something other than the here and now. He turned to his mam, a quizzical look on his face, as if to ask 'What now?'

"Mam?" Flo said gently.

"Yes, love," Marion said, turning to her slowly, as if drawing herself back with great difficulty from somewhere else. "What is it?"

"I'm just going to take our Jack to have a look at Central Pier," Flo replied. "It's only a few hundred yards away. You and Dad stay here for now, and we'll pick you up in a while, if that's OK with you?"

"Course it is, love. You go on and enjoy yourselves," Marion insisted. "We'll be all right. I might just rest my eyes for a bit. Your dad's already there, I see."

She leaned back in her deckchair, closed her eyes, and as soon as her head touched the canvas she drifted into a comfortable and quiet snooze.

"Mam?" Jack whispered, a look of disappointed alarm invading his little face. "What…?"

"It's all right, chick," she said as they crept away. "They're tired, and the pier is only just down here. We'll be back before they wake up."

Jack wasn't sure. He wasn't happy leaving his grandparents alone and unattended, making it feel like a betrayal, a desertion of the ones he loved. He enjoyed Central Pier, with its rickety entry turnstiles and grand pagoda-roofed turrets. For him they were a fascinating gateway to a bygone age, an age he would experience only through anachronistic edifices such as this. Dating to around the same time as the Tower, it provided changing entertainment for the mass holidaymakers wishing to escape their daily grind of work and life for a week. For them this was a different world, where their food was provided and their entertainment stretched along the Golden Mile. They only had to choose.

Unbeknown to her son, Flo had already booked for them all to see a show at the Tower Circus for later in the week. This would thrill him to bits, she was convinced. She couldn't wait to see his face when the animals came in, and when the clowns Charlie Cairoli and Paul did their tricks. *Theirs* were ringside seats which, Flo hoped, would prove to be very eventful.

-o-

"You've been very quiet during tea," Flo said to her son once they had closed their bedroom door behind them. "What's the matter? Cat got your tongue?"

"Not really, Mam," he answered slowly, neither seeing the point of nor understanding *that* comment … obviously it hadn't, because it was still in his mouth.

"Well … what, then?" she insisted. "Didn't you like your tea?"

"Not really," he answered eventually, screwing his nose at the thought.

"But, wasn't it one of your all-time favourites?" she went on, puzzled. "Meat and potato pie?"

"It is," he said, not one for pulling his punches, "but not how Mrs Ridge cooks it. Her pastry's not as crisp as you do it, and *her* meat is too…"

"I *get* it," Flo sighed.

"Fatty. Not my cup of tea at all," he added finally.

Flo smiled. Even in his down moments he could bring out humour. She recognised so many grown-up sayings that he had taken as his own but always used correctly, in the proper context.

"It's bedtime for you, young man," Flo pointed out. "Another busy day tomorrow … enjoying yourself."

"Mam?" he asked slowly, as he put on his pyjamas.

"Yes, dear?" she said, waiting for the impossible question, which *always* followed this particular introduction. "What is it?"

"Am I in trouble?" he went on.

"Why on earth should you be in trouble?" she asked,

quite surprised. "*Should* you be in trouble?"

"Well," he answered, with a yawn, "you called me 'young man', and that usually shows I've done something you don't like."

"It's just a saying," she said, smiling that he hadn't quite got a handle on all terms of endearment yet. "Now into bed and asleep. I'm just going to the lounge to spend half an hour with your grandma and granddad before I come to bed."

"What are you going to talk about?" Jack asked through another yawn.

"Well …" she said, tucking him in. She didn't finish what she was going to say. As she turned to kiss him goodnight his eyes were closed, he was curled into his favourite position, and his breathing had slowed to a contented sigh.

Such a lot he knew, this little man, yet still so much to learn.

"Night night, my little soldier," she added, as she closed the door quietly. "Sweet dreams."

-o-

Eric sat on his own, hunched behind a small table in a dim corner of his club, staring into the depths of an almost empty pint glass. A half-smoked Woodbine smouldered in a pitted ashtray overbrimming with foul-smelling cigarette stubs of various brands. He drained his drink and, dragging himself up on to numb legs, he staggered an unsteady course to the bar.

"'Nuther, 'Arry," he muttered to the barman.

"Doesn't tha think tha's 'ad enough, our kid?" the barman suggested, concerned at Eric's state. "I just thought…"

"Do what tha gets paid for," Eric growled. "Tha's not paid to think."

"I were only concerned about…" Harry continued, holding placatory open hands up in front of him.

Eric laid his money on the counter, gripped his full glass, and tried valiantly to guide his beer back to his lonely stool. A trail of brown splashes on the floor – and down his trousers – hailed his lack of success. Wisps of blue smoke from the dying cigarette stub grabbed hungrily at the new, thick stream of fresh smoke drifting lazily out of his nose and mouth to join the fug concentrating in Eric's corner.

He couldn't think straight. How was it, again, that he wasn't now lying in warmth and comfort with the woman he had loved from childhood, a full belly persuading his eyes to close, and his whole being beginning to rejoice in his good luck? What was it she had said? Don't come back? Why, the ungrateful bitch. Who does she think she is, telling *him* what he can and can't do? He'd show her. Show her what, though? *She* had all the cards stacked in her favour. She had said it, and she could be a stubborn bugger when she set her mind to it.

Two choices, then. Kowtow, throw his cap in the door, and do as she asked, or…

His eyes closed and his head slumped forward on to his arms on the table: the result of too much ale, no food, and not enough sleep. Harry beckoned to a couple of Eric's mates. They could see to it that he got home, to sleep off the drunken stupor he found himself in more often than not these days.

-o-

Dotty French sat in her favourite chair by the back window, nursing her little Eric, wondering whether she had done the right thing. Of course she had … hadn't she? Her little boy deserved better than a casual visit now and then, when he never got to see his dad. No: he had to commit to his son, otherwise he would be like a shadow drifting in and out of his life, never knowing when he was going to see his father.

She owed her son that much.

Yet how would she manage without the extra money Eric brought to her? Just like the hordes of other women who found themselves without support for their fatherless children, she supposed. She needed to earn.

Dotty wasn't afraid of work. She had worked throughout pregnancy with all her children. She couldn't go back to her previous job, though, as the firm had closed a few years before. There was always her dad's greengrocery. He was forever short of reliable paid help, and he was a good boss. But did she really want to work behind the counter of a cold, unheated shop? Beggars couldn't be choosers, really, she supposed. She would *have* to do something, both to prove she didn't *need* Eric Ingles and to put food on the table for her son.

"You can bugger off, Eric Ingles," she muttered, a determined, steely look growing in her eyes. "I don't need you. You had your chance, and now *we* are moving out and on. My family is more important to me than you ever could be."

She drew little Eric closer to her breast, burying her face in his sparse thatch on top of his head as a tear formed, drifted down her cheek, and disappeared into his hair.

Dusk began to sneak around door frames and to form little puddles of dimness in corners away from windows. Except for the occasional drowsy sigh from her son all she could hear was the gentle hiss of complete silence as the early evening gloom stalked – hunted – her. It seemed to want to warn her that soon she would need to turn on the gas mantles to give her at least the small amount of light she *could* afford. Until she began to earn her own money bedtimes would continue to arrive early.

-o-

"Mam?" Jack's gruff little voice crept from under his bedcovers.

"Yef, chicken?" Flo gargled, as she spat her mouthful of toothpaste into the sink. "What is it?"

"How many days have we got left?" he asked. Little Jack asked rhetorical questions a lot. They were the sorts of questions which could easily trip up the unsuspecting, because he knew their answers. He simply wanted – needed – corroboration of what he already knew.

"What do *you* think?" she answered, following their usual protocol in such situations.

"I think yesterday's was our first breakfast," he began. "Today's will be our second."

"What, day?" Flo asked. She knew he wouldn't be either tripped up or stumped.

"No, silly," he smiled. "Breakfast. Then there will be five left, and I'm sure there still won't be any porridge."

"Very true," she answered, absent-mindedly, combing her hair.

"I wonder if they'll all have been the same," he mused, knowing probably they would.

"Now, then, young 'un," Granddad Jud greeted Jack, as he settled into their breakfast table. Brilliant nine o'clock summer sunshine strode through the window, covering the white tablecloth in a warming light. "'Ow's tha doin' today?"

"Ah'm all rayt, Granddad, tha knows," Jack answered. "Is *thy* all rayt, owd cock?"

The other guests smiled at each other, marvelling at this incongruous conversation between a sixty-something-year-old and a tot of six, who were talking as if they'd been pals for decades. Flo smiled at her mam, pride swelling in her bosom, at how this scrap of humanity took every day in his stride, and was able to be calm and matter-of-fact about every situation he encountered.

"I told you so, Mam," Jack turned to Flo.

"Told me so what, our Jack?" she said, not quite sure what he was talking about, although she *did* have a slight inkling. She found that, if she tried to trace back his thought-line to some earlier conversation, she might come up with one or two possibilities. Mostly it was too much like hard work, and if she took the trouble it usually turned out to be something quite obscure – almost as if he was testing her deductive skills.

"Porridge, Mam," he answered simply, while buttering a piece of toast.

"Porridge?" she puzzled. "What about porridge?"

"Yes," he went on. "There isn't any. I said so in bed this morning. It'll be the same tomorrow as well. You mark my words."

His granddad was already finding it hard to cover his mirth, even behind *his* huge hands.

"So may I have the same as yesterday, please?" he asked politely. "Except … may I have beans instead of tomatoes?"

"Well, go on then," she agreed. "But why the change? And since when did you have cooked tomatoes? You've never had them at home."

His brow furrowed in deep thought for a moment or two, as if trying to decide upon the right words, being mindful of where he was. Then he said, deliberately,

"Unlike beans, tomatoes make me trump – usually at school, after dinner."

The breakfast room erupted into huge guffaws, rattling cups and saucers so much the other guests had to put them down for fear of dropping them through their uncontrolled laughter.

-o-

By eleven o'clock they were out on the street, walking up

Central Drive towards the Tower, which was only a short distance away. The warm sunshine lifted their spirits, and tried to persuade them to tarry a while at one or other of the tables outside various cafes on the front. The further they walked, however, and the nearer they came to the Tower, Jack became quieter and more withdrawn into himself. A seriously worried frown began to draw his brows towards his eyes, and he started to drag his feet.

"Not much further to go now, our Jack," Flo said, trying to cheer his growing mood of disquiet.

Then … there it was. An ominously dark giant iron finger, pointing towards the wisps of white which flecked an otherwise clear blue sky.

Jack stopped, turned towards the Tower – his gaze being drawn slowly up towards the uppermost platform – and began to shake his head slowly as a grimace formed on his face.

"What's up, young 'un?" his granddad asked, puzzled at the change wrought on the lad's face. "Is ter worried, or summat?"

Jack didn't answer straight away, but simply stood gazing upwards.

"Jack," his mam insisted, "what's up?"

"Well," he began slowly, his hands resting on his hips, "I don't think I can do it, does tha know, Granddad."

"Do what, lad?" Jud asked, still none the wiser as to what troubled him. "What does tha mean?"

"Climb up all that way, Granddad," Jack continued. "It's too far, and I wouldn't be able to reach all those crosspieces of iron. Besides, my arms and legs aren't long or strong enough."

"You don't have to climb up the *outside*," Flo laughed, tears rolling down her cheeks. "There are steps and a lift *inside* the Tower. So you won't be tired at all."

"Oh, all right then," Jack answered, relieved once that bit of welcome information had sunk in. "What are we waiting for?" With that he launched himself towards the entrance, a huge grin on his face.

"Come on, you slowcoaches," he went on, "let's go. Can't hang about. We've a tower to climb."

Chapter 13

Although William's return from Bochum trailed a successful athletic tour his summer was fraught with worry about his exams. He knew he hadn't done enough to secure the passes he needed to further his ambitions to go on to the sixth form, and from there to college. Yet there was always an outside chance, always hope. It was August, the eve of results day, and he hoped he had done enough, but an enormous dose of reality told him he hadn't.

"Good luck, love," his mam wished him as he set off to trudge the mile or so to school to collect his future. "I'm sure it'll be OK. You'll see."

A myriad of thoughts crowded his confused mind as he dawdled his way through the estate. If the worst came to the worst he could stay on and resit those where he failed to get a decent mark. Surely it wouldn't come to that? If only he could do exams in his favourite subject: sport. Sadly, it was not to be.

The rest of the world, oblivious to William's anguish, was going about its mundane daily business. If the people he had passed on his way to his sure doom had known about his demise they still wouldn't have given him a second thought or a second's pity. His family had advised him often that his future was in *his* hands, no one else's. Now his time of reckoning had finally arrived. Doomsday scenario: pass and move on, or fail and reassess?

"William Ingles," his form teacher announced in the assembly hall, cutting through the milling throng of expectant and excited adolescents as if drawing his name closer to the tumbrils of eighteenth-century Paris. The envelope handed to him, he hoped, wouldn't sign *his* death warrant.

Taking a deep breath through dry lips and even drier mouth, he slipped his finger under the flap and drew out the dreaded note.

-o-

"Mam?" Jack asked Flo as she stood in front of her brand-new electric washing machine. Wow … gleaming white, modern technology, a mystery to all who beheld it. "Do you know how it works yet?"

"No, chick," she hesitated, not really sure what to say, "but I've tried reading the instructions, and … I still don't understand what to do with it. I've asked your grandma, because she has one, and she *does* know. She'll be up later this afternoon."

"Is Granddad Jud coming as well?" he said, excited at the prospect.

"If he's not still in his allotment," she answered, not taking her eyes from this wonder of machinery, "he might."

"Mam?" he said again, after a pause, while watching her stroke its sleek sides and polish it once more – for the fifth time – with her cardigan sleeve.

"Yes, dear?" she answered again.

"Where's our William gone?" he queried. "Only I saw him going out a bit ago, and he wasn't in a good mood."

"He's gone to school," she said, absent-mindedly.

"But why's he gone to school in the holidays?" he went on. "If the grammar school doesn't have holidays like everybody else I don't think I want to go. Is he going to find out if he's passed his exams?"

"How on earth did you work that one out?" she gasped, astounded at his perception.

"I heard you talking to him earlier," Jack said, chewing on an apple he'd left the day before. "He's not going to pass, is he?"

"Of course he is," she said, tutting at his incessant stream of questions. "Your questions will be the death of me."

She picked up the instructions booklet for her shiny new English Electric washing machine to see if, magically, it might have turned into understandable, plain English.

"Mam?" Jack piped up again once he'd finished sucking what was left of his apple core.

She sighed, resigned to being bombarded by questions from his annoyingly, insatiably questioning mind.

"Yes?" she said. "What is it now?"

"What's 'pass' mean?" he asked. "Is it like walking past somebody in the street? You know, like when you told Grandma you'd seen Mrs Butterfield and you had to pass by her quickly because she smelled? Or like when you said I have to ask our William to pass me some bread at table when we're having fish and chips? Or…?"

"It's to do with school exams, which you'll find out about soon enough," she said, exasperated by all this talk about stuff she didn't understand fully. "Now enough about all that. Go and play on your bike for a bit. Fresh air's what *you* need."

"But there's a nasty smell outside," he replied. "Granddad says it's caused by Farmer Borril spreading his poo on his fields. He must have to do a lot—"

"Mam," Flo interrupted him, not comfortable where this line was taking them, as Marion walked through the door. "Come in, please."

"Nasty smell out there," Marion said, a look of disgust

crossing her face. "Must be Farmer Borril muck-spreading—"

"Don't *you* start," Flo interrupted, hurrying to change the subject. "This washing machine…?"

"Oh, aye," Marion started. "It's easy. All you have to do is…"

Their voices trailed away as Jack made for the wash house side door to get his bike. Now that his mam had a new machine, which was supposed to make his clothes clean magically at the turn of a switch, what would she be doing with the old wash house? Would he have to sleep there if William had any more Germans to stay? He hoped not, because there was always a fusty smell when he went in. He'd get used to it, he supposed, but he'd prefer not to have to.

"Hello, our Jack," his granddad's cheery voice cut through the mustiness of the wash house.

"Granddad…" Jack's face lit up as his most favourite person on the planet swam into *his* orbit. "What's tha doing here? 'As tha come to 'elp me mam wi' t' new washing machine?"

"I don't need to, does tha know," Jud said, a grin on his face. "Thi grandma knows better than me how to do it, so I leave well alone. No, I just wondered if tha wanted to come up to my allotment for an hour or so?"

"Your allotment? Me?" Jack gasped, eyes wide and hands clapping each other. "Yes, please. Are we going now?"

"Just got to ask your Mam," Jud said, "and then we're away. All rayt?"

"Aye, Granddad, me owd flower," Jack replied, taking a lead from the old man, "tha's rayt enough."

-o-

Eric Ingles had spent as little time as possible in his family's company, maintaining a low profile by tailoring his shift pattern so that he could spend his downtime either alone or in his club. This suited Flo and Jack fine, and William had so much more on *his* mind to make his father irrelevant.

Dotty French, true to her word, had locked her door to little Eric's father, refusing to let him near to his son. The little lad knew no better but, although he wouldn't dream of admitting it, it crucified his father. He had tried to see them both twice, but to no avail. Had he tried a third time Dotty might have relented, but his innate stubbornness wouldn't allow it. As far as he was concerned she would only refuse him twice. He would get over her, and one day he might see the lad again. If he didn't life wouldn't stop. He wouldn't be able to repair the damage he had wrought on his first family, but no matter. There would be other fish in the sea, of that he was sure. In the meantime he would keep himself to himself, allow Flo and her brood to get on with their lives, and save as much money as his drinking habit would allow.

-o-

The house was quiet, except for the throbbing hum of the new machine, which was in process of returning the family's soiled clothing to pristine clean once again. The first load was in, enduring the untested washing cycle, the results from which Flo eagerly anticipated.

Her dad had taken Jack off to his allotment to show him the magic tricks he performed with nature's harvest. She felt sure he would be captivated, and would regale her with all the joyous secrets he would learn from his granddad. She had decided to put a few pies and cakes in the oven, so she had an excuse to watch the washing machine.

The door snecked and her elder son sidled in, a glum expression fixed to his face. He crossed the room without a word and slumped into the armchair by the passage door.

"Hello, love," she greeted him, as she closed the oven door on her last tray of pies. "Any luck?"

She knew instinctively her last comment was irrelevant, because his countenance said it all.

"Never mind," she added. "You'll be able to improve on the few subjects you need in November, won't you?"

"That would be all of them, then," he sighed, after a lengthy pause.

"All of them…?" she frowned. "Does that mean…?"

"Failed them all but one," he said, shuffling his feet and staring at the floor. "Looks like that job down the pit is coming closer, eh?"

"Not the way to talk, our William," Flo said forcefully. "That's not like you. Where's that passion, that 'carry on until I win' attitude you always have in your athletics? I'm sure it's the same with everything else. Besides, your granddad would never forgive you."

"Granddad?" he puzzled, looking up from the floor. "How's he involved in all this?"

"You wouldn't understand what he's done to make sure you have the chances *you* want to choose from," Flo said sternly, steely hazel eyes fixing his. "And I'm not going to tell you what. You owe it to *yourself* to carry on, to have the chance to do what you always wanted to do. You need to stop feeling sorry for yourself, and do something about it to make sure this doesn't happen again. September at school will be a new start. OK?"

"You're right, Mam," he said, after a moment or two, lifting himself out of his chair of despond. "I'll make sure November brings a very different result."

"That's ma boy," she smiled.

"Just nipping next door to see Peter," William ventured. "I need to talk to him about the next step."

"Next step?" she puzzled. "Next step to what? And what has Peter Gittins to do with *your* plans?"

"Like me, Peter didn't do very well in his exams," William

said. "Just a couple fewer failures. So if I can persuade him to carry on we could help each other. What do you think?"

"Excellent idea, I'm sure," she answered, "but will it work?"

"We'll have to see, won't we?" he replied, as he made for the door. "Be back in about an hour."

"Don't be any longer," she shouted as he headed for the Gittins's house. "Tea won't be long."

-o-

"What do you do in your allotment, Granddad?" Jack asked as they closed the huge gate to the Corporation's allotment complex. "And why is it here?"

"Well, young Jack," Jud started, "it's where I grow me flowers for thi grandma, and it's where I grow me prize tomatoes. Tha might want to 'old thi nose in a sec, because if tha doesn't…"

"Pooh," Jack protested, making a grab for his nose while screwing up his face. "Dat's a 'orrible ftink."

"Tha'll get a noseful," Jud continued, a broad grin on his face as he watched his grandson dance about in discomfort. "Now that's Tommy Stoke's pig muck. Next time tha comes up here – just before yon black hut – tha needs to remember to squeeze thi nose."

Either side of a cinder track, which was wide enough to take an ordinary-sized tractor, ran parallel hedges of tall elder. In full leaf and flower, they were dense enough to afford a certain degree of privacy to the allotments beyond. The track continued for a hundred yards or so, and disappeared round a sharp right-hand bend.

"What's that, Granddad?" Jack asked, pointing out a low black building on the bend which seemed to bar their way.

"That's owd Tom Smith's duck shed," Jud replied, a smile on his face.

"Duck shed, Granddad?" Jack puzzled, asking the obvious. "Does he keep ducks in it?"

"No, lad," Jud went on, his grin spreading. "The door is so low that, every time tha goes in, thy has to duck thi head so as not to bang it."

"Granddad," Little Jack laughed, "tha's 'aving me on."

This incongruous couple turned the bend, chuckling and enjoying each other's company, all the while Jud pointing out which allotment belonged to whom. They stopped suddenly, as Jud crossed his lips with his forefinger in a sign for Jack to listen.

"What is it, Granddad?" Jack said, in his hoarse gruff little whisper.

"Listen," he replied, "quietly."

Faintly, through the vague rustle of the hedges surrounding them, could be heard the insistently unmistakeable voice of a cuckoo.

"What *is* it, Granddad?" Jack urged, a faint smile growing across his intent little face.

"It's thy first cuckoo," Jud said quietly. "She's a bit late, but a cuckoo nonetheless. She's a bird that doesn't build her own nest, does tha know, like all other birds."

"Then where does she lay her eggs?" Jack asked. "On the floor?"

"Nay, lad," Jud went on, "she borrows a nest which isn't hers, and lays her one egg in someone else's home. Cheeky, eh?"

"Aye, it is that, Granddad," Jack answered slowly, another question growing in his mind. "But whose? I mean, how does she choose? Is it the first one she comes across?"

"Usually smaller birds like dunnocks or warblers, I think," Jud said. "I don't know an awful lot abaht it, but to me she seems like summat of a bully, really."

"We've not learned anything about birds in school yet,"

Jack said, a slight frown furrowing his brow, "only robins, and we did a poem about a blackbird once."

"'Ow does that go, then?" his granddad asked. He liked it when Jack was confident enough to want to perform, which seemed to be mostly when his audience was small and known to him.

"'In a far corner, close by the swing …'" he started, feet planted firmly, and hands clasped behind his back, finishing off with a flourish of his right arm.

"Excellent," his granddad congratulated him, clapping his huge hands together. "Tha's a clever lad."

"Oh, it were nowt, our Granddad," Jack replied, a mischievous look in his eye and a huge grin spreading across his face. "Are we there yet? Which is *your* allotment?"

"Well, if tha turns to the right and opens yon gate," Jud said conspiratorially, "tha'll see what we've come to do."

Steadily and very gently Jack pressed the latch and opened the gate. The scene which jumped out at him stopped him in his tracks. Mouth agape and eyes like saucers, he couldn't help but wonder at what assailed his senses. A plot of land a quarter the size of a large football pitch, sliced into two lengthways by a red brick path, lay before him. The one side was covered by row upon row of specimen flowers of many colours, ranging from huge in and out curved chrysanthemums to glorious multicoloured shrub roses, at the end of which stood two magnificent greenhouses.

The other half of the allotment seemed to be a small market garden on its own, with enough different types of vegetables to ensure a round-the-year supply for a whole family. At the gate end, red and black currant bushes provided not only luscious fruits, but also an important windbreak to protect Jud's produce from the sometimes keen wind. To the other side open fields formed a huge welcome buffer against grey and intrusive pit slag heaps beyond.

"Granddad," Jack spoke at last. "Which is yours?"

"Both, our Jack," Jud said with pride. "Is tha going to give me a hand, or what?"

"What does tha want me to do, Granddad?" Jack asked eagerly.

-o-

"She is, you know," Peter Gittins insisted. "Has been for a long while. Well, a couple of weeks, at any rate."

"Don't talk daft," William guffawed nervously. "How could you know, anyway?"

"Jenny Vicars told me," his friend replied. "Seriously."

"But I don't even know Val McDermot," William protested. "Besides, I…"

"Tha'll miss out again," Peter insisted. "I'm telling thee, Will Ingles. Think back to Judy Grace. Remember? And now who's she going out with? Jack Brogdan is who."

William fell silent for a few minutes, deep in thought as to whether he should ask Val McDermot out or not. He liked her a lot, but he'd never asked a girl out before. He'd never even *spoken* to a girl before. So how would he fare now? If he wanted to ask he needed to do it sooner. She would probably say no, and there would be an end to it. But what would happen if he was wrong? He knew the answer to that one. It didn't take an Einstein to work it out. Where would he take her?

"Pictures is usually a good place," Peter butted in to his thoughts.

"Have you been reading my mind?" William said, surprised by his incredibly accurate interpretation of what was in William's head. "I was just about—"

"To say that?" Peter interrupted. "Of course I knew what you were thinking. It's logical, and, anyway, you're my best mate. It's what *I* would have been thinking."

"Do you—?" William started.

"Think she might say yes?" Peter hit the bullseye again. "Course she will. Why wouldn't she? Get in there, my son. I'll be close by."

"I don't know where she lives, for a start," William pointed out. "So how would I ask her? I know she goes to the high school, but we're not back there for another couple of weeks or so."

"Tell you what," Peter suggested, "I'll ask Jenny, and she'll ask Val. Sorted."

"And how would you see Jenny Vicars?" William puzzled. "She's the same as Val, surely…?"

Peter touched the side of his nose with his forefinger, a sly smile on his face and a glint in his eye.

"You sly old dog," William went on. "You're going out with her, aren't you?"

"What do *you* think?" Peter grinned.

"How long has this been going on?" William asked, punching his friend's shoulder playfully. "And how come I didn't know?"

"You've been away, old man," Peter said, "gallivanting in foreign parts, cavorting with strange women and eating funny food."

"I wish," William replied with a heartfelt sigh. "In bed every night by eight, and up every morning by six? Yeah, right."

"Have you got enough money to take us to the flicks or not?" Peter said nonchalantly.

"Yes, course—" William started. "Hang on a bit. What's this 'us' thing about? I've enough for me and … Val … if it happens. You can pay for yourself."

"It was worth a try," Peter sighed, "seeing as I will be the one to set it up. But if you want to be tight…"

"All right, all right," William agreed. "Seeing as I will

owe it all to you, and…"

"The fact I'm skint," Peter added with a laugh, as he slapped his friend on the back, and dodged away into the street.

"You … I'll get you, Peter Gittins," William shouted as he gave chase, laughing as he followed his mate down the road.

Chapter 14

"What the bloody 'ell has tha done that for?" Eric snarled at his wife. "Tha knows full well that when I'm on afternoons I don't like heavy food to go to bed on. So why, for God's sake, does tha put stew and dumplings in front o' me?"

"You've always eaten it before," Flo snapped back. "Awkwardness, that's what it is. You awkward bugger. Well, what do you bloody well want? Salad wi' watercress and sliced cucumber sandwiches, to suit your delicate constitution?"

"Tell thee what," he said, "hows about I gi' thee short money next week instead?"

"Thy always gives me short money," Flo shouted back. "And the rest, where does that go? Don't forget, Eric Ingles, I know down to the last penny how much wage tha draws each week. If tha gives me any less … tha doesn't get fed. Bairns have to come first, so don't give me any of thy bloody nonsense."

"Well, I can't eat *that* muck," he growled.

"Not to worry," she replied quietly unconcerned. "I know someone who will."

"I'm going to bed," he muttered, slamming out of the kitchen.

"What's the matter with him?" William asked as he

came in, catching sight of the untouched casserole on the table. "Complaining about your food again? Any chance of, you know, a plate of that delicious-smelling stew?"

"Course there is, love," Flo answered, reaching for the ladle. "Your father doesn't want it, so why not?"

"This is lovely, Mam," William said, his muffled voice trying to fight its way through a mouthful of dumpling.

"Mam?" a gruff little voice floated in from the passage doorway.

"Jack?" Flo said. "You all right? Why are you in the passageway? It's OK, your dad's not here. You *can* come in, you know, although it is a bit past your bedtime."

"Couldn't sleep," Jack answered.

"I'm not surprised," she laughed, "you've still got your clothes on. So how do you know you can't sleep? Have you tried yet?"

"I didn't get changed into my pyjamas because I *felt* I wouldn't be able to sleep," Jack replied slowly, after a bit of thought. "Besides, the smell of Dad's stew and dumplings was disturbing me."

"Disturbing you because your dad was going to eat it and you wouldn't be getting any?" she asked.

"No," he answered seriously. "I *knew* he wouldn't want it – he never does – but I didn't want it to go to waste."

"It wouldn't have gone to waste, silly," Flo reassured him. "I would have warmed it up for tomorrow's dinner for us all…"

"Except for Dad," Jack corrected her.

"Yes, well, of course," she continued, a little flustered at her six-year-old's perception and quick reasoning. "But … how did you *know* your dad wouldn't want his supper?"

"Because I know he eats somewhere else before he comes home," Jack said, dropping his bombshell. "May *I* have some, please?"

"Course you may, chick," Flo agreed, beckoning him to a seat, astounded at what he had just said. She knew that he wouldn't be making it up, because he was a truthful little boy. "But … how do you know that, if you're not making it up?"

"I heard Dad talking to Mr Gittins next door, over the back fence behind the wash house," Jack said, once he had finished his first mouthful of dumpling.

"And when was that, pray?" Flo asked, a murderous look in her eyes towards her husband.

"About two months ago, I think," he answered hesitantly. "Am I in trouble, Mam?"

"No, love, of course you're not," Flo assured him, kneeling next to him and putting her arm around his shoulders. "Did you hear *where* he has his supper, by any chance?"

"At Lizzie Oakenshaw's, I think," Jack answered after dispatching another mouthful of stew. "She lives—"

"I know where she lives," Flo butted in. "The hussy."

"Another to add to his tally then, Mam?" William joined in when he had finished his supper. "That meal was lovely, and I'm glad he didn't get to have any. Let him eat where he likes. We get to save on his meals *and* cut out the aggression. I wouldn't let on if I were you."

"Lizzie Oakenshaw, eh?" Flo muttered as she cleared the pots into the sink. "Mmm … Bed then, young 'un, if you've finished your *second* dinner … and you, William?"

"Got a bit of reading to do before September jumps out at me," he replied. "I'm serious about these resits, you know, Mam. Peter and I have worked out a joint plan to get what we want, and…"

"And does your plan include Val McDermot?" Flo said, eyebrows raised in mock surprise.

"Val McDermot?" William returned, genuine surprise circling his face. "How did you get to know about her?"

"A little bird told me," Flo answered smugly.

"Our Jack?" William ventured. "I'll..."

"Nothing to do with him," she said firmly, "although he probably *does* know. I wouldn't put it past him. There's nothing much he *doesn't* know. He surprises – and worries me – sometimes."

"No need, really," William answered. "He's the smartest one in this family, and he'll go far. Further than me, that's for sure."

"Just make sure you're not distracted again, that's all," Flo warned him. "No third chances, you know."

"Don't worry, Mam," he replied, putting *his* arm around *her* shoulders. "I know."

He put his supper things into the sink and headed for the front room. His birthday and his exam showdown were only about three months away. He just couldn't countenance failing again, but all the while he tried to read his image of Val McDermot wouldn't let him. Perhaps it was too late at night, and perhaps he had just had too much of his mam's fantastic stew and dumplings to allow his brain to function unimpeded. Perhaps bed *was* the only option, and then he would be able to dream of this new girl without interruption.

-o-

"Mam?" Jack asked, in that tone that told her his question might be one of those which started as one thing and ended twenty minutes later as something unexpectedly different. There was no way of telling. So she took them all in the same spirit, with equanimity and good grace.

"Yes, love?" she said from her easy chair in the corner of the kitchen. Her view of dark grey skies and scything rain didn't do much to lift her spirits. "What do you want to ask?"

"Is it summer or autumn?" he asked, taking her entirely by surprise. "Only I know it's nearly not either – but if it's summer why does it rain so much, and if it's autumn why isn't it raining *enough*?"

"I beg your pardon?" Flo asked, surprised that such a simple question was very difficult to answer. Once she had thought about it she said, as she usually did, "Why don't you ask your brother? He should know."

"Actually," he said, "I do know the answer."

"Then why ask?" she puzzled, carrying on with what she was doing. She liked these sorts of questions the least: the ones where he knew the answers but never shared them with her.

"It was an observation, really," he added, looking away from the window, and inching towards the back door on hands and knees. The floors were always clean because Flo didn't allow anyone into the house unless they took off their shoes in the doorway.

This strange little boy loved crouching in the doorway with the door ajar when it was raining. He loved to feel the cool breeze which inevitably accompanied such a wet day, and to watch the drops bouncing from the paths and changing the grey soil to a rich black. He would never dream of standing outside in the rain and jumping aimlessly into puddle after puddle like most other little boys of his age. He loved to watch wet weather, but from the warmth and safety of his house doorway.

"Mam?" he asked again. His mind could pose a dozen different questions and you wouldn't be able to forecast even one, or why it had come, or where it had come from. "What are you doing?"

"I'm darning William's woolly socks, love," she said, surprised at such a mundane request.

"What's 'darning', Mam?" he asked again, a genuine desire for answers firing his eyes.

"I'm mending a hole so that it won't get any bigger," she smiled.

"If there's a hole in his sock doesn't that mean it's broken and can't be mended?" he suggested. "When Granddad has a hole in his watering can he usually says, 'Time to get rid of yon bugger', and he throws it away. Can't you throw yon bugger away, Mam, and get another?"

"That'll do for swearing, young man," she warned him. "And who's going to pay to replace it, might I ask?"

"Well," Jack continued, "you can't ask Dad, because he will say no. So can't our William pay for it out of his paper round money?"

"No, love," Flo said, an indulgent smile on her lips. "Don't worry. When he *needs* new socks, I'll find the money from somewhere."

"Won't his foot be sore when you've mended his sock?" Jack asked, this time a puzzled frown beginning to wrinkle his brow.

"Why's that?" she asked, not sure where this was leading.

"Well, you seem to be darning a piece of wood into his sock," he observed, "and that will rub his foot."

"Silly," she guffawed. "That's my mending mushroom."

"So it's a magic mushroom, then?" he offered naively. "If it's made of wood, and is sewn into William's sock, how can we be expected to eat it?"

"Eat it?" Flo said. "Why on earth would you want to eat my mending mushroom? It's called a mushroom only because it's shaped like one. It helps me to steady this floppy woollen material while I'm … darning it. Like to have a go?"

"Er, no thank you," he refused quite firmly. "I don't like mushrooms much, anyway. Do you think it's going to stop raining any time soon?"

"Why, have you got a date?" Flo quipped, not sure whether he might understand the inference."

"Fourth of January 1946," Jack threw back at her, a broad grin of satisfaction spreading across his face, although in his naivety he hadn't understood her initial reference.

"Good one, Jack," she laughed.

"You didn't really mean that, did you, Mam?" he said, realising from her facial language and her response that there was more in her remark than he had understood. "Does 'date' mean something else that I haven't learned about yet?"

"Well, er," she began, feeling a little embarrassed that she had used an image he couldn't have experienced at his age, and that she felt she needed to explain the concept to him. "It's when a boy spends time with a girl together, and…"

"Like when I'm at school sitting next to my friend Joyce Jones?" he replied. "Is that a 'date'?"

"No, not really," she said, feeling that she shouldn't be trying to explain this to him yet. "It's when a boy arranges to see a girl on their own, with no one else about," she went on. "*That's* called a date."

He became pensive for a short while, and then said, "Is our William having a date with Val McDermot, then?"

"Jack!" she gasped. "How did you know about that?"

"Jenny McDermot's in my class at school, and *she* says that her sister likes our William," he explained. "Val is her sister. I've been having dates with her at playtimes in the playground. Is it still a date if the girl makes the arrangement?"

"Dates?" Flo asked, not quite getting what he meant. "With Jenny McDermot? How come? What do you mean?"

"Well," Jack replied, "we often play together when nobody else is with us. *You* said…"

"No," she laughed, "it's something different from that. It's not a date if you're playing together. I'll explain it to you later, but not now. I think it's stopped raining. You going out?"

"I'd rather go into the front room and read my library book," he said, "if that's all right."

"Course it is," Flo said, relieved that their 'talk' had ended.

Yet it was very likely the subject of their conversation would resurface in the near future. Little Jack wouldn't forget, that was for sure. She would just have to deal with it when it happened. She always did.

-o-

There was never a dull day when her Jack was around. He reminded her often of her brother at that age: the things he used to get up to, his mannerisms, and his ways. But *her* Jack was so much deeper and yet much more open than anyone she had ever encountered. If he even felt something wasn't quite right he would say so – sometimes in a roundabout sort of a way, which you would have to work at to understand. He possessed an innate sense of morality, which he hadn't inherited from his father – a morality which obliged him to stand up for honesty and justice.

"Mam," he once said when they were in town shopping, "that man over there has just dropped this pound note. Quick … let's catch him up."

"Which man, love?" she replied, not wanting the effort of finding him. "I think he's gone. Put it in your pocket, and let's move on. I've got your dad's tea to get ready."

"Mam." he insisted. "I can still see him. Come on. He's only over there, by the Co-op."

"Jack, wait," she had shouted.

"Mister," Jack had said when the man was before him, "you dropped this."

"Hello, young Jack," the man said, surprised he'd been stopped by a tot waving a pound note in front of him. "It *is* Jack, isn't it?"

"Yes, Mister," Jack answered. "But you dropped this over the road by Kappas's Butchers. How do you know my name?"

"I know your granddad, Jud Holmes," the man answered. "I'm Allan Todd."

"Hello, Mr Todd," Jack said finally. "Would you please take this? It's yours – and yes, I am sure. I saw you pull it out of your pocket with your handkerchief. I picked it up from the pavement and followed you. It *is* yours."

By this time Flo had reached the scene and recognised the man.

"Flo Ingles," Allan said as she drew near. "Not seen you for a while. Is this young man yours?"

"He is indeed," she sighed. "And if he says the money belongs to you … you'd better believe it. Small world, eh, Allan?"

"Well, young man," Allan said, turning to Jack. "I thank you for your politeness and good manners. Would you please take this half-crown for your honesty?"

"I don't need rewards," Jack said politely. "It's your money, and that's that. It's only fair it should be returned to you."

"You saved me a lot of money," Allan returned, "so *I* think it's only fair I share my good fortune with *you*. Please?"

"Thank you very much, Mr Todd," Jack had said, accepting the reward, finally. "I'll put it towards me mam's birthday present."

-o-

"You know when we met Mr Todd in town the other day?" Jack asked his mam as she sat down in the front room to continue her darning.

"Now let me think," she said. "What day is it today?"

"Thursday," he replied, ever sure of himself. "It was last Saturday, the day we had to get me some new pumps and PT shorts for the new school term in eleven days' time."

"Ah, yes," she recalled. "What about it?"

"You said it was a small world," he went on, eyebrows moving up and down as if on strings. "What did you mean?"

"Did I?" she asked, never quite sure what she had said

and when.

"Yes, you did," he assured her. "We were in front of the Co-op, just before he offered me a bribe of half a crown for finding his pound note."

"A reward, dear," she corrected him. "It was a reward he was offering you. A bribe is when someone offers you money to do something you wouldn't normally want to do."

"Well," he pointed out, "I didn't want to take the money, so it could have been a bribe."

"All right, dear," she agreed quickly. She had learned from experience that, occasionally, it was expedient to agree with Jack's 'technical' exactitude to save a prolonged explanation later.

"Did you mean what you said?" he asked again.

"Did I mean *what*, dear?" Flo said, rapidly losing track of the original question. "That the world was small?" she asked again, slowly this time. "Oh, I see what you're getting at now."

"Any rag bones?" the rag-and-bone man's raucous cry thrust its way into the room. "Good prices paid for all metals, clothes, good quality goods… Any rag bones?"

His voice drifted away, accompanied by the steady rattle of his horse's hooves and the clatter of his rickety cartwheels as they rumbled over the rough concrete road surface.

"It doesn't mean that the world *is* small at all," she began to explain, "just that when some things happen unexpectedly it seems that the world is a small place. It's just a saying."

"Or is the world getting smaller because there are more people living in it?" he offered as she finished her darning. "Mr Penny, our stand-in teacher, said last term that the earth was losing some of its size because of volcanic eruptions, so you could be correct."

Chapter 15

The year 1953 was a good one for William Ingles. Not only did he pass all his GCE resits in the previous November, but many of them were top or close to top marks. Even better than this, though, was his first date with Val McDermot.

"Stop fretting, Will," Peter advised him. "Finally, after months of shilly-shallying you've managed to ask her out. Hallelujah."

"The asking was hard," William confided. "But what do I do now? I've gone and done it, and—"

"Done what?" his friend butted in nonchalantly. "You've done nothing yet, my friend. Until you've done … the business … you've accomplished nothing."

"What do you mean by 'the business'?" William asked, anxiety taking over at what Peter might be suggesting.

"You're going out on a date with the girl of your dreams, for goodness' sake." Peter sighed. "You're not going to ask her to marry you. Jenny and I will be there as well, so just follow my lead. Val will know what to do."

"What films am I taking you to see, pray?" William said, his question laced with sarcasm. "*Bambi*?"

"*From Here to Eternity* with Burt Lancaster and Deborah Kerr," Peter started, "followed by *The Robe* with Victor

Mature. A double-header. Excellent."

"Not heard of either of them," William replied, curling his bottom lip and shrugging his shoulders.

"Well," Peter said, starting his spoiler, "the first one takes place—"

"Stop," William ordered, jamming his fingers into his ears. "I don't want to know."

"There," Peter grinned as he leaped over their adjoining fence, "you're interested already."

Unfortunately he caught his trailing foot on a loose paling, which tipped him into the sharp, penetrating spines of a shrub rose. William burst into fits of uncontrollable laughter as he witnessed his friend's frantic but useless efforts to disentangle himself from the rose's sharp barbs.

"I hope it doesn't spoil your looks for tonight, Pete," William laughed as tears streamed down his face. "Don't worry, though. I'll bring some of me mam's Pond's face cream. That should have you coming up smelling of roses."

"Ha bloomin' ha," Peter replied, grimacing as he pulled the twigs out of his clothes. "You're becoming a thorn in my side, don't you know, Will Ingles. See you at five. Put something decent on."

"And what do you mean by that?" he shouted back.

"Just look in the mirror," Peter's fading voice drifted back at him.

"Cheek," William muttered as he turned to sample his mam's cooking. Meat and potato pie for tea. How good did it get?

"Hello, our Jack," William greeted his brother as he went into their shared bedroom to get ready. "Doing a bit of reading?"

"Yes," Jack replied, raising his eyes momentarily from the page. "Homework."

"How many's that you've read so far, then?" William

asked again, casually, as he flicked through his clothes in the wardrobe.

"Two," Jack said, without looking up this time.

"Two this year?" his brother queried. "That's not a lot. I think—"

"This week," Jack interrupted.

"But it's only Tuesday, and…," William puzzled, not sure whether he had heard correctly. "Which ones?"

"*The Lion, the Witch and the Wardrobe*," Jack started, "and *The Hobbit*."

"Wow," his brother hissed, impressed and astounded he could read so quickly. "You must like reading."

"I do," he replied. "White shirt, dark brown trousers, brown shoes, and your dark brown bomber jacket with the fur collar."

"Eh?" William asked, not really sure what he was hearing. "What was it you said about clothes?"

"You're going out with Val McDermot tonight, aren't you?" he said, quite matter-of-factly, "and you need to make an impression. You always look good in those clothes, so I thought…"

"What do *you* know about fashion, and taking girls out?" William scoffed. "You're only six…"

"Seven," Jack corrected.

"Seven, then," he went on. "You've never taken a girl out in your *seven* years."

"Neither have you in your *seventeen* years either," Jack replied, quick as a flash. "But you look good in those clothes, better than the old stuff you usually wear."

"How do you know about Val and me, anyway?" William asked. "Good guessing, eh?"

"Stands to sense," Jack replied, touching the side of his nose with his forefinger. "You've fancied her for ages, and only just plucked up courage to ask her. As that new film

From Here to Eternity has just come to the Empire cinema it makes sense that *that's* where you'd be going."

"There's more to you than I understand, our Jack," William smiled. "You'll be prime minister one of these days, I don't doubt."

"A letter in a brown envelope came for you today," Jack said. "Looks offi … offish … important. Besides, Gordon Gittins told me his brother Peter was going to the pictures with *his* girlfriend, so I put two and three together to make…"

"Two and *two* together," William corrected. "Two and two to make four. You need to brush up on your addition, or…"

"Two and three together to make five," Jack continued, ignoring his brother's comment. You didn't get one over on Jack Ingles easily.

"Yes," William corrected again, "but the saying is 'putting two and two together' *obviously* to make four, but you don't need to add the 'to make four' bit."

"Why not?" Jack asked simply. "It's true. Two and two *do* make four."

"Yes, but…" William tried to explain but on seeing his brother's set little face he knew it would be futile, so he shrugged his shoulders and ruffled Jack's hair.

"Don't you want to see what the letter says?" Jack asked, straightening his hair.

"I'm sure our mam will be able to see what's inside without me helping her," William said, not in the slightest bit curious.

"She says she won't open it, because it's addressed to you," Jack went on, "and, as you *are* seventeen, you must attend to your own affairs. Shall I go and get it for you?"

"Oh, well, go on then – if you must," William replied, voice muffled inside his best shirt as he gave in to his brother's incessant whining. "But be quick, mind, Jack. Did you hear me, Jack?"

"Yes, I'm here," he replied, waiting for William's head to emerge from his shirt.

"Well, go on then," William urged. "I don't have all night. What's that in your hand?"

Jack held out a small brown official-looking envelope which had OHMS printed across the front. A puzzled frown on his face, William took it and turned it over several times before scratching his head.

"Well?" Jack urged, eager to see what delights the envelope might hold. "Are you going to open it, then?"

William felt for the envelope's corner, and without taking his eyes from his little brother's face he tore open the flap, slid out a neatly-folded piece of paper, and let the envelope waft gently to the floor.

"Mam?" he called as he headed for the stairs, a puzzled furrow stitching his brows together. "What does 'national service' mean?"

-o-

An urgent knocking at the back door forced Flo's eyes from the paper in her hand as Ada Gittins bustled in, a similar frown on her face and piece of identical paper wafting about in her hand.

"Our Peter has received—" she said, a hoarse rasp escaping her throat.

"His national service call-up papers," Flo finished her sentence.

"What does it mean, Mam?" the two seventeen-year-olds asked in unison, a note of panic rising in their throats.

"That you've been ordered to join the army for two years to serve your Queen and country," Eric Ingles butted in as he came in from work. "Two years away from home learnin' discipline and 'ow to behave proper. It'll be t' meckins of both of you."

"Hate to say it, but he's right," Flo added, once he'd disappeared upstairs. "Effective from September the first. Peter'll be just eighteen, and you'll be close."

"And keep yer bloody voices down," a harshly raucous voice from upstairs cut through their shocked gabble. "Can't a working man have a bit of quiet when he comes in from work? I'm going to have a nap, so bugger off somewhere else to do yer yappin'."

William's shocked, uncomprehending face betrayed his ignorance about this sort of growing up. His baptism into real adult life was about to sweep him off his feet, threatening to submerge him in his own personal font of fear.

"What does all *that* mean when it's at home?" his pal Peter added, not understanding anything that had just been said, either.

"It's the law, I'm afraid," Peter's dad, Harry said, as he joined the party by the front gate. "All young men from seventeen *have* to join the army for two years. It's called national service, and I did mine just after the war. It means you have to live, eat, and sleep army from this September for two years."

"Can we – er – live at home and, you know, travel to the army every day?" William asked naively.

"Ha ha," Peter's dad grinned. "You certainly don't live in a real world, do you? You'll probably go to Catterick in the North Riding for your initial training, and then be sent somewhere else in the world – wherever there's a trouble spot or fighting, or something."

"Fighting?" the boys asked, looking at each other, faces becoming ashen. "With guns and stuff?"

"Soldiers," Peter's dad said. "It's what they do. Live ammunition, bigger guns, and … *even* bigger guns."

"But, we can't do that," William insisted. "We might be

… killed."

The last exclamation drifted to a slow whisper, as he began to understand the implications of this foolish act. He could see from his mother's face that she was worried too.

"Don't join the infantry," Peter's dad advised them. "They are the sloggers, the first into action. Cannon fodder, we used to call 'em. They were the ones who got shot first, and…"

"That's enough now," Ada Gittins warned. "You'll be frightening 'em to death … you and your stories."

"They're not stories," Harry Gittins insisted. "They'll need to be prepared, wi' their wits about 'em. The Royal Signals is what they want to be in. They do their fightin' behind the scenes. Intelligence is what they're about, you mark my words."

"September…" Peter mused once they were on their own. "Tha's not got long to woo yon Val, tha knows – because if tha doesn't she'll be away wi' somebody else once we're off to Catterick or wherever. She won't wait."

"Then what's the point in going out with her at all?" William replied, puzzled at his friend's idea.

"Because, my dear boy," Peter confided, "there's fun to be had between now and then – and besides, it weren't going to be permanent … were it?"

"No, course not," William said, after a moment's thought. "But…"

"But *nothing*, my lad," Peter smiled. "Enjoy."

"What about you and Jenny?" William asked. "Will you…? You know…?"

"She were fun to be with, and all that," he replied with a grin, "but it were never going to last. Run its course, I think. We're only young."

"Then flicks still on?" William asked.

"Course it is," Peter said, a wicked grin decorating his face. "Come on, get your glad rags on. We've only got a quarter of an hour, and…"

"These *are* my glad rags," William insisted quietly. "What more do you want?"

"OK," Peter replied, casting his critical eye over his friend's attire. "If you say so. You'll do, I suppose. Coming?"

He turned to set off up the avenue towards their old houses, making sure this time that he left enough space between his trailing leg and the top of the gate as he leaped over. What he hadn't allowed for was the ample form of Mrs Hambleton as she staggered home with two bags of shopping in each hand. He hit the pavement directly in front of her and pivoted deftly off his leading foot to his right, missing her by a shaving. *He* skipped across the road and was saved from the Carters' rubble-strewn garden by their – for once – closed gate. She didn't break stride, not noticing what had just whizzed past her nose.

William opened the gate, barely able to keep a straight face as he joined his friend.

"Afternoon, Mrs Hambleton," he greeted her. "Do you need a hand with those heavy bags?"

"No, thank you, William," she replied as she passed him by, "but I thank you all the same. You *are* a polite young man, and it's a pity there aren't more like you hereabouts."

Her last comment was delivered with a sharp look towards Peter as she continued on her way.

–o–

"Mam?" Jack asked as he stared into the fire. He loved to imagine monstrous faces and fabulous animals among the roaring flames and its spitting, white heat. Their coal fires had always held a fascination for him, particularly on a cold winter's night when the hint of spring was just around the corner.

"Yes, love," Flo answered, swapping one flat iron for the

other, as it threatened to leap into the fire from the blackened swivel rest by its side. "What is it?"

Tuesday late afternoon and early evening was time for ironing in the Ingles household, following washday the day before. The kitchen was always steamy and damp and warm, with laundry festooning clothes horses and ceiling racks.

"Will our William *really* be in danger when he goes to the army?" he puzzled.

"'Fraid so, chick," Flo answered, not taking her eyes from the ironing. "Or, at least, according to Mr Gittins."

"Can't he just not go?" Jack asked, naive to the workings of the larger world around him. "Can't he just … refuse?"

"Doesn't work like that," she tried to explain. "He can't just refuse. It'll get him into serious trouble."

"But he doesn't get into *any* trouble when he refuses to go to school," Jack insisted. "You always say he'll get into serious trouble, but he never does."

Flo smiled, and tried to ruffle his spiky hair. He was a deep thinker, was her little boy, and his reasoning never seemed to be like other people's. She worried how he would cope with the unexpected as he became older. She wasn't sure whether he would be able to handle anything like national service but, hopefully, when *he* reached seventeen it wouldn't be an issue. It upset her, too, that he didn't have a father with whom he could enjoy all those things most little boys did with *their* fathers. In fact she was desperately upset that *his* father neither wanted to be with him nor would even acknowledge his paternity. Yet her Jack accepted everything his little life had thrown at him so far, and never seemed fazed by the unexpected, the unforeseen, or the unexplained.

"I don't really want him to go," Jack added finally, his eyes downcast. "I might not see him again, and I might have to find someone else to sort Norman Carter out for me. Do you think our William would do that before he went to the army, Mam?"

"I'm sure he would, love," she answered absent-mindedly, as she guided her iron missile around the creases in her bedlinen. "Why would he need to do that, anyway?"

"Long story," Jack said, as he made for the door. "Going down to Granddad's for a bit. I promised I would help him lift some of his taties out of his garden before tea. He's getting on a bit now, you know."

Her smile broadened as the back door clicked shut. No, he'll be all right, her Jack. Of that she had no doubt.

Chapter 16

The new unseasoned logs cracked and spat in the fire grate, launching Roman candle-like cascades of orange and red sparks up the chimney. William had never seen a fire like this because coal was all he had known, with its pungent smell of sooty carbon and sulphur. This was something … exciting and different, almost like sitting round a campfire in the forest. Only he had never sat around a campfire in the forest.

Val's house was bigger than William's, much bigger. One of those huge Edwardian semis on Cambridge Street just behind the Girls's High School, it oozed quality and expense, both of which William had never experienced in his relatively short life. The lawns were shaved within an inch of their lives, and the herbaceous borders – back and front – sowed thoughts of a rich riot of tropical foliage in his mind. This was in stark contrast to the chewed front lawn and the veg- and rhubarb-covered back garden at home. What would he do if she wanted to…?

"Are we going to … you know?" Val asked as she rested her head on his ample shoulder. Her face was beautiful in the red glow of the fire. "Mum and dad are at my sister's in Castleford. So…"

"How can we?" William said, after a moment's

embarrassed thought. "It's your mam's house, and…"

"Don't you want to?" she answered, expecting him to want to do what *all* boys want to do with a girl.

"I like you a lot, Val McDermot," he replied, drawing her closer to him. Her smell filled his nostrils, making him realise how lucky he was to have her as his girlfriend, "and I love being with you. But … I don't think it's right. Not yet."

"Don't you find me attractive?" she said, puzzled at his hesitation.

"Of course I do," he insisted. "It's not that. I don't think anybody should do … you know … *it* until they're married. I'm sorry, but it's something I feel strongly about. And besides, what would we do if you became pregnant?"

"Are you trying to tell me you want to marry me, William Ingles?" she teased, feeling him shuffling a little uncomfortably in his seat.

"Who knows?" he said honestly, looking into her eyes. "I'll be going away very soon for a couple of years into the army. You might get fed up of waiting, and find someone else."

"*You* might find someone else better than…" she said slowly.

"There isn't anyone else better than you," he insisted quietly.

"One of the reasons I like you so much," Val said, snuggling further into him. "I only asked because it's what boys seem to want, and the reason I didn't have a boyfriend – until you. You see, I've never done … *it*. I feel the same as you."

"I haven't, either," William answered, gripping her more tightly, "and I won't find anybody any better, because I won't be looking."

He drew her close and kissed her gently on the lips. The logs in the fire cracked and settled back into the iron grate, sending a great mushroom of multicoloured sparks up the chimney again.

"But," she stammered, her face glowing in the dull light of the fire, "how can you – we – feel like this? We've only known each other ... weeks. Surely we can't...?"

"Trust me," William interrupted, a firm believing tone underlying his words. "I *know* we've got something special, Val. Shall we trust to our instincts, and see where it takes us? I've a feeling I *know* where it's going to take us."

He drew her close again, rejoicing in the intimacy of their closeness, hoping that what they had would still be there when he returned.

"So this is your young man, Val?" a light, cheerful voice echoed from the kitchen door.

William, taken completely by surprise, shot to his feet and straightened his mop of blond hair. He turned to face the voice, and caught sight of a slim but heavily breasted figure as she slipped back to the kitchen.

"Mum?" Val said, a catch of surprise in her voice as she tracked the voice's owner into the room. "I thought you were staying at our Grace's tonight. Is she not well?"

"Oh, she's well enough," Val's mum answered, "but you know what your father's like with his girls and any interloping males. Not good enough by half. *He* started a heated argument, and *we* had to come away early."

"Who started the argument?" Val insisted, thoroughly confused. "Grace's husband, Barry?"

"No, of course not," Val's mother replied, stamping in frustration. "Your father. Who else could turn a pleasant evening into a slanging match?"

"I should be going..." William said, creeping up on the first convenient lull.

"No, you must stay," Mrs McDermot insisted. "I'm sorry for drawing you into our family difficulties. Cup of tea, er...?"

"William, Mrs McDermot," he replied. "William Ingles. I…"

"Not Eric Ingles's lad?" a rasping male voice growled, as its owner latched the back door.

"Yes, sir," William answered. "That's my dad."

"A real trouble-causer *he* is," Mr McDermot huffed. "Nothing but trouble at the pit."

"Dad's the colliery manager," Val said, catching a puzzled look on William's face.

"He *is* my father, Mr McDermot," William said firmly, "but I am *not* him."

"Well said, young man," Mrs McDermot butted in. "Now William, that cup of tea … and a piece of Victoria sponge to help it on its way?"

"Of course he will," Val said, sliding her arm through his. "William's been called up to do his national service, Mum."

"So I should think," Mr McDermot interrupted. "All youngsters ought to be called up. Teach them discipline and…"

"Actually, most of us do know how to behave, Mr McDermot," William pointed out quietly and calmly. "Most of us will look on it as an opportunity to do something different before settling back into ordinary life. Hopefully, Val and I will be able to write to each other while I'm away, and…"

"Over my dead body." Val's dad growled very firmly. "She's too young to have a boyfriend, and I won't hear of it. She can't possibly know her own mind at her age. Look what happened to our Grace. She…"

"I think I'd better go," William insisted calmly.

"I'll see you out," Val agreed, leading him quickly to the front door.

"Straight back in, mind," her father's voice followed them out.

"I'm sorry you had to hear all that," Val said, drawing closer to William. "He means well, but he's a bit old-fashioned really. It won't put you off …?"

"Don't worry," William reassured her. "My father's ten times worse. He's got a fancy piece, and we don't talk to him at all. He'll not put *me* off. *My* worry is he'll put you off *me*."

"Not going to happen," she said, as she reached up to kiss him, a smile starting to grow as she felt the warmth of his firm lips on hers. "See you tomorrow?"

"Try to keep me away," he grinned as he reached the gate.

The late June evening was balmy but welcoming, and all the better because there was no school the following day. His part-time job with the local butcher had given him enough money to take his girl to York for the day, although she didn't know it yet. He'd been once with his school's athletics team, but never to spend time in the city centre just doing … things. So this he was looking forward to.

-o-

"And where have you been, young man?" a vaguely familiar voice jolted William out of his fireside cosiness with Val and plans for the day after as he rounded the corner of Cambridge Street on to Wakefield Road. "Up to no good, I'll be bound."

"Pete," he gasped. "What are you doing apart from wandering the streets with no home to go to?"

"On my way home after a very pleasant and productive evening, I'll have you know," his friend replied.

"Yeah, right," William guffawed. "You wouldn't know productive if it bit you on the arse. Come on … where *have* you been?"

"Jenny's," Peter answered slowly. "Been sorting a few things out."

"Jenny's?" William puzzled. "But I thought you'd…?"

"Decided she's the girl of my dreams," his friend said, his

simple, stark reply slid out of his mouth slowly and quietly. "Can't live without her, and it seems like she feels the same. What's happening to me, mate? I feel like I'm becoming me dad, for God's sake."

"Been watching too many sloppy movies, I should think," William smiled, understanding how his friend felt.

"I thought it would be easy," Peter added, "what with going away for a couple of years. But it was the hardest thing I ever tried to do."

"Does Jenny know that you … you know…?" William asked, genuinely nonplussed at his friend's surprising revelation. He had thought they were solid.

"Course she does," Peter said. "Told her straight away. Seems to have brought us closer. She thinks I was trying to do it so she wouldn't have to wait if she found someone else. The weird thing is she tells me she's wanted me from late primary school. If you remember, she was a late starter. Came here when her dad took over one of the local pits. He's a bit of a case, really."

"I know the feeling," William interrupted. "Same with Val's dad. We've crossed swords already. Nobody's good enough for *his* daughter."

"Snap," Peter laughed. "What is it with these people? Think they're better than everybody else. Jenny's mam's lovely, though. She had a right go at him for being so stuck-up, and…"

"This could be an exact rerun of my meeting with Mr McDermot," William gasped. "What, are we twins now?"

They both dissolved into fits of laughter as they rounded the Hark to Mopsey pub close to home.

"Doing anything tomorrow?" Peter asked as he unsnecked his gate.

"Taking Val to York," William replied as he closed theirs behind him. "Though she doesn't know it yet."

"Sounds like great fun," Peter said. "Any room for two little 'uns?"

"Fantastic idea," William agreed. "How are you for funds? Don't want to show you up, but I've more than enough for us all."

"Just got paid for my first week's part-time at the Co-op," Peter bragged, puffing out his chest. "I've got more than I know what to do with. I was going to treat Jenny, anyway, so now I've got the perfect excuse. Thanks, mate. You sure we won't be intruding?"

"Course you will, but I can cope with that," William said with a laugh. "You're my best mate, and what are best mates for if not to …. take the mick out of each other? It'll be a blast. See you at half eight."

"Half eight?" Peter said, throwing up his hands in mock shock horror. "What sort of a time is that?"

The evening closed in as both doors snecked at the same time. Perfect timing.

-o-

"Are you listening to me, Jack Ingles?" the teacher's voice fell about his ears.

"I am, Mr Smith," Jack replied immediately without hesitation. Mr Smith was newly out of college, and felt he had to show his authority in class.

"Then why are you staring into the beyond, my lad," his teacher asked again, "and not writing down what I've been saying?"

"I was thinking about my answer, really," Jack explained.

Mr Smith was never sure how to take the lad's answers, but he *was* sure he might regret pursuing this line of questioning. He knew Jack wasn't a time-waster and he knew, to his cost, that he always had a polite, pertinent answer to *all* his questions. He wasn't sure in himself … so why he was about to pursue this line?

"Then what *was* I talking about, and why were you taking such a long time to formulate your answer?" the teacher went on, hell-bent on putting Jack on the spot.

"The history of our town is complex, and so I needed to think about why the railways were brought here and what the people did in the town that persuaded the railway folk to come," Jack replied slowly, without any feeling of antagonism or cheek towards his teacher.

A suppressed snigger raced around the room. Jack's classmates always recognised when there was sport to be had at the expense of this particular teacher, usually when he fell into the trap of trying to trip up Jack Ingles. He was odd, was Jack, but clever with it.

"And have you arrived at a wise conclusion, Jack Ingles?" the teacher said, sarcasm being the only weapon left in his armoury.

"Coal, Mr Smith," Jack replied, after a slight pause, which made the scene all the more comical. "You know: the black stuff we throw on the fire. My granddad says that although our town is mentioned in the Domesday Book it wouldn't have lasted long without the discovery of coal, and…"

"Yes, Jack," Mr Smith butted in, his throat and neck beginning to redden. "Thank you for your lesson. Hands up those who think Jack is right."

A dense field of swaying arms and waggling fingers, including Jack's, shot into the air in support of their friend. *Their* Jack was always right, and all the *other* teachers recognised it. They wouldn't dream of challenging his knowledge, as they knew him very well.

"Very well done, Jack," a different voice cut through from the door. It was Mr Tomlinson, the head teacher. "You show an excellent understanding of the question, and I bet your granddad has some wonderful tales to tell as well."

"Thank you, Mr Tomlinson," Jack replied. "Yes, he does, and he knows a lot about gardening too, and how to snare rabbits, and…"

Fortunately for Mr Tomlinson the bell's strident clang drowned the rest, and stopped Jack in his tracks.

"OK, children," Mr Tomlinson went on, relieved that he wasn't about to be regaled with the gory details of how Jack's granddad caught and prepared his supper. "Coats on, and out to play."

"A word, Mr Smith, please…" the head teacher said quietly once the youngsters had cleared the room. "Jack Ingles is a very polite and even little boy, whose sense of justice and rightness are very deeply rooted for a boy of seven. He would never be cheeky or antagonistic towards you – or any of his teachers, for that matter. He is very smart and thoughtful, and always thinks through his responses carefully. He would rather remain silent than give an answer he isn't sure of. In other words … he is an excellent pupil with unlimited potential who, hopefully, will go far. Sarcasm or any other lame linguistic ploy will never work with him. He doesn't understand it because it doesn't rest well with him. He will always try his best, no matter what you try to teach him. He *will* succeed despite the adults who may cross his path from time to time."

"I was only…" Mr Smith attempted a limp explanation, embarrassment beginning to affect his speech.

"I simply wanted to alert you to his foibles and to be aware that, although you may feel undermined by the likes of Jack Ingles," Mr Tomlinson continued, "he will not deliberately do so. If you are trying to enter into a power struggle with Little Jack you won't win. Use him to your advantage, and bring him along by trying to find out his strengths and interests. He has a very intriguing life history and an extremely interesting granddad, whom he adores.

You might like to give *him* a try…"

"A try?" Mr Smith stammered. "I don't…"

"He was a coal miner," the head explained, "until he retired recently. He started work at the colliery when he was eleven. Just a thought for when you get on to the coal industry topic next term…"

"Ah," the young teacher said quietly as the head's suggestion began to make him think.

"Cup of tea and a biscuit time, eh, Mr Smith?" Mr Tomlinson suggested, turning smartly on his highly polished brown brogues. "Don't be late back to lessons, now."

"Don't worry, lad," Mr Hardwick soothed with a smile, as Mr Smith stumbled into the staffroom. "He's a lovely, genuine little lad, is our Jack, and most of us have fallen into the trap of underestimating his knowledge and putting him down as a daydreamer. You'll get over it. Just take on board what the head has said to you and you won't go far wrong. Don't treat him with kid gloves, but just be aware. He *could* be your greatest ally and asset."

-o-

"Mam," Jack shouted as he pushed his way through the back door. "Mam, I'm back."

"Hello, chick," Flo said as she emerged from the bowels of the house. "Good day? Who's your friend?"

"This is Jenny, my friend from school," he replied. "We have dates in the playground. Remember?"

"Oh, yes," his mam smiled. "Hello, Jenny. It's nice to meet you at last. Our Jack has told me all about you. Cup of tea or glass of pop, Jenny? Our Jack always has a cup of tea and a piece of cake when he comes in. You?"

"Pop and cake please," Jenny said, a huge grin of anticipation splitting her face.

"Jenny's our William's girlfriend's sister," Jack added,

once his first mouthful of cake had disappeared.

"Yes, I know," Flo said, her face displaying a smile of satisfaction at knowing *something* about her sons. "Do you live around here, Jenny?"

"Not really," she replied quietly. "Cambridge Street. I'm going to my nana's until Mum picks me up. She does a part-time job at Dr Twist's surgery."

"Well," Flo went on while the youngsters tucked in, "you're always welcome, Jenny McDermot, whenever you're in the area."

"I'll just go and put my pumps on, Mam," Jack said, heading for the stairs, "and then I'll walk around to Jenny's nana with her."

"He's a good boy, really, is our Jack," Flo said as they waited. "He needs to change out of his school things as soon as he gets home. Feels more comfortable."

"I really like Jack," Jenny said quietly. "He's funny, and so clever. He never has a bad word to say about anybody, and he's the most honest person I've ever met. I really like him."

"Aw, that's very kind of you to say so," Flo said, tears beginning to fill her eyes. She had carried a great deal of worry about her little boy's chances of leading a happy life. He was a strange one, that was for sure, but the world would have been a lesser place for his not having been a part of it.

Chapter 17

Was it really normal for someone to rationalise as intensively emotional a happening as losing a brother in such a relaxed, pragmatic and accepting way? Jack's logic in his soon-to-be-eight sort of a way was that William would be back from the army soon enough, and nothing he could do would make the slightest difference. He had all sorts of things to get on with, and worrying about an eighteen-year-old brother didn't feature in that at all. As far as Jack was concerned his brother could take care of himself, and *he* would look after their shared bedroom as if it were his own.

His mam, of course, had cried buckets. Her son was going away to join a man's army even though he was still only a boy in her eyes, and that meant he was turning into a man. Would she be able to cope with *that*? Why wouldn't she? She had endured all that her pig of a husband could throw at her, so seeing her firstborn rather less frequently should be no sweat. Famous last words?

"Mam?" Jack started on Monday breakfast before school.

"Yes, love," she replied cheerfully as she poured out his porridge. "What is it today?"

"Why did our William have to go to his army by coach?" he asked. "Why not the train? It's quicker and…"

"No train to Catterick where he's gone," she answered, pleased there was something she *could* answer for him.

"But why Wakefield?" he went on. "And why midnight? Didn't they want people to know he was going? Is he going to be a spy?"

"No," she laughed, cheering up with his quaint little questions. "It's nothing like that. The coach had to pick up lots of soldiers from lots of places, and Wakefield was the last call. Mr Lee's taxi was very handy, because there were no buses at that time. Your dad had to pay Mr Lee quite a bit. Remember when we went to Bridlington – a year or two since – and Mr Lee took us to the station?"

"Mmm," he replied quietly, face screwed as if drawing back an unpleasant memory. "I didn't like it much."

"Didn't like it?" Flo asked, surprised. "What didn't you like about it?"

"It smelled of mothballs," he said, after a moment's consideration. "You know, like that smell in me grandma's wardrobe. Why are they called mothballs, Mam?"

"Something for you to find out, my lad," she said quickly. "Time for school. Come on, or you'll be late. You don't want Mr Hardwick to keep you in now, do you?"

"Mam?" he piped up as his last mouthful of porridge slipped down his throat.

"Yes, chick," she sighed, stacking the washed plates and dishes on the draining board.

"What's St Vitus's dance?" he asked, taking his time over the pronunciation of unfamiliar words.

"Why on earth do you want to know that?" she gasped, not sure where he might have got that from. His strangest questions always came out of the blue when she was least expecting them.

"Well," he ventured, "Grandma said I had it the other day. Is it an incurable disease? Can anybody catch it? Does it mean I have to learn to dance? Does it…?"

"School," she said sternly. "Now … Upstairs, and brush your teeth and hair. St Vitus's dance, indeed. I'll St Vitus's dance you if you don't get a move on."

A reedy little voice greeted him as he fastened the back door. "Eh up, Jack. Is thy off to school?" It was his friend and next-door neighbour, Gordon Gittins.

"Course I am," Jack answered. "Where else does tha think I'll be off to? Scarborough?"

"It's that Mr Smith again today," Gordon moaned as they approached the main Wakefield Road. "I don't like him. He tries to boss you about, and doesn't listen to what you have to say."

"Take no notice," Jack advised. "He's only trying to be a teacher and, if you listen to what he has to say, he *does* talk a bit of sense. Anyway, it's only one lesson after dinner. History, I'm sure. Coal mining. I think we probably know more about that than he does. Don't you?"

"Aye, 'appence," Gordon agreed. "You'll put him straight, our Jack, I'm sure. Playing out after school? I fancy going up Goosehill Fields to chase Farmer Borril's bull, Arthur."

"It's not called Arthur," Jack said, throwing a disbelieving frown Gordon's way, "is it?"

"No. Course it's not," Gordon laughed. "It's just that to me it looks like it *should* be called Arthur. All docile and soapy, and that. You know."

"Don't let him hear you calling him soapy," Jack replied, a serious look on his face. "He'll have thee, tha knows."

The smile on Gordon's face was swept away by a concerned frown, as Jack burst out laughing.

Gordon threw his pump bag at him as he dodged through the school's wrought-iron front gate, just missing Mr Tomlinson's head in the process.

"Gordon Gittins," he boomed, "come here at once."

"Yes, sir," Gordon answered sheepishly as he approached the head teacher, chin slumped on to his chest. "Sorry, sir. Didn't mean to throw it at *you*, sir. It was meant for—"

"Enough, Gordon," Mr Tomlinson interrupted, his grave voice not reflecting his sparkling eyes. "What would you have done if you'd hit me, eh? Laugh?"

"No, sir," Gordon answered, trying to suppress a smile. He was good, was Mr Tomlinson: always smiling – and never told you off, really. Just liked to remind you, in an amusing way, who was in charge. "Sorry, sir."

"Go on. Clear off into class," the head ordered. "Miserable, mischievous miscreant." The two pals ran off round the corner into the boys' playground.

"Phew! That was a close thing," Jack gasped as they skidded to a halt in front of the boys' cloakroom door. "Daft beggar. You nearly hit *him*, of all people. Don't do things in half measures, you, do you?"

"He's all right, is Mr Tomlinson," Gordon sighed. "He can take a joke. Besides, it *was* an accident. I didn't mean to nearly hit him."

"And what 'ave we got 'ere?" a gruff voice invaded their ears. "Tweedledum and Tweedlebloodydee?"

"Get lost, 'Arry Snot," Gordon hissed, as he turned to face the much bigger boy. Harry Snodd was the school bully, who didn't like being called 'Snot' at all. "Or me an' Jack here will…"

"You'll what, you little…?" he growled, as his face began to turn crimson. "And what was that you called me?"

"I think – actually – he called you 'Arry Snot, Harry," Jack said, much to the great amusement of his friends and a few more from their class.

"'Arry Snot, 'Arry Snot," they all began to chant, winding him up to such a pitch that he swung out at the nearest boy, who ducked just in time. As his hand hit the door frame Harry Snodd let out such a wounded squeal that Mr Hardwick ducked outside to see what the fuss was about.

"What on earth's the matter?" he said, confronted by a high-pitched wail gushing out of Harry Snodd's doubled-up body. "Have you hurt your hand, lad?"

"It … were … 'im, … sir," he sobbed, pointing at Gordon with his uninjured hand, who was trying hard to hide his mirth.

"Don't be so soft," Mr Hardwick advised him. "He's *much* smaller than you, so how do you expect me to believe *that* tale?"

"But…" Harry complained.

"But nothing. Into line now," the teacher ordered. On the first clang of the school's handbell little bodies scattered and miraculously snaky class lines began to grow, ready to move off to class. As Gordon slid past Harry Snodd he pulled out his tongue in defiance of the bully's mouthed threats of the hellfire and damnation he would visit on the little boy.

-o-

It was worth a try, anyhow. If she'd been in she might have listened to him. She had before, and almost every other time she had relented. So why shouldn't she now? She didn't mean what she had said – threatened – about not letting him see his lad. She couldn't do that. He had rights.

He stopped for a moment, just before the door. He couldn't see any lights, no matter how he craned his neck. Curtains? That was it. Thick, drawn curtains. What was she trying to hide at five o'clock on a September evening? Who was *he* kidding? He knew what she was like. Awkward bugger when she wanted to be. He *knew* she wouldn't be there. Neither would his lad.

It couldn't harm just to see, though, could it? Just a little tap, so as not to disturb the bairn. A rough, rasping voice broke into his delicate thoughts.

"What d'yer want, mate?"

"Nowt," he growled, turning on the newcomer. "I want nowt."

"If it's yon Dotty French tha were after," the voice softened, taking pity on the pathetic shadow in front of him, "she's gone. Moved. Shifted. Tecken t' bairn wi''er."

"Does tha know where?" he asked in return, not really knowing why.

"Back to 'er parents, I think," the other man replied, tipping the peak of his flat cap while he scratched his head. "Though I'm not that sure, tha knows. Her dad's got yon greengrocer's down Wakefield Road, and…"

Eric didn't stop to listen. The words faded away as he made slowly for home and his tea, his clogs clacking on the cobbles as he clattered down the snicket.

He wondered if Lizzie Oakenshaw might be in. Should he call round on the off chance? No. He didn't feel like Lizzie Oakenshaw tonight. She was good-hearted and a reasonable cook, but she gabbed too much … and you never knew who else she might share your business with.

A couple of pints and then home? Sounded like a plan.

A friendly voice drew him in and ushered him to his usual cushioned booth.

"Eh up, Eric owd cock. 'Ow's tha doing? Not seen thee for a while. Been hiding, working or holidaying? Usual?"

"'Ow do, 'Arry," Eric replied quietly. "Nay, I've come in for a bit of peace and quiet, so if tha doesn't mind… Pint of Tetley's, when thy has a minute."

"All rayt," Harry said, touching the side of his nose with his forefinger. "A pint of Tetley's coming up."

A familiar voice assaulted him as he settled back into the cushioned bench with his pint.

"What's thy doing here? Shouldn't thy be at home wi' thi

wife and bairn?"

Eric looked up from the rim of his glass to see a slightly older and rounder image of himself looking back at him. It was rather like looking into a fairground distorting mirror: him, yet not him … a disturbingly familiar image, without his customary six pints to soften the edge of reality.

"What does thy want, Harold?" Eric asked gruffly, returning to the bottom of his glass. "I've nowt to say to thee."

"Well, perhaps tha'll listen instead, then," his brother replied, equally sternly. "Our Blanche and Allan are concerned – *we* are concerned – about the situation wi' Flo."

"None o' thy bloody business," Eric said through gritted teeth. "I thought I made that clear last time thy tried to stick thy bloody nose in. So – now tha's had thy say – bugger off back to them two and keep away. Now can I have me drink in peace?"

"The only trouble is," Harold insisted, "that *I* know how much thy really earns, and how short tha's keeping her and Jack."

"And what's that to do wi' anything?" Eric snarled, clenching and unclenching his fists.

"And is *that* supposed to frighten me?" Harold sneered. "Don't forget, I know all your grubby secrets from when you were little, and I know *all* your scams from when you were a teenager. I'm pretty sure all the folks you have screwed might be interested."

"Is tha threatening me, Harold Ingles?" Eric snapped, leaping to his feet, fists clenched and flecks of spittle flicking from his mouth.

"If that's how tha wants to view it," Harold countered, taking a step towards his incandescent brother. "But I'm telling thee this… If tha doesn't do something about yon lass and bairn *I'll* start talking to a few folks who would like to hear what I have to say. And if they come a callin'…"

Then without a backward glance he was gone, leaving his brother stunned and fuming. What brought *that* on? Something he'd said? But he'd not seen his brother in months. Why this? Why now? He always was a sanctimonious git, with his violin playing. They never got on – but then, Eric never got on with anybody. They were all out to do him over, so he always got in first. What's so wrong with that? Rule of the jungle.

His mind began to drift back to his earlier days, to the times he didn't have much – not with his skinflint of a father. So when opportunities presented themselves he took what he needed, without compunction or thoughts of morality. Most of his shady dealings gave him a great deal of satisfaction, convincing himself he was being true to the Robin Hood principle. He took from the better off, and gave to the poor: himself.

Big Alf Lee hijacked his thoughts, making him draw a sharp intake of breath. Now Eric wasn't afraid of a fight, but Big Alf Lee…

Harold wouldn't tell Big Alf, would he? No, course he wouldn't. Yet he had never seen his brother like this before. That glint of defiance warned him about change. Now he wasn't so sure, so cocky. Perhaps he needed to be careful. Perhaps he needed to pay more attention to Harold's demands. He didn't have any particular desire to spend the next six months in intensive care.

A wheezy voice startled him from his thoughts.

"Deep in thought, owd cock? Penny?"

"Just one or two knotty problems I need a bit of help with, Cyril," Eric replied.

Cyril Sykes was his oldest acquaintance from early secondary school. They'd been involved together in one or two deals, which had been mutually beneficial, so if anyone understood situations like his it was Cyril Sykes. Whether he would be prepared to share all his problems yet, however, Eric wasn't sure.

"I've – er – a little deal I'd like to share wi' thee, Eric my lad," Cyril stated quietly, looking warily around them as he shuffled into the seat opposite Eric. "A little deal which tha might be keen to hear abaht."

He moved his shifty eyes closer to his co-conspirator and dropped his voice to a thin, reedy sigh.

"Don't go any further, Cyril," Eric warned before he wouldn't be able to take the detail back. "I've enough on me plate just at the moment."

Cyril shuffled back in his seat, a look of disbelief and surprise crowding his lowering brow.

"But…" he stammered, nonplussed.

"No buts, old friend," Eric started to explain. "Normally I'd be interested… You know me. But I just can't…"

"Owt I can help thee with?" Cyril offered.

"Maybe," Eric replied. "But not just now. I'll let thee know. All rayt?"

"Aye, lad," Cyril nodded. "Whenever tha's ready. Got to go."

-o-

"Why do these days have to come round so quickly?" Flo muttered. She always hated rent day. This was the day she handed over a large chunk of the meagre housekeeping Eric left for her in the sideboard drawer. She always took the money out, counted it several times to see if had grown, sighed, and put the rest back for essentials during the week.

This day was no different.

"Nine, ten … eleven? Twelve? Thirteen?" she puzzled. "Thirteen? Can't count, Flo lass. Wishful thinking."

The second time of counting produced the same result.

If she hadn't counted wrongly, then what? Who had…? Couldn't have been her skinflint of a husband, could it? Should she tell him he'd left her too much? Too much? What about all the times she had had to borrow from her dad? No. She wouldn't tell him. Best to wait and see for next week. If the amount reverted, she'd know. But what if it stayed the same? What then?

No matter. She'd cross that bridge when she reached it. As for now, she could heave a sigh of financial relief. She could pay her dad back *and* clear the slate at the Co-op… Heaven. It was the only act of decency her husband had ever done, even if it was absent-mindedly.

Yet was she judging him harshly? Did he at least deserve the benefit of the doubt? Perhaps he had had a change of heart and mind towards their son, and he had decided to get to know him better.

Although she desperately wanted all this to be true she had known Eric Ingles for far too long to believe any of this fantasy stuff. *She* knew the extra money had been either forgetfulness or a brief rush of conscience. Yet she didn't believe he had one. She dreaded to think what might happen next week.

Chapter 18

"Do you realise," Mr Abbot, the stand-in teacher said, "that you're now in the top class? And what does that mean?"

"That we're top dogs, Mr Abbey?" Jimmy Wood, clown of the class quipped.

"Not quite yet, Jimmy Wouldnot," the teacher answered to a wave of titters rolling round the room. "My name, by the way, is Mr Abbot. The blackboard bears the clue, young man, if you are able to read it."

Jimmy's cleverness soon turned into embarrassment as the class recognised the teacher's jibe at the lad's expense.

"That we'll soon be doing our scholarship exams, Mr Abbot," Jack piped up, willing him to get on with the lesson.

"Well done, Jack Ingles," the teacher praised. "Your eleven-plus is very important to you, because it alone will dictate where you spend the remainder of your school life – secondary modern or grammar school."

A murmured buzz rolled around the room as the children recognised the words that had been echoed in hushed and disappointed tones in many homes, where 'life-changing' and 'life-determining' were the sentiments often expressed. Some families knew already that their youngsters would not be entering the hallowed halls of the grammar school, but an air of hope and optimism always skulked around dark corners and in the deeper recesses of their minds that they might be proved wrong.

"What you won't be doing in your eleven-plus," Mr Abbot continued, "is this."

From a large brown paper carrier bag he drew a sheaf of oversized black-and-white photographs, which he proceeded to hand out to every child in the class.

"Been taking photographs Mr Abbey – er – Abbot?" Jimmy Wood asked, a cheeky grin growing on his face. "But we ain't got no cameras, Mr Abbot."

"Any, Jimmy," Mr Abbot corrected. "We haven't got *any* cameras."

"Sir," Jimmy answered.

"I want you to look at these photographs very closely," the teacher explained. "Think very carefully about what you see, and then describe that in your exercise books."

"But, sir," Jimmy butted in again, "I don't see nothin'. It's all blurred and grey and fuzzy. How can I…?"

"Use your imagination, lad," Mr Abbot insisted. "I'm sure you'll think of something."

"But, sir…" Jimmy whined on.

"Yes, Jack?" the teacher turned to Jack's waving arm. "What do *you* want?"

"Sir, if you wish," the lad offered, "I'll swap with Jimmy. Mine's an aerodrome or something. He can have that, and I'll have his fuzzy picture."

"If that's what you want, Jack Ingles," Mr Abbot sighed, eyes ascending to the heavens, whence most people seek inspiration, hope, or relief.

"Thanks a lot, Ingles," Jimmy said, his hoarse whisper not conveying the same sentiment as his words. "Now I'll 'ave to do some thinking. Not what I wanted."

"Shouldn't have complained, then," Jack replied. "I *was*

trying to help."

Yet, now he had kindly offered to let Jimmy off the hook, what was he going to do with a fuzzy black-and-white photo of … black-and-white fuzziness?

"It's a picture of a bridge taken in thick fog," Mr Abbot whispered as he passed, raising his bushy eyebrows in recognition of Jack's dilemma. "Can you see the lights? You can just make them out with … a little … imagination. Don't describe what you *can* see. Just imagine what you can't see."

This last comment plunged Jack into deep thought about what might be going on under and around the bridge. Once thoughts had been opened to his fertile mind ideas began to flood in.

Recognising the moment of truth, Mr Abbot stood at the back of the room, arms folded across his ample chest, a smile dithering around satisfied lips. He had recognised Jack's smartness in the short time he had been in the school, and was keen to exploit and develop it.

-o-

"Wow," Mr Abbot exhaled slowly as he put down the last of his marking on the staffroom table.

"Problem, Mr Abbot?" the head enquired over his steaming teacup at afternoon playtime. "Top class?"

"No – and yes, Mr Tomlinson," the teacher replied. "No problems with the top class. I was simply expressing my admiration at the depth of imagination those youngsters display, particularly…"

"Jack Ingles?" the head continued.

"How did you—?" Mr Abbot asked, taken aback by Mr Tomlinson's astute guess.

"We've had young Jack since he was five," the head went on, "and in all that time he has never ceased to amaze, confound, surprise, and … puzzle us. He has displayed levels of maturity and dispassion beyond his years, when we least expected them. He is one smart, complex little boy."

"I can see that in his writing," Mr Abbot agreed. "Will he pass his scholarship test, then?"

"Undoubtedly," Mr Tomlinson said. "I know it's a commonly expressed platitude, but I believe he could be either prime minister or an author – or both – one day. We've just got to make sure his wastrel of a father doesn't corrupt him. I don't think our Jack will allow him to do that, though."

"Father?" the teacher asked.

"That's a story for another day," the head insisted, turning towards the door. "The bell's about to go for end of play, and it *will* be rung exactly on time. Jack's the bell monitor."

On the first clang of the handbell all activity in the playground stopped, and children began to make their way to the doors.

"What did I say?" Mr Tomlinson smiled at the new teacher, as youngsters began to jostle around their coat pegs. "On the dot."

"Jack…" the head broke off. "Jack Ingles."

"Yes, Mr Tomlinson," Jack said as he turned back to his head teacher.

"How's William these days?" he asked. "Did I hear he was in the army?"

"He's home now, sir," Jack replied. "Starts teacher training college when I start at the grammar school."

"Oh, you've decided you're going to pass, eh?" Mr Tomlinson joked.

"Stands to sense," Jack pointed out seriously. "My practice results and all the tests we've done this year say I can't fail … and I won't. Must go, sir. Mrs Crossley won't like it if I'm late. Intelligence test practice, you see."

"OK," the head said, suppressing a slightly indulgent

smile. "You go to it, young Jack. Can't keep Mrs Crossley waiting."

"He's a natural, that boy," he muttered again as he made for his office, and the second cup of tea and digestive which beckoned him from his desk.

-o-

Although William enjoyed his spell in the army relatively, he was glad to be back home. He was pleased to be eating real home-made food again. Oh, how he'd longed for his Mam's meat and potato pie. More than anything else he was dying to see Val.

They had seen very little of each other over the previous two years, mostly because he had been posted away in the Far East for the last ten months of his service. This meant, of course, no home leave – and no Val. Although they wrote to each other frequently he had had to admit to himself that he was afraid she might have found someone else, even though they had promised to stay faithful. She was almost at the end of her two-year teacher training course away in Leeds, and this weekend was the first time they would have spent together since his return from Malaya.

He was nervous … very nervous. Much more so than on their first date. *This* date could be make or break for their – so far – long-distance relationship. He had decided that the *Pal Joey* matinee at the Empire would be good, allowing them to be close in the dark. An early evening walk in Haw Hill Park would then give them talking space. He wasn't sure whether he was looking forward too much to the park, which held many warm memories but which might prove to be their last. He couldn't help these thoughts flooding his mind, because they had been apart for what seemed like a lifetime.

"Seeing Val today, Bro?" Jack asked as he tucked into his

toast and marmalade.

"Bro?" William puzzled, as he sat down next to his brother. "Where on earth did you get that from? Not been in the army, have you?"

"Everybody uses it at school," Jack replied, a frown growing on his brow. "Why? What do you *want* me to call you? And why do you ask if I've been in the army? You know I'm too young."

"It just so happens – *Bro* – that everyone in the army calls everyone else 'bro'," William laughed, "So as usual, little brother, you seem to be ahead of the game."

"Well, are you?" Jack persisted after a short pause.

"Am I what?" William asked, not quite understanding what Jack was getting at.

"Going to the pictures with Val?" he answered, perturbed that his brother didn't seem to understand the conversation they were having.

"How on earth did you know we were going to the pictures?" William gasped.

"Stands to sense," Jack sniffed. "Where else is there to go, except the park?"

"Suppose," William said quietly. Wow. He'd forgotten how his brother's reasoning could leave you reeling if you weren't paying close attention. And yet, if you *were* listening carefully, he could go off on a relevant tangent at any time, leaving you none the wiser.

"I take it you are, then," Jack said, putting his half mug of tea down carefully on his Mam's best white tablecloth. He couldn't remember ever having a dirty one. Always brilliant white – and always fresh, every morning. "What game were you talking about before?"

"Game?" puzzled his brother, unable to keep up. "I didn't mention any game."

"You remember, surely?" Jack insisted. "You know, the

one you said I was ahead of."

William smiled as Jack disappeared out of the back door to somewhere … interesting, no doubt. You never could tell with Jack. No sooner had the door snecked than he turned his mind back to Val McDermot. If she had decided she wanted to move on, what then? He honestly didn't know. His feelings for her would lessen significantly the longer they were apart, his mates had assured him. No reason, then, not to play the field, *they* had said. Being in the Far East nobody would ever know, anyway. On the contrary, *he* would have known. His feelings for her had deepened and intensified, making it harder to bear. He *had* to sort things out today. He needed to know where he stood, so that some sort of life could go on.

A familiar voice rang in his head as he closed the back door behind him.

"Will, I didn't know you were back."

"Peter?" he replied, swinging around to face the friend he'd not seen for six months. They'd been posted to Malaya at the same time and had spent a month or two together initially until Peter's posting to Singapore, some thousand or so miles away. They spent the rest of their service neither seeing nor communicating with each other because of the sensitivity of their work.

Yet here they were – two big, bronzed young men with the world at their feet, ready to take the first steps along a chosen path each had been preparing a lifetime for.

"How's Val?" Peter asked.

"Seeing her tonight," William said, taking a nervously deep breath.

"And…?" Peter said, raising his eyebrows, willing his friend to fill the gap.

"Don't know," William replied with a sigh. "Not sure whether she'll still want me."

"Don't be soft," Peter guffawed. "She's crackers about you. OK, you've not seen each other for a while, but the old spark will be there when you get together again."

"What about you and your Jenny?" William changed the subject. "Are you faring any better than me?"

"Not my girlfriend any more," Peter said quietly, head slightly bowed.

"No … Pete!" his pal gasped, a horrified look on his face. "How come? I'd have put money on you two."

"Well, then," he grinned mischievously, "it's a good job, because I've asked her to marry me, and … she said yes."

William growled in relief.

"You bastard. I'll get you back for that one."

They shook hands and hugged each other, both delighted that things had worked out for one of them at least.

"Growing up at last," William continued, slapping him on the back. "You owd … bugger."

-o-

"Frank Sinatra was fantastic, Will," Val said, as she slipped her arm through his. "Thank you for bringing me."

Early summer was a wonderful time in the park, when late spring flowers had begun to take over the afternoon shift from the crocuses, snowdrops and primroses. The heady, heavily perfumed night-scented stocks had started already to broadcast their presence as the youngsters ambled around the lake, caught up in each other. For them, at the moment, the rest of the world didn't exist. So many months had been spent thousands of miles away from each other that they felt they *had* to make up for lost time.

"I missed you, you know," William said, "a lot."

"I thought you might have been too busy," she replied slowly, gently, waiting to see his reaction. "You know? Protecting the world."

"The army never gives you too much free time, it has to be said," he agreed. "Free time breeds idle thoughts, according to their propaganda. But I set aside time each day to go through everything we've done together … every detail, every moment shared."

"Will," she sighed, drawing closer, "I never dreamed you'd feel so strongly. I thought…"

"No," he chided gently, "you didn't think about the things that matter to me. I want to be with *you*, and have ever since that first meeting, that first date…"

"You realise," she replied, "that we'll still be apart because of where we are in our lives. I have a job already agreed in Leeds from September. And you go to college…?"

"In Leeds," he said quietly, looking into her puzzled eyes.

"But I thought you had applied for a college down south somewhere?" she said, more confused than ever.

"I gave backward," he went on, wondering if her mild protestations were because he'd chosen to be nearer to her. "I got a letter of acceptance two days ago. I start at college in Leeds in … late September."

"Will," she whooped, throwing her arms about his neck. "Then—"

"We needn't be apart any more," he finished off.

"So will you be in halls of residence?" she asked, tentatively. "First year, and all that?"

"Not really," he said, a slight smile creasing his mouth corners. "Can't see myself wanting to live with a bunch of youngsters… So I've rented a house just round the corner from the college."

"How on earth can you afford that?" she said, taken aback by the suggestion. "A college grant doesn't stretch … that far…?"

Her words slowed to a halt, because she had begun to understand where he might be going with this.

"For a single man – no, of course it wouldn't," he agreed. "But a *married* man would command a higher grant, and he *would* be able to afford it, especially if his *wife* had a job too. Something like a … teacher?"

A look of complete surprise invaded her face, and a smile began to creep up on her.

"Will Ingles?" she asked, squeezing his arm, not quite sure how he was going to receive her words. "Are you asking me to marry you, by any chance?"

"Well," he continued unabashed, courage swelling in his breast, "as a matter of fact, I am … and this will seal it, I hope."

He pulled a small maroon velvet box out of his pocket and, to an excited look of joy from Val, he opened it and slipped the most beautiful diamond and sapphire cluster ring on her finger. His worry had been that she might pull her finger away, but instead she threw her arms around his neck and said, "Yes, yes," over and over, as if she couldn't believe the man of her dreams wanted to spend the rest of his life with *her*.

"I thought we might catch the early train in the morning to have a look at the house," he suggested. "You might not like it."

"If it's where I think it is," she said, "of course I'll like it. But a day in Leeds would be excellent. Mrs William Ingles. Just think…"

"Mrs Valerie Ingles," he corrected. "You will be my wife, but still your own person."

"Come on," she urged. "Let's go and tell my mum and dad. Mrs Val Ingles … wow."

Chapter 19

"Hospital, Mam?" Jack asked, a little lump of disquiet rising in his throat. "But you can't…"

"It's all right, love," she reassured him. "It's a routine operation, and I'll be out in no time. Your grandma says you can stay with her for the time being. William's in Leeds doing stuff to his new house and *will* be for a few weeks, and your dad can … look after himself."

"But what about you?" he pleaded, putting his breakfast spoon back into his empty porridge dish. "What will they be cutting out? Will it be safe, and do they know what they are doing?"

"I can't tell *you* exactly what it is," she replied, throwing her hands in the air, "but it's what women sometimes have to have done. I'll be fine."

"But why four weeks?" he persisted. "Why do I have to spend four weeks with Grandma and Granddad?"

"Because," she explained, "*you* can't look after yourself, and William won't be here."

"Four weeks?" he asked again, more slowly and calmly this time.

"I will need to spend a little time in convalescence, at Lytham St Annes," she sighed.

"What's 'con-val-esc-ens'?" he asked slowly, not able to

get his mouth around that one easily.

"It means I'll be going somewhere for complete rest, so I can recover from the operation," she explained calmly. "Do you understand?"

"Course I do," he replied. "It means that the operation is so serious you need complete rest away from everybody to make sure you get better. You *will* get better, won't you, Mam?"

"Of course I will," she said, trying to allay his fears. "You'll see."

"You're not just saying that to shut me up?" he went on, pushing her patience to the edge with his insistence as he usually did.

"Enough now, Jack," she said a little sharply. She knew how he functioned, having to get things straight in his head, but sometimes she had to be firm for sanity's sake. He did have the capacity to go on, saying the same thing in several different ways, and she knew she could break the cycle only by being sharp with him. He would then take away the problem and assimilate its implications. Generally this was enough, but Flo wasn't so sure with any perceived danger to his mam. He couldn't be left with his dad. He would rather live with Mrs Gittins next door.

Saturdays were usually great for Jack. He visited his grandparents, and spent some time with his granddad 'allotmenting'. Today's adventure into tomato cultivation had suddenly become shrouded in a cloud of worry that his mam wasn't going to be with him much longer.

"What is it, love?" his grandma asked, while they waited for Jud to change into his allotment clothes. "Something's bothering you."

Jack thought for a moment.

"It's me mam, Grandma," he replied gruffly.

"Hospital? Operation?" Marion asked, knowing what

might be perturbing the lad.

"Hmm," he said quietly. "I'm sure she's not telling me all of it. She thinks I won't understand – but I've looked up the only operation she could be having, in the encyclopaedia, and I do. That's why I'm worried. I know all about hyst … hysteri … hysterical rectums."

"And if I were to tell you not to worry," Marion continued, a smile splitting her face at his mispronunciation, "I know you wouldn't listen, and that's all right. But, if I were to tell you that *I* had the selfsame operation before you were born, would *that* help? Would you realise that, although it *is* a major operation, it *is* entirely safe these days. Although you are probably wary of hospitals, surgeons *do* know what they are doing … usually."

"Ah well, you see," he went on, picking up on her words, "it's the 'usually' bit that bothers me. What if…?"

"Jack, love," she interrupted, an indulgent smile on her face, "the operation is as safe as it *can* be. Nothing's completely sure in this life. You just have to … trust, and believe. Women have *that* operation all the time."

"Well," Jud interrupted, as he walked through the lounge doorway, "is tha comin', or what?"

"What?" Jack replied, in a reply of their first interaction of the day. "Tha's all rayt, Granddad, owd cock. I'm wi' thi when tha's ready."

Marion raised her eyes to the heavens and sighed, as she returned to the washing up. "Don't be late, mind," she shouted as they left. "Tea'll be on t' table at five, and at quarter past it'll be in t' bin."

"What're we abaht today, Granddad?" Jack asked, crossing the field behind their garden and heading for the snicket between the houses of Hope Street. "Are we rebuilding yon second greenhouse?"

"Aye, lad," Jud replied, "we are that."

"Why did that one blow down, and yet t' other stayed firm?" Jack asked as they crossed the main road to Goosehill Road and on to Ellins Terrace.

"Because *I* built the one that's still standing," Jud said, a note of pride decorating his words. "When I took ower t' allotment there were only one greenhouse – a right 'otchpotch of a building. A bit of a brick wall here, and a bit of wood and glass there. I'm only surprised it lasted *so* long."

"Were it 'ard, Granddad?" Jack asked. "You know, to build it – cos you weren't a brickie, were you?"

"It weren't too 'ard, really," Jud said, as they reached the top of Ellins Terrace, before the gate to the allotments. "All you've got to do is to use your brain: think it through, and work it out logically. Easy, really."

"Is that what we're going to do now, Granddad?" Jack said, knowing what the answer would be. "Think logically, and work it out before we build it?"

"First things first, our Jack," Jud chuckled. "We're going to inspect all me rabbit traps to check for tomorrow's dinner. Then we're going to have a sit-down for a bit – thinking and planning stage, if you will. Only *then* will we make a start on clearing the site and cleaning the bricks."

"Cleaning the bricks, Granddad?" Jack puzzled. "Have we brought some soap and water? And why do we need for them to be clean? I don't mind getting me hands a bit mucky, tha knows."

Jud burst into a loud guffaw at his grandson's naivety.

"Nay, lad," he explained. "Cleaning t' bricks in this case means chipping all the old mortar off 'em so they're ready to be made into a new wall when time comes."

"Are the new frames and glass here as well?" Jack said, wanting to impress his granddad by his knowledge of what material they would need.

"Good 'eavens, no," Jud said. "We're not building today.

All *that* comes later. If we get a couple of dozen bricks cleaned today we'll have done well.

"All rayt, lad, we're 'ere. Let's check for dinner, and then it'll be sleeves rolled up, ready to use a bit of elbow grease."

"Elbow grease, Granddad?" Jack asked, scratching his spiky head. "What's elbow grease?"

"I've a big tub in me second greenhouse, our Jack," Jud answered, trying not to smile. "You rub it on your elbows, and it makes you slip through the work you're doin' easily and without getting too tired."

"I think I must need some of that, Granddad," Jack said, rubbing his hands in glee. "I think we'll be able to clean two dozen and one bricks at least with your elbow grease."

-o-

"Well, our Jack," Marion greeted her grandson as they took off their gardening boots at the porch step. "And what sort of a day have you had?"

"Excellent, Grandma," Jack enthused. "Granddad's taught me all sorts of things – how to trap rabbits for dinner, how to grow tomatoes, how to clean owd bricks quickly, even without elbow grease, and…"

"Elbow grease?" she puzzled, looking up at her husband's face, which was covered in mock surprise.

"Aye, Grandma," Jack went on, enthusing about the new skills he had learned. "It's stuff you rub into your elbows to make you work easier and quicker. We worked very well, even though Granddad had run out of *his* elbow grease."

"Jack, dear," she began to explain, her hands planted firmly on her hips, "there is no such thing as elbow grease. It's one of your granddad's sayings, that's all, and it means to work hard."

"But…?" Jack stammered, turning towards his granddad, who shrugged his huge shoulders, raised his bushy eyebrows, and grinned. Jack burst into fits of laughter at his granddad's joke. "You got me then, owd cock. I won't forget that one, and I *will* get you back … one day."

Chapter 20

"Mr Tomlinson?" Jack said as he looked up from his blanketed seat on the front lawn in the warm, late May Saturday sunshine. "Come through, please."

"Hello, Jack," the head teacher greeted as he unsnecked the gate. "Is your mother in?"

"Yes, she is," Jack replied, leaping to his feet as he turned to find her.

"What's happened to your nose?" he asked, perturbed that it looked swollen and bruised. "Been fighting?"

"No," Jack replied, as he disappeared round the house corner, followed slowly by his head teacher.

"Mr Tomlinson," Flo greeted him, wiping her hands on her pinny before offering one to shake. "Would you like to come in for a cup of tea?"

"Sadly, no, Mrs Ingles," he sighed. "I would like nothing better, but I have quite a few calls to make before lunchtime – and it is rather warm work, me not possessing a motor vehicle."

"What can I do for you?" Flo asked, slight anxiety catching at her breath. "Nothing wrong, I hope?"

"Not at all," the head teacher assured her. "Rather a pleasant task, really. I have to tell you that your Jack here has been offered a place at the grammar school."

"You mean," she gasped, "that he's passed his scholarship?"

"Indeed he has," he replied. "It was never in any doubt, as the young man himself told me on the odd occasion. Second highest mark in the district. You should be very proud."

"We are – I am," she corrected herself. "Thank you for all you've done for him."

"It's been a pleasure," the head said, "I can assure you. There was never a dull moment with this youngster. Could I ask what's happened with Jack's nose? I'm puzzled because he would talk himself out of any confrontation situation he might find himself in."

"Billy Goodison is what happened," she huffed. "Big fat bully."

"You mean the Billy Goodison who's in his late teens?" he frowned. "Rather large young man with no sense of normality?"

"That's the one," she bristled. "Punched him in the nose out of the blue, in passing. Should be strung up. It's a good job for him our William's at college."

"I know he does need understanding because of his low esteem and special needs," Mr Tomlinson agreed, "but there was no need for that, I'm sure. Did you speak to his parents?"

"Yes, I did," Flo replied, "but they're as bad as him. Shouldn't be allowed. Anyway, our Jack will learn from it and know what to do if there's a next time."

"Lovely talking to you," Mr Tomlinson said, as he turned towards the gate, "and I would have loved to take you up on your offer, but I've quite a way to go yet, I'm afraid. William doing well?"

"Yes," she answered. "He's getting married soon ... Val McDermot, his childhood sweetheart. Now there's another Woodhouse success."

Pushing through the hugely overgrown privet hedge he snecked the front gate and was gone, puffing his way down the street, his jacket over his arm and sleeves rolled to the elbows. Ever the professional man, his tie flapped loosely over his shoulder in the warm late spring breeze.

"Well," she said to Jack, smiling broadly, "now who's a very clever young man? Second highest in the district, is what your head teacher said. You couldn't get better than that."

"Best in the district?" Jack mused, though that wouldn't have mattered to him at all.

"Aren't you pleased with yourself?" she asked, puzzled that he didn't want to make much of his achievement.

"Yes, but," he said slowly, hoping she might understand, "all that matters is that I didn't find the tests hard, and I passed. So now I'm off to the grammar school, as I always knew I would. My next problem will be how to succeed when I get there. But that's not now. Is it all right if I go to Grandma's to tell them the good news?"

"Course it is, love," Flo agreed, watching him skip round the corner and through the gate. This was her Little Jack, who had caused her so much concern – and not a little joy, into the bargain. How could he have grown from that quiet little scrap into this clever, pragmatic thinker, who was mature beyond his years?

"Grow up so quickly, don't they?" a familiar voice cut into her thoughts. "Exciting and worrying at the same time, eh, Flo?"

"Hello, Ada," Flo said as she turned to talk to her next-door neighbour.

"I remember having a similar conversation about our eldest," Ada went on, "all those years ago, and look at them now. Both about to get married and ... grow up. Was that Mr Tomlinson I saw floating out of your front gate?" Ada asked.

"Aye, it was," Flo replied. "I assume he'd been to tell you

about your Gordon first?"

"Yes, he had," Ada agreed "Alphabetical order or summat, I should imagine. It's funny, isn't it? Here we are, talking about them going off to grammar school in a quiet, matter-of-fact sort of a way, when last time we were all whoops and shouts and laughing."

"Mmm," Flo started, "perhaps it's because we know what's to come – homework, sleepless nights worrying, expense – deciding what's important and what's not…"

"Them growing up and leaving home, more like," Ada interrupted, a tear in her eye. "Then what do we do? Wait for grandkids?"

"Cup of tea, Ada, lass?" Flo suggested softly, recognising the anguish she had gone through with *both* her boys, hoping beyond all hope she would live to see them both grow up and be settled.

"Aye, go on then," Ada agreed. "Plenty of time. Mine's on afternoons, so 'e won't be bothering me for quite a while."

"I've no idea *where* mine is," Flo said, resigned, "let alone know what shift he's on. Not what I signed up for, but it suits me."

Flo would dearly love to wait for grandkids, never really believing she would achieve children, let alone anything more. Life had thrown all it could at her in her all too short forty-four years, and yet she was still here. By the skin of her teeth, though, she felt increasingly. Her heart had become more troublesome of late, causing her concerns about her boys.

William was OK. He was settled, and would get on with his life no matter what. But what about her darling Little Jack? They had been through so much together in *his* little life. Was it too much to ask that she could see *him* settled too? Still, it didn't matter how much she might worry or protest. God in his own way – his own time – would call her, and *that* she accepted.

The impending operation was preying on her mind somewhat. A great many what ifs crowded her conscious hours – uncertainty which she couldn't shake, but knew she would have to control somehow. Easier said than done, she understood. The problems with her husband had saddened her significantly, although she didn't like to admit it. Yet she had become stronger through it, where she had had to do many of the tasks a partner might have taken on. Unfortunately, in the society she inhabited, usually the man worked and the woman did everything else. There *were* isolated relationships, however, where the man did most things. In such cases there existed an imaginary queue of hopeful women waiting for any sign of a breakdown. Circling vultures, Jack's granddad used to call them.

"You're very quiet, Flo," Ada noticed, over her second steaming refill and her third digestive. "Worrying about your operation?"

"Aye, lass," she replied, after a moment's hesitation. "Just thinking about … what if…?"

"I know it's easy for me to say," Ada interrupted, "but you'll worry yourself to death if you carry on like that. One of your bairns is gone, and t' other will be well looked after by your mam and dad while you're away. Just think on it as a welcome rest. Two weeks' recuperation at Lytham St Annes… Heaven."

"I suppose," Flo said quietly. "But I can't help thinking about … what if the operation goes wrong, and…"

"Flo," another familiar voice drew her attention as she heard the back door open. "You all right, love?"

It was her mam.

"Hello, Ada," she smiled, turning to Flo's friend. "Has your lad passed as well?"

"He has that, Marion," Ada grinned. "Like peas in a pod,

our two sets of lads. What one lot does, the others aren't far away. Well, I'd better…"

"You're all right, lass," Flo insisted. "Stay where you are. I'm just going to make a fresh pot for me mam. Not in any hurry, are you? It's good to have time to have a chinwag for once. Dad and Jack…?"

"Guess," Marion replied, casting her eyes to the heavens. "Our Jack loves to help his granddad with the allotment. 'Allotmenting', *he* calls it. I'm sure those two have become joined at the hip."

"It's good he has a male adult influence in his life," Flo said. "The one who should be spending time with him doesn't give a toss whether he's alive or not."

It was hard for her not to become overwhelmed by the bitterness she felt towards Eric, but Jack seemed much happier with his granddad. She knew *he* would never let anything happen to her lad, and whatever he did with him could only be to Jack's benefit.

-o-

"I've told you already," Dotty French insisted through clenched teeth, knuckles white with suppressed anger. "If you're not prepared to commit to me and our son you will never have a place in our lives. How did you find us, anyway? Who told?"

"It were only a matter of time, lass…" Eric tried to explain quietly.

"Don't you bloody well 'lass' me," she interrupted violently, throwing the daffodils he had just given her back in his face. "Now get off my step before I call me brothers out to move you. You remember Len and Johnny?"

"All rayt," he muttered as he turned on his heels. "'Ave it yer own way. But I won't be back, and yon bairn'll be nowt to me from now on."

"He's better off wi'out thee, anyway, Eric Ingles," she shouted after him, as tears trickled down her face. "And so am I … you rotten bugger."

Her voice tailed off as he rounded the corner, head down and hands jammed into his coat pockets. This was really the end of her troubled association with the only man she had ever really loved and, fortunately for her, she *knew* he would never return.

"What to do now then, Eric lad?" he mused as he headed towards the only woman he knew wouldn't let him down.

"Pint, Eric, my old son?" Harry Springer asked as he sidled to the bar.

"Aye," Eric grunted, as he wiped away the froth from the first one to greet him, "an' keep 'em coming, 'Arry lad."

-o-

"And where's yon husband of yours?" Marion asked once Ada had gone, disdain painting her face at having to mention his name. "He's not at work today. I know he's not."

"One of two places, I should imagine, though I don't care where he is," Flo replied, a vague frisson betraying her feelings. "Staring at the bottom of a pint glass for one, and the other? Doesn't bear thinking about. That floozy Dotty French's kicked him out, I know that for a fact. As for the rest, I don't care – as long as he brings money in for my bairn and keeps issen away from me."

"I'm sorry, love," Marion said quietly, as she drew her daughter to her. "I wish it could have been better, but he never was good enough for you. We all knew that, but nobody should be allowed to behave as he did to you. I hope the bugger rots in hell."

"Mam…" A gruff voice filled the room as the door opened. "I'm back."

"Hello, our Jack," Flo smiled as he rushed in and flung

his arms round her and buried his face in her wrap-around pinny. "I'm still here. Have you had a good time in your granddad's allotment?"

"I 'ave, that," he answered, joy and excitement colouring his words in equal measures. "We've had a grand time. Did you know that some of Granddad's chrysanths have flower heads as big as footballs, and…"

His voice tailed away as they headed for the front room to hear about his escapades with his granddad. Flo knew that at some stage their peace and happiness would be jolted by the return of his father and the false sense of euphoria his absence encouraged would evaporate, but until then they would rejoice in being together. Their sense of enjoyment and joy in each other's company had made them blissfully unaware of the dire troubles that lay ready to ambush them around the next metaphorical corner.

Chapter 21

"But you love your grandma and granddad, don't you?" Flo asked her worried son.

"Course I do," Jack replied, a slight quiver in his voice betraying the upset he felt, "and I would love to stay with them for four weeks. But I want you to be here as well."

"If I *don't* have this operation *now*," Flo insisted, "I may not be here for your next birthday. I'm sorry to be blunt, but it's the only way."

Lifting his face from the floor after a few moments of silence, he fixed her with his deep green eyes and said calmly but with conviction,

"Then you'd better make sure you come back safe and well."

She drew him to her bosom, a deep well of love swelling inside. She'd never had this depth of feeling with her elder son, whom she loved, but felt she had had to share him with his father. Yet Jack was hers alone. They had been through so much together, and now she was afraid for the future ... *his* future. She *had* to see him grown-up, at least, didn't she? The Almighty wouldn't be so cruel, would he? To see her Jack off her hands and on his way to a successful life wasn't too much to ask, was it?

Flo knew instinctively what her mam's view on this

would be, having lost two good men out of her life. What had she ever done so wrong to turn him against her? In her low moments she would question whether he was a God of love at all.

Although her real dad had died before she knew him Flo would have loved the opportunity to have spent more time with him. This, she understood, carried a double-edged sword because if he had lived she wouldn't have had her beloved half-brother Jack, who was Jud's son – and therein also lay her mam's dilemma. Flo finally recognised why her mother held so much bitterness. She knew that she would never have been able to have both husband and son. But which would she have chosen? Beyond question. The only outcome was a deep pain whichever path she might have chosen, and a lasting hatred of the German race in its entirety. Was this an outlet for her grief, or was it a convenient excuse so she wouldn't have had to make that intellectual – and pointless – decision?

"When are we going then, Mam?" Jack asked as he sat down at the kitchen table.

"We?" she asked, eyebrows raised in surprise at the question. "*I* am going to the hospital in five days, my little one. *You* will be staying here with your grandma."

"Mam," he insisted, knocking over his chair as he leaped to his feet as if to emphasise his insistence.

"No argument. No choice," she added firmly. "Your granddad is taking me in Mr Lee's taxi, and…"

"No he's not," a deep voice interrupted from the other side of the partially open outside door.

"William!" Jack gasped, as he shot to the door. "I'd recognise *that* voice anywhere. How come…?"

"A little bird told us we might be needed round about now," William laughed, as he tried to ruffle his brother's spiky hair. "Ouch. Your head should come with a health warning."

"Will and Val," Flo butted in, "it's wonderful to see you both, but don't think you're going to—"

"For once in your life, Mother, you *will* do as you are bidden," William interrupted. "We have a car, and we're not taking no for an answer. It'll seat four, so our Jack can come along too. No ifs or buts: settled. It also means Granddad doesn't have to spend unnecessary money lining Mr Lee's pockets, and he can spend his time productively in his greenhouse."

"How long are you going to be here?" Flo asked eagerly. "Please say it's not just an overnighter. We'd love to hear about Leeds, and how things are – wouldn't we, our Jack?"

"Not sure, really," Jack answered slowly, a glum, serious look on his face. "Especially if it means I have to go and stay with Grandma and Granddad, and give up *my* room here."

"Jack," Flo began to remonstrate. "That's not like you. Why are you…?"

"Mam," William winked, "our Little Jack's growing a sense of humour. You had us going there for a time, owd cock. Do I detect our granddad's influence there, then?"

Jack burst out into a throaty chuckle as his mam wafted her tea towel over his head.

"So?" Flo asked again. "How long?"

"Until after you go into hospital," William answered. "Until you've had the operation. We'll be staying at Val's parents', if that's OK. Don't want to boot our Jack out of his room now, do we?"

"But," Jack insisted, "will you be coming to see us?"

"Of course we will," Val said, a gentle smile on her face. "We need to see me mam and dad, but we'll be backwards and forwards."

"Not as if it's a million miles away," William added. "It's Cambridge *Street*, not Cambridge the town."

-o-

"We can't tell them yet," William whispered to his wife once they were at her parents' house. "None of them, really."

"Too right," Val agreed. "You know what my mum's like – and yours – perhaps too much excitement and expectation too soon before she goes in. Besides, it's early days. Another couple of months? When it's a bit more sure?"

"Can't be too careful, really," William said, drawing his prize closer to him. "Got to look after you."

"William." she sighed, a smile of satisfaction flicking from eyes to mouth. "I'll be—"

"Doing as you are told." he interrupted firmly. "You're all I've got, and I'm taking no chances. Don't be drawn by your mam, either. You know how she tries to wheedle information from you. And certainly not your Jenny. *She's* as sharp as our Jack, and would blow it straight away."

They began to unpack the few things they had brought with them as they looked around the room, which hadn't changed at all since it had been Val's as a youngster.

"She's even kept the teddy I won as a prize at my first infant school sports day." Val whispered. "Look…"

"What a shame," William said. "It's almost threadbare. Look at its ears. What did you do to it? Try to eat it?"

They both laughed, nostalgia building a comfortable cushion around Val's memories.

"William?" she asked quietly, after a moment or two's silence. "Are you sure we can afford the house until next September, when you start *your* job? I mean, my teaching salary isn't that great, and we've had no time at all to save. How are we going to manage?"

"It isn't a problem, love, really," William reassured her. "I've more than enough stashed away from what I earned in the army. Besides, my little office job before college also gave us more than enough to pay for the car and … other things we are going to need before long. Your teaching job is the difference between poverty and living in luxury and idle decadence."

"Right," Val snorted. "And when … you know…"

This was an innocent use of words to the casual observer, but it bore a wealth of hidden meaning for *them*.

"I'll carry on with the part-time holiday job until you…" William explained.

A gentle tap at the door drew warning glances, and urged them to leave their conversation unfinished.

"Come in, Mum," Val said, as a forefinger across her lips urged silence upon her husband. "We're decent."

"I wasn't…" Mrs McDermot said quickly as she bustled into the room, embarrassment clouding her face.

"She's pulling your leg, Mrs M," William smiled, as he hugged his mother-in-law. "She's such a tease."

"I just wanted to ask how things are at home, William," she replied, still flustered, as she straightened the imaginary creases in her skirt and picked the imaginary bits from her cardigan. "How's your mum bearing up? It must be a very trying time."

"She'll be fine, Mrs M," William reassured her. "It's not the first time in her life she's had to put up with hardship. With our support, she'll be … fine. Does anyone fancy a takeaway for tea? We've had such a busy day."

"William Ingles," Val gushed in mock enthusiasm. "You do know how to sweep a girl off her feet."

"I think that's an excellent idea," Val's mother chipped in quickly before he had time to withdraw his offer. Cooking wasn't the first love in her life, and she grabbed any excuse not to with both hands. "Fish and chips, or Chinese?"

"Or both?" William offered quietly.

"That's just…" Val laughed.

"Gluttony?" he suggested with a grin. "It was a joke,

but…"

"Joke? I don't think so," Val sniggered, a look of mock disbelief crowding her face.

"Fish and chips for me," William said, ignoring his wife's attempt to discredit his veracity, while trying to tickle her into submission. "A large portion. I'm a growing lad."

"That's what I'm concerned about," she giggled helplessly, while trying to escape his usual attempt to silence her.

"I'll set the table," Mrs McDermot said, as she slid out of the room. "You children can carry on your games later. Tea first?"

William wrapped his long arms around Val's body and drew her gently into a soft lingering kiss, which she gave herself up to willingly.

"Last person to the car's a wet haddock," she shouted as she slipped from his arms and sidestepped neatly to the bedroom door, down the stairs, and out to the front gate before he had even opened his eyes.

A grin splitting his face, he launched himself after her, only to find her sitting in the passenger seat as he reached the gate.

"Slowing down, William, my boy," she said, a smug self-satisfied smile creasing her mouth corners. "It must be all that food you say you need."

"Sly and underhand you've become, Val Ingles," he laughed as he slid behind the steering wheel. "I'll get you back … one day."

"You'll need to get up a lot earlier, our William," she replied, "if you want to outdo me."

Chapter 22

Fear of the unknown played a large part in Flo's pre-op routine. Second nature to the nurses and theatre staff, it was so entirely and frighteningly new to her that she found it hard not to let it betray her darkest fears. Her future, and that of her sons, lay entirely in their hands. If she hadn't agreed to the operation she would have been dead within six months, they had said. If she agreed to having her vitals removed she might die anyway. Lose–lose situation, which didn't inspire confidence. What should she believe? If only…

No looking back now, as her hospital trolley sped her, drowsy, towards her impending doom.

"Not to worry, Mrs Ingles," soothed a gentle, softly spoken Irish lilt, once the rickety-click of unoiled wheels had ceased to jar. "Not long now, and then you can start your new life."

New life? What did she, a mere slip of a lass, know about *her* life? A life which, had it not been for her boys, would have been a living, breathing disaster. Why did she have to choose such a worthless, dissolute pig for a husband, when she could have had her pick? What if she … had … been…?

A dreamless, drug-induced sleep wiped the discords from her troubled mind, and – for the following few hours – would keep her in oblivious ignorance of what was happening to her body and, potentially, her life.

Still, everything was going to be different when her physical problems had been settled, *they* said. Who was *she* to gainsay the professional carers who would give her life back to her? But for now her future was on hold.

Her two sons were concerned, Jack more than his brother. He was like an ill-sitting hen at his grandparents'.

"Granddad?" he would ask.

"Aye, lad?" Granddad would answer. "Probably in theatre about now."

"How did tha know what I were going to say?" Jack would return, quick as a flash.

"Because," his granddad would reply, "tha's asked me the selfsame question four times already. Stop frettin'. She's in t' best hands there are. They know what they're doin', and she'll be out sooner than tha knows. If tha's short o' summat to do, yon wash house out back needs clearing out, and…"

"It's all rayt, Granddad," Jack would smile. "I'm not that … desperate, tha knows."

Flo's operation, unfortunately, had had to be postponed until the school summer holidays, giving her and her Jack longer to brood on its outcome. Fortunately William and Val were able to fit that in with their busy schedule, with weekends at her mum's. The change to the summer holidays made it more convenient all round, and gave them both space to relax and time to spend together.

Mid August was glorious: floor to ceiling sunshine, and only a hint of a breeze to take the extreme heat out of their Mediterranean summer. Shrubs wilted and lawn edges distanced themselves from surrounding paths, while assuming a similar, sympathetic light brown colouring. Gardens suffered from hosepipe and water bans in general, except for those whose owners had had the foresight to install water butts. Old gardeners really *did* know what they were doing.

Jud Holmes had the best gardening of his life. His crops of outdoor veg and greenhouse tomatoes were the best ever, even by his high standards. Unfortunately, becoming increasingly irritated and bored with seeing him only during hours of darkness, Marion had begun to think he had more on his mind than gardening.

"Jud Holmes…" she said after tea, her folded arms decorating her already ample bosom. He knew instinctively she had something on her mind, taking apart the clipped way she spat out his name, the disconcerting frown on her face, and how she had planted her four feet eleven and a half inches in front of his easy chair.

"Aye, lass?" he replied hesitantly, not wishing to experience the sharp edge to her tongue, which had been known to flay the nerves out of his body. "Summat on thi mind?"

"You're spending an enormous amount of time with yon plants and stuff these days," she said, after a moment or two's pause. Marion had developed that hiatus to a fine art. It gave the maximum of threat from the minimum of effort, and although the years of fielding this weapon had given Jud a degree of experience in its handling, he was never sure whether he had got it right any time.

"Aye, lass," he replied quietly. No aggression. No tension. No lump at the back of his head. He knew that he would lose any battle of wills with his wife, big man though he was. Aggravation from her could last for days, and he wasn't prepared to risk it. Life was too short. "Tha likes me veg and stuff, doesn't tha? Best around, thy said. Can't grow stuff wi'out putting time in, tha knows that."

"Are you sure it's yon allotment tha's wedded to?" she chuntered, straining her neck to look into his eyes.

"What's tha trying to say?" Jud asked, puzzled at her line of questioning. "Is there summat else tha's got on thi mind?

The only other thing that's worth anything in *my* life is four foot eleven, and is standing in front of me now."

"Well," she muttered, placated at last. "Just make sure it's always like that."

"Is it all rayt if I carry on wi' gardening, then?" he grinned.

"Get on wi' thi," she laughed back, throwing her wet dishcloth across the room at him, which he ducked under just in time.

"Jud?" she drawled as they sat down with their mugs of tea.

"Aye, lass?" he said slowly, not taking his eyes from his *Daily Mirror*.

"Has there ever been … anybody … else?" she added deliberately. "You know … you might have liked better?"

"Better than what, lass?" he said, lazily flicking over his pages. "Better than what? Me tea? Me garden? Thee?" he grinned, tossing his paper into the corner near the fire grate, ready for burning. "Tha's all I've ever wanted, Marion. Tha knows that."

"Then why doesn't tha tell me more often?" she teased.

"But I do," he complained playfully. "I told thee on thy birthday last year. How much more does thy need telling?"

He put his huge arm around her shoulders and drew her barely resisting body to him to plant a wet kiss on her mouth. He loved her with all his Yorkshire heart, but it wouldn't do to tell her in so many words. She wouldn't expect him to, but she liked to tease and cajole and prod his ribs. They had had their lows, but now they were solid. It was such a shame Jack – her Jack – wasn't here to share in what they had grown into.

"I can allus turn yon back garden into an allotment instead, if tha wants," he suggested, a wicked smile on his face. "All it takes is…"

"No fear," she protested. "On your way, you big lummox.

I couldn't do with *you* under my feet *all* day *every* day. I'll put up with it as it is, thank you very much."

-o-

Flo's operation hadn't gone to plan. There had been complications, they had said. Whenever hospital staff weren't sure of surgery outcomes, it was always put down to unforeseen complications. Folks hereabouts usually assumed death would be the inevitable outcome, with no one knowing why. However, general everyday explanations were no comfort to Flo's alarmed family – who were in the waiting room, eager to see her.

"What does that mean, Granddad?" Jack asked, impatient to see his mam. "Why can't we go in?"

"She's probably tired and sleepy after the operation," Jud tried to explain to the lad, though even he found it difficult to understand. If anyone should have understood it would have been him, after the length of time he'd spent in recovery following his pit accident. But an accident was different, wasn't it? Putting things back together again, not taking anything away, surely?

"It probably means things haven't gone to plan, and…" William began, but stopped after a hefty nudge in his ribs and a glower from Val. He shrugged his shoulders and mouthed a 'sorry' to her. She was definitely the compassionate one in *their* relationship. *He* jumped in with his size twelves without thinking, usually.

"Might as well settle down," Marion said. "It might be a while."

"Oh, er—" Jud jerked to life following Marion's timely poke in the side and nod towards the cafeteria. "Anybody want anything? Cup of tea, pop, or owt else?"

"Thank you, Jud," Marion said as if it had been his idea. "Very kind. A cup of tea and scone for me."

"Nothing for us, Granddad, thank you," Val replied with a smile, recognising Grandma's hand – or elbow – in this.

"Cup of tea and a bun, Granddad, please," Jack piped in, not eager to miss anything which might fill a little gap in his belly. "Will it be long?"

"About five minutes," Jud answered. "Just as long as it takes me to get through yon cafeteria."

"No," Jack insisted. "Not that. I mean until we get to see me mam."

The door swung inward before Jud had time to complete his errand. A bewhiskered and bespectacled ageing doctor shuffled into the room, a permanently worried frown adorning his face. His crumpled white coat and lopsided surgical hat betrayed a less than assiduous attention to personal tidiness.

"Mr and Mrs Holmes?" he uttered gruffly, interested only in conveying information without compassion. "Your daughter's condition is … critical … but stable…"

He paused momentarily, his inadequate person skills not allowing him to take them gradually through the trauma that they might lose Flo. Panic began to set in as his eyes flicked wildly from one shocked face to another.

"Well, erm," he continued slowly, wishing his personal hell to be over as quickly as possible, "if there's anything else you need to know Nurse Haskey here will tell you what you … need … to know."

His last few words tailed off as he hurried out of the room and down the corridor, leaving the nurse – who had only just arrived – to handle their inevitable questions.

They stood, dumbfounded, uncomprehending eyes desperately seeking support and answers from equally stunned faces.

"And what did he just try to tell us?" William turned to the nurse slowly. "Did he say that our mam was – is – in a serious condition?"

"Serious but stable," the nurse answered quietly, understanding their anguish. "But…"

"Never mind your 'buts'," he continued sharply. "What about 'routine operation' and 'as safe as it could be'? Or were they just platitudes to cover what damage your inept doctors might have done?"

"Nothing is 100 per cent certain, Mr Ingles," the nurse added slowly. The only thing worse than a complaining relative was an articulate one who could work out something might have gone amiss. "We will do the best we…"

"May we see her?" Marion added, ignoring whatever the nurse might want to say. "Is she awake?"

"She's not," the nurse stammered, "but you may have a short time with her. Follow me."

She turned on her polished heels and swished out of the door, her white starched apron rattling the jamb as she passed. Although saying nothing, she was rather irritated by patients' relatives who seemed to know everything, and in fact needed to be agreed with but ultimately ignored. The soft shush of her regulation black rubber-soled shoes, and the clinical swish-click of her starched ultrawhite apron were quite mesmeric as they were bustled through the labyrinth of pale green corridors to Ward 4 in the women's unit.

The shock they felt as they hurried through the double swing doors into the ward was absolute. Ten beds – some with wheeled screens – contained ten female bodies, each in a different physical and medical state. Some comatose, some barely awake, they all wore the same post-operative paraphernalia. Tubes sprouting from hidden orifices festooned each patient bed like weirdly tangled tree trimmings left over from Christmas.

Flo was unconscious, although the hospital euphemism was somewhat kinder and more patronising. This 'self-induced period of recuperation and regeneration' was entirely normal and would last for several days, they said. Collective common sense and wisdom would explain it as unusual and worrying. Marion and her friends had personally experienced enough hysterectomies to understand that this was not how such operations usually ended. If only the staff would be honest a good deal of aggravation and mistrust would be avoided.

"I'll leave you here," the nurse said, turning to go.

"But," William interrupted before she had time to become swallowed up by the anonymity such a large establishment cultivated, "we need some answers before you go, and…"

"Sorry," she shot back over her shoulder, "but duty calls. Someone will be here soon to answer all you have to ask."

The flack-flack of the swing door heralded her descent into oblivion, leaving the family unable to comprehend the possible reasons why such a standard operation should have gone so wrong.

"Why's me mam not awake?" Jack whispered. "And what are all those … those … line things doing around her? Won't she trip up if she gets up to – you know – go to the toilet? How…?"

"Enough, Jack, love," Marion hushed him. "You can ask yon doctor when – if – he comes to talk to us. You can sit down and talk to your mam a bit if you want."

Jack was puzzled by this. Why would he want to do that? He could see she was asleep, and his mam had always taught him not to disturb people when they were asleep.

"It's OK, lad," his granddad added. "She's asleep from the operation, but we'd like her to be awake soon. So thee talking to her might decide her to talk back, si thi."

A quiet lad by nature, Jack didn't really know how to respond to that suggestion – so he simply sat and held her hand, somehow hoping a touch would be just as good as a word.

"How about that cup of tea now, then, Jud?" Marion suggested, "seeing as we'll be here for a bit?"

"Aye, lass," he agreed, jumping to his feet. "Tea, scone, and a bun for these two. William? Val?"

"I think we'll have a couple of coffees, if that's all right, Granddad," William said, following Val's nod. "I'll come and give you a hand."

"Thanks, lad," Jud replied. "That'll be a rayt good help."

"Little Jack," a weak voice whispered, as Jud reached for the door handle.

"Mam," he replied gruffly, squeezing her hand as a sense of elation and relief invaded his body. "Me mam's awake, Granddad, just like you said she would be. I whispered stuff to her, and … she heard me. Mam…"

Jud swung his huge frame around again, mission aborted once more … tea and cake a memory, but in a good way.

"How are you doing, lass?" Marion soothed, grasping her daughter's hand with passionate urgency.

"I've seen better days," Flo murmured. "Though I've not witnessed worse. Have I been out long?"

"A little while, love," Marion replied, a slight smile of relief creasing her eye corners. "We're all here."

"All?" Flo replied quickly, raising slightly on one elbow, a note of panic edging her tone.

"With one exception, naturally," Marion reassured her. "So there's no need to worry … All as love you."

Flo sank back with a relieved sigh as she looked over at her elder son and his wife.

"William … Val…" she said. "Thank you for coming, and for looking after this lot. It's…" A grimace of pain ambushed her conversation, causing her eyes to glaze and her clenched knuckles to blanch.

"Mam?" Jack's hoarse whisper betrayed his concern.

"You…?"

"I'm all right, love," she sighed, relaxing visibly. "Just twinges now and again. Any chance of a cup of tea, Dad?"

"Rayt enough, lass," Jud nodded. "Anybody else? Third time of asking."

"Coming to give me a 'and, our Jack?" Jud asked, quite obviously wanting to leave Flo with the older people.

"No, Granddad," Jack muttered gruffly. "I'll be all right here, cos…"

"Jack?" Jud asked again. "I can't manage doors and things on me own, si thi. So come on, our lad … an 'and?"

"It's all right, love," Flo whispered to her little lad. "I'll be fine. You go and help your granddad now. I'll still be here when you get back with my cup of tea."

"If you're sure," Jack said, following his granddad to the door. "Three teas, two coffees, two scones and one bun. Anything to eat for my slightly larger brother and my sister-in-law?"

"Well, go on, then," William nodded. "A couple of scones with butter – and jam, mind you."

"We'll join you to help," Val suggested, nudging William as she headed to the door.

"But…" he protested, quickly realising he needed to follow his wife's unsaid lead. "I think … Val's right. Granddad does need a hand. Can't be easy when…"

"Steady now, young William," Jud said, a grin beginning to form. "Be careful tha doesn't say anything tha might regret, or I'll set our Jack on to thee."

"Right, lass," Marion started, once the last of the family horde had retreated, "now tell me."

"I don't know, Mam," Flo sighed. "I remember the trolley with the rickety wheel taking me to theatre, and then … here. It seemed all so quick. I thought they'd done nothing until the pain kicked in, and then it was obvious they had."

She paused, eyes closed, discomfort obvious as she tried to ride the waves. Women's lot, eh? Marion understood, as all women understand. What they have to bear is painful for them … and for their menfolk, in different ways.

"Is our Jack all right, Mam?" Flo asked, once the crest had passed and the trough embraced her once again. "He's not taking things too … hard? I know what he's like. A brooder, until it all pours out. He needs…"

"He's fine, love," Marion assured her. "Trust me. Your dad's so good with him. Knows all the right things to say and do to keep him occupied. He loves that bairn. Reminds him of his own Little Jack."

Tears began to trickle their erratic way down her worn face as memories of *her* son hijacked her thoughts. Little Jack was the image of her lad at that age, except for the hair. No spikes with *her* Jack, only curls and waves.

"Mam?" Flo whispered, pain edging her concern, as she tried to lift herself to comfort *her* mam.

"It's all right, lass," Marion assured her, dabbing her cheeks. "I just closed my eyes and there he was, that loving smile on his face. You know, just like yon bairn of yours. Anyway, your dad's spoken to t' powers that be, and you'll be convalescing in Lytham as soon as you're well enough to travel. Two weeks by the sea. Champion."

"But, I can't…" Flo protested. "Jack needs…"

"Jack's needs are catered for with us. Don't you fret," Marion went on. "He knows what's about, and he's good with it. Looking forward, he says. His granddad's got a few things planned. 'Projects', he calls 'em, and William's promised to take us all to see you when you're well enough in the home."

"Home?" Flo gasped. "Makes me sound like I'm old and helpless."

"Look at it as a home from home, lass," Marion smiled, "and you won't go far wrong."

"And what about Eric?" Flo asked. "Hasn't he said anything? Upkeep of me home? Rent?"

"All taken care of," her Mam smiled. "Seen very little of him, really. Keeping a low profile, your dad says – whatever that means. Anyway, he seems to be paying the rent and all necessary dues. Obviously he's on the make because he doesn't have to give you anything while you're in here, and Jack's being looked after by us. So God's in his heaven, and all's right with the world."

Chapter 23

"Mam?" Jack said. "Can I go for a paddle wi' me granddad?"

"Paddle?" Marion frowned. "Why on earth would anybody want to do that?"

"We did it every day when we went to Blackpool with you and Granddad," Jack reminded her. "Are the sand and sea any different here from at Blackpool? Only, I think it's the same water, same sand, and same coast. Seawater's supposed to be good for you, or so Granddad says. If…"

"Oh, for goodness' sake." Marion threw her hands up in supplication. "Anything for a quiet life, Jud Holmes."

"Goody," Jack whooped, face glowing with excitement. "Shall we explore yon sandy hills, Granddad? They're only just down the road."

"Dunes, lad," Jud corrected.

"Is it painful, Granddad?" Jack asked, a mischievous glint in his eyes. "Perhaps you can get some cream from the chemist for your dunes."

"Smart-arse," Jud laughed. "Dunes are…"

"Piles of sand held in place by grass. I know, Granddad," Jack added quickly. "Do you know that if it weren't for the grass these dunes would be blowing about the town?"

"Aye, lad," Jud replied. "It were me as told *you*."

"I knew I'd heard it somewhere," Jack laughed. "Well?"

"All rayt," Jud said, prizing himself out of the comfortable chair which gripped him. "Coming, William?"

"Come on, then," Jack urged. "Us lads together."

"Not joining them, Val?" Flo asked from her cushioned lounger.

The west coast clean air seemed to be doing her good, as she had taken on a much healthier look to her skin.

"Don't feel like it really," Val said. "Rest here and a cup of tea will do me more good than tramping up and down sandy hills. Besides—"

"You're expecting, aren't you?" Marion interrupted. "Only I've been wondering for a while that you looked…"

"Fatter? Healthier? Thicker hair? Better complexion?" Val smiled. "Yes, we are."

"Val Ingles," Flo gushed. "You kept that one quiet."

"Just waiting for the right moment, Mrs Ingles," Val said, a satisfied and comfortable look growing around her eyes.

"Oh, for goodness' sake, call me Flo. We're all girls together," Flo insisted. "When's it due? This is so exciting. Something good to look forward to. I'm going to be a grandma."

"Steady, Flo," Marion advised. "You know you're not well enough for too much excitement."

"Excitement?" Flo gushed. "It's the best news I've had for many a year, and I'm allowed to be excited as long as I don't try to leap over the table. Does your mam know yet?"

"Yes," Val smiled. "My little sister had worked it out, so we had to tell Mum before *she* did. She's rather like your Jack, is our Jenny: sharp and clever, but speaks it as she sees it. No chance to keep secrets in our household. We were going to tell folks this week, anyway, so I had to swear her to secrecy until we could tell."

"And I'm going to be a great-grandma," Marion burst

out, suddenly realising the importance and impact of what she had just heard. "When am I going to see my first great-grandchild?"

"Early spring, we think," Val said, not having given a great deal of thought to the endgame. "Not made exact calculations yet, if it's possible to do that. But we're happy with early spring."

"And William?" Flo ventured tentatively.

"Over the moon, really," Val said, a little more confidently. "He was quiet at first, because his view of our first few years together was establishing our base and building on our earning ability as teachers before starting a family. Our priorities now, of course, have changed somewhat, and he has really become excited and positive about our family, as have I."

"What about your job, and your home?" Marion asked. "Will you have a job, and will you be able to afford to live? I only ask because I've seen youngsters like you before in similar situations not being able to afford … after—"

"Don't worry, Grandma," William interrupted, as he came back into the room. "Everything's taken care of. We can afford everything we need. Val will work until Christmas and take time off over and after the birth, and we'll play it from there. The money I saved from the army will give us enough for rent for the two years I'm at college, and then I'll have a job without a problem."

"But what if you don't get a job?" Flo asked. "What then?"

"There aren't enough teachers to fill the posts available," William said. "So I won't have any trouble getting one. Just don't worry. It's all sorted out and planned, as far as life can be planned."

"You know that if you need a bit of … you know … help … at any time, your granddad and I have a bit put by," Marion offered. "So don't be afraid to ask."

"That's very generous of you," Val smiled, "and we *will* ask if there's a need. But as far as we can see things will be tight for a couple of years, but that's part of the fun: managing."

"And are you happy, lad?" Marion asked pointedly.

"Ecstatically, Grandma …" he assured her, putting his arm around his wife and drawing her to him. "Ecstatically. Who wouldn't be?"

"Where're your brother and Granddad?" Flo asked. "I suppose he's teaching Little Jack something dodgy."

"Actually," William replied, "they're paddling, would you believe it? Granddad's trousers are rolled up to his knees, socks in his pocket, and shoes tied together over his shoulder. They're like two old men reminiscing about past times and pointing out stuff to each other as they go along."

Flo smiled and settled back in her lounger, satisfied that she would live long enough to see her little boy grow up. William was already a man and settled with his childhood sweetheart, so she had no worries there. Her William soon to be a dad … where had all those years gone? Frightening, how swiftly time seemed to have passed her by. She knew in her heart of hearts she wouldn't have long left, despite doctors' views to the contrary. Perhaps she *would* survive her recent operation, even though it had been touch and go. She *was* on the mend. No doubt about that, for sure. But, underneath it all, her serious illness at fourteen and all her years of aggravation and discord with Eric had taken their toll. She would have needed a reasonably even life to have overturned such a serious prognosis.

Still, enjoy the rest and recuperation, Flo, lass. Keep your strength up, and see your Jack on his way. That's the most important task.

And then? Just wait and see, eh? What's meant for you won't go by you. That's what *you've* always said.

Chapter 24

"It's a girl this time. Val's had a little girl," Flo shouted as she bustled into her mam's. "Just had a letter from our William. He says Val and daughter are doing fine, and now that's his family complete."

"I should think so as well," Marion tutted. "Three's enough in anyone's eyes, surely?"

"Fantastic," Jud agreed. "And what's our Jack think about it all?"

"Well, you know our Jack," Flo joined in, as she mashed a fresh pot of tea. "Mam? Dad?"

"Aye, lass," Jud rubbed his giant hands together in glee. "Tha knows I'll never say no to a fresh pot. Yer mam were just saying as it might be nice to have a holiday together again. A bit like Blackpool before our Jack got so ... big."

"Is Mrs Ridge still with us, then?" Flo asked. "Only she wasn't so good last time we heard."

"Course she is," Jud said, becoming animated at the thought. "Better than ever. Apparently doctor's put it down to allergies."

"Aye," Marion chipped in, "allergic to her second husband, truth be known. As soon as she were rid, her health bucked up no end."

"Jack's just ... Jack," Flo shrugged. "Does his own thing,

which you would expect at sixteen, and doesn't cause any bother to anybody else. Just finished his GCEs, and so he's earning a bit of spending money in case."

"In case of what?" Jud asked, his renowned bushy eyebrow frown almost covering his eyes.

"In case anybody decides to book a holiday, he says," Flo laughed. "Then he'll have some money to treat whoever takes him."

"That's our Jack," Marion smiled indulgently. "Always thinking about other people. But then, we've known that all his life … little bairn."

"Lord a mercy me," Flo said, throwing her hands in the air. "Not so little now, Mam."

"Where's he working, then?" Jud asked. "I've not seen him out on a weekend, except of course to play his rugby, and weekdays are out because of school. So what and when?"

"Ah," Flo said, dropping to a whisper and touching the side of her nose with her forefinger while looking either side to check nobody else was listening, "nobody's supposed to know this, but he's taken the occasional day off school to join other folks in the pea fields pulling peas."

"Pulling peas?" Marion puzzled. "Do you mean shelling peas, by any chance? If he did that out there peas wouldn't be fresh, would they?"

"Nay, lass," Jud tried to explain, "they pull the pods of the plants and stuff 'em in sacks. Then they get paid by the bag load: about three shillings for half a hundredweight or so, I think."

"It is all right, isn't it?" Flo said, becoming confused and a little less sure by all this talk of earning money and taking time off school. "He's finished his exams, and there's not long left to the summer holidays."

"Got his head screwed on right, has yon lad," Jud added. "He knows what he's doing all rayt. Wanting to get some brass behind him? Good on him, I say. Can't fault his thinking."

"So this is where you are, is it?" Jack's happy voice swooped into his grandma's kitchen. "Thought you'd emigrated."

He kissed and hugged Mam and Grandma, with a special man hug for his granddad.

"All rayt, me owd cock?" he greeted Jud. "'Ow's tha doin' today?"

"All rayt, ta," Jud replied. "Gorra job, as tha, lad?"

"Aye, I 'ave that," Jack said. "Pay's all rayt as well. Gives me a bob or two for me 'olidays."

"Is thy off anywhere nice?" Jud continued.

"Wherever tha's offering to teck me," Jack said, to guffaws from his granddad and smiles from his mam.

"You're not going to get into trouble, are you, love?" Flo asked seriously.

"What for, Mam?" Jack said. "Done nothing wrong. With whom, anyway?"

"School," she explained, "for not being there."

"We've all finished our exams," he replied, "and so the school recognises there's nothing productive for us to do. Some are going on to do A levels, some aren't, but some haven't decided yet. So the teachers have nothing positive they can offer us. I'd rather earn a bit of money from time to time than waste my time sitting around playing games. We're allowed to leave officially at the beginning of July, anyway."

"So that's that, then," Jud said, nodding at the others. "I *said* he had his buttons sewn on."

"And your next day in the pea fields?" his mam asked.

"Tomorrow, early," he said. "Six o'clock start, if that's OK with you, Mam? I won't wake you, cos I bought myself a cheap alarm clock today."

He drew out of his pocket a traditional portable windable clock, which seemed to have seen better days because of its peeling red paint.

"It's got a quietish bell and luminous hands, so I can tell what time it is in the dark," he enthused, winding it up and setting the alarm with more than a little difficulty.

"How much?" Jud asked.

"How much what, Granddad?" Jack replied.

"How much did tha pay t' dustbin man to allow thee to dig it out of the dustcart?" his granddad went on.

"Nay," Jack protested. "I bought it from Jimmy Smith in our class, for a tanner. Cheap at half the price, if it works … and it does."

Flo watched her little boy interacting so naturally with his granddad with wonder in her eyes. Could this be the little boy whom she brought home through the snow from Wakefield hospital all those years ago, tucked under her coat, close to her breast? Now almost a man, he was behaving as if he was ready to take on the rest of the world. Would that she might see him grow into that man she knew all along he would become. Only the Almighty could sort that one out.

"How did you latch on to that job?" Flo asked, not sure where he might have found that out. Jobs like that were never advertised. They were usually word-of-mouth jobs, which needed contacts. But where in *his* social group did he come by such information?

"Gordon Gittins's mate's dad's uncle has a small farm out Glasshoughton way where, of all things, he grows … peas." Jack answered, munching on a chocolate digestive while sipping his tea. "He needs pea pullers, and we're good workers. Pay's all right, but you've just got to learn to be quick."

"But," his granddad said, a wicked glint in his eye, "thy's too precise to be quick. Thy'd have to make sure every pod pointed in t' same direction, with the stalks exactly the same length, and…"

They all burst out laughing at the amusing picture Jud had painted of his grandson.

"You have to learn to overcome such ways, I'm afraid," Jack said, shrugging his shoulders. "It's hard, but it won't do in today's quick society to take too long doing stuff that other folks depend on. Speed's money these days, unfortunately, Granddad, owd cock."

"It's all rayt to fit other folks' needs in," his granddad replied, "but you can't beat careful attention to detail … one of the things I've always admired in you, our Jack, so don't change too much. Your own values are more important than earning lots of dosh."

"Thanks, Granddad," Jack replied with a smile. "I appreciate that, but you've no need to worry. *This* job's a one-off, and it won't affect me at all. These digestives are lovely, Grandma. Did you know that…?"

"Aye, lad," his granddad interrupted, "tha's already told us where, when, and by whom they were made."

"Am I *that* predictable?" Jack smiled, almost apologetically.

"Aye, thy is, but don't ever change," Jud added quickly. "There's a comfort in being able to guess what tha's going to say occasionally. Tha's all rayt as thy is, our Jack."

"What are you trying to say, Granddad?" Jack replied, a huge grin on his face.

"Has tha thought what tha's going to do when tha's got thi exam results?" Jud said. "Carry on with thy education, like?"

"I'd thought I'd go down the pit," Jack said, serious-faced. "It's not the same as when *you* started, and there are lots of opportunities. Do you know…?"

"You're not serious?" all three gasped at once. "You're going to waste your education on that?"

"No, course not, but I told you I'd get you back, our Granddad," Jack laughed. "Elbow grease, indeed."

"You bugger," Jud roared with laughter. "You did me right and proper there. You're just too quick for me these days, our Jack."

"I don't know what I want to do really, Granddad," Jack told him honestly. "Sometimes I fancy doing what our William's doing, but then I'm not sure about the pay and holidays. Thirteen weeks sounds a bit too long for me."

-o-

About the Author

Born in 1946 in the West Riding of Yorkshire's coal fields around Wakefield, he attended grammar school, where he honed his love of writing stories, but enjoyed sport rather more than academic work. After three years at teacher training college in Leeds, he became a teacher in 1967. He spent a lot of time during his teaching career entertaining children of all ages, a large part of which was through telling stories, and encouraging them to escape into a world of imagination and wonder. Some of his most disturbed youngsters he found to be very talented poets, for example. He has always had a wicked sense of humour, which has blossomed only during the time he has spent with his present wife. This sense of humour also allowed many youngsters to survive often difficult and brutalising home environments.

He retired almost ten years ago, after forty years working in schools with young people who had significantly disrupted lives because of behaviour disorders and poor social adjustment, generally brought about through circumstances beyond their control. At the same time as moving from leafy lane suburban middle class school teaching in Leeds to residential schooling for emotional and behavioural disturbance in the early 1990s, changed family circumstance provided the spur to achieve ambitions. Supported by his wife, Denise, he achieved a Master's degree in his mid-forties and a PhD at the age of fifty-six, because he had always wanted to do so.

Now enjoying glorious retirement, he spends as much

time as life will allow writing, reading and travelling.

'Jack', the second volume of the saga, will be released towards the end of 2016.

Lightning Source UK Ltd.
Milton Keynes UK
UKOW02f1227040716

277655UK00001B/5/P

9 781910 077825